GONE WITH THE WOOL

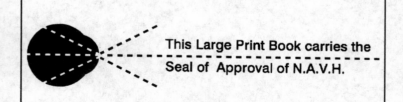

A YARN RETREAT MYSTERY

GONE WITH THE WOOL

BETTY HECHTMAN

WHEELER PUBLISHING
A part of Gale, Cengage Learning

GALE
CENGAGE Learning®

Farmington Hills, Mich • San Francisco • New York • Waterville, Maine
Meriden, Conn • Mason, Ohio • Chicago

GALE
CENGAGE Learning®

LIBRARY OF CONGRESS CATALOGING-IN-PUBLICATION DATA

Names: Hechtman, Betty, 1947– author.
Title: Gone with the wool / by Betty Hechtman.
Description: Large print edition. | Waterville, Maine : Wheeler Publishing, 2016. | Series: A yarn retreat mystery | Series: Wheeler Publishing large print cozy mystery
Identifiers: LCCN 2016042834| ISBN 9781410495594 (softcover) | ISBN 1410495590 (softcover)
Subjects: LCSH: Knitters (Persons)—Fiction. | Murder—Investigation—Fiction. | Large type books. | GSAFD: Mystery fiction.
Classification: LCC PS3608.E288 G66 2016 | DDC 813/.6—dc23
LC record available at https://lccn.loc.gov/2016042834

Published in 2017 by arrangement with The Berkley Publishing Group, an imprint of Penguin Publishing Group, a division of Penguin Random House LLC

ACKNOWLEDGMENTS

I want to thank my editor Julie Mianecki for all her help in getting this book into shape. My agent Jessica Faust keeps steering me through the changing publishing world.

Thank you monarch butterflies for your amazing ability to come back to the same spot every October. What is most astonishing is the butterflies have never been there before. Somehow they inherit the ability to come back to the same location. In my book, their destination is Cadbury by the Sea, but in real life, it is Pacific Grove, California. The town does celebrate the return of the butterflies, but I'm pretty sure it is more subdued than the events and hoopla I came up with for this book.

When I saw the silver crown Amy Shelton crocheted, I decided it was possible to crochet anything — even a butterfly. I am very proud of the pattern for a monarch butterfly that I created for this book.

Thanks to my knit and crochet group Rene Biederman, Alice Chiredijan, Terry Cohen, Trish Culkin, Clara Feeney, Sonia Flaum, Lilly Gillis, Winnie Hineson, Linda Hopkins, Reva Mallon, Elayne Moschin and Paula Tesler for the friendship and yarn advice.

A special thank you to Linda Hopkins. She is so generous with her time, and her help with the patterns is invaluable. The support from Roberta and Dominic Martia is much appreciated. And of course, thanks to my family, Burl, Max and Samantha.

1

Why hadn't I realized this problem before? The bright red tote bag with *Yarn2Go* emblazoned on the front fell over as I tried to cram in the long knitting loom for my upcoming yarn retreat. My selection of round looms rolled across the floor before falling flat. The other long looms scattered at my feet. Julius, my black cat, watched from his spot on the leather love seat in the room I called my office as I gathered up the odd-looking pieces of equipment.

I might be able to get them into the bag for my meeting, but it would simply not work to hand out such ungainly and heavy bags to my retreaters as they registered.

Julius blinked his yellow eyes at me. "I know what you're thinking," I said. "This is the fourth retreat I'm putting on, and I should have figured this out already." The plan had been that after my meeting, I was going to pick up the boxes of looms and stuff the bags for the retreaters.

I looked around the small room, as if there might be an answer for me. There were reminders of my aunt's handiwork with yarn everywhere. My favorite was the crocheted lion who patrolled from the desk, though his face was too amusing to appear threatening. And then there was the sample of my handiwork that I was the most proud of. It had taken me a while, but I'd finished making the worry doll from the last retreat. I loved the doll and the concept. You were supposed to give her your worries, and she would take care of them. I'd given mine a face with an attitude, which made her appear up for the job.

"Worry doll, how about some help with this?" I pointed at the bag, which I had smartly propped up at my feet when I'd refilled it. It fell over on its side anyway.

"I'm talking to cats and dolls," I said, shaking my head in disbelief as I grabbed the handles and lugged the bag out of the room.

Julius followed me to the kitchen, making a last play for a serving of stink fish. I started to ignore it, but such a little effort made him so happy, and eventually I gave in. The can of smelly cat food was wrapped in plastic and then in three layers of plastic bags, yet somehow the strong smell still got through. I held my nose before giving him a dainty portion and then starting the involved job of rewrapping and resealing it. He was busily chewing as I went out the back door.

Julius and I had only been companions for a short time, and he was the first pet I had ever had — though I was beginning to think he viewed me as the pet. He had definitely chosen me, and he seemed to be doing a good job of training me to give him the care he desired. I'd wanted him to stay inside initially, but he'd had no intention of being strictly an indoor cat and had pushed open a window to show me how to leave it open just enough so that he could come and go as he pleased.

Outside, the sky was a flat white. That was the average weather here on the tip of the Monterey Peninsula. White sky, cool weather, no matter the month. It just happened to be October, though you couldn't tell by looking around. There were no trees with golden leaves — mostly there were Monterey pines and Monterey cypress, which never lost their foliage and stayed a dark green year-round. The cypress tree on the small strip of land in front of my house had a typical horizontal shape from the constant wind. Somehow it made me think of someone running away with their hair flowing behind them. It seemed funny, since I had run here to Cadbury by the Sea, California.

My name is Casey Feldstein, and to make a long story short, I'd relocated to my aunt's guest house in Cadbury when I was faced with moving back in with my high-achieving parents (both doctors) because I was once again out of a job. Sadly, my aunt had been killed in a hit-and-run several months after I moved in. She'd left me everything — a house, a yarn retreat business and, as it was turning out, a life.

I might have moved almost two thousand miles away from Chicago, but that didn't mean I had severed my ties with my parents or, I was sorry to admit, my need for their approval. It still stung when my mother ended our conversations with her usual, "When I was your age I was a wife, a doctor and a mother, and you're what?"

So, maybe I was thirty-five and it was true that I'd had a rather spotty career history that, until recently, seemed to be headed nowhere. Of all the things I had done, my two favorites were the temp work at the detective agency, where I was either an assistant detective or a detective's assistant, depending on who you talked to, and my position as a dessert chef at a small bistro. I would have never left either of those jobs — they left me.

Though my mother had a hard time acknowledging it, these days I did have an answer for her usual comment. I had taken over my aunt's yarn retreat business, even though I hadn't known a knitting needle from a crochet hook when I'd started. And I'd turned my baking skills into a regular job as the dessert chef at the Blue Door restaurant, plus I baked muffins for the assorted coffee spots in Cadbury.

I started to walk past the converted garage that had been my home when I'd first moved here and then made a last-minute decision to go inside and check the supply of tote bags, as if the new ones I'd had made up might somehow be bigger than the one I was carrying.

The flat light that made it through the cloud cover was coming in the windows and illuminating the interior. The stack of bags sat on the counter that served as a divider between the tiny kitchen area and living space. I folded one out and measured it against my stuffed one. No surprise, they were the same size. As I flattened the bag and put it back, I noticed the worn manila envelope that had been sitting there for months. I still hadn't figured out what to do about its contents.

I hadn't told anyone about the information the envelope contained, not even my best friend Lucinda Thornkill, who owned the Blue Door with her husband, Tag, so there was no one to go to for advice.

There was no reason to deal with it now, except to procrastinate from dealing with the bag issue. I guess there was *one* person I could go to for advice. It was two hours later in Chicago, and even though it was Saturday, my ex-boss at the detective agency was probably leaning back in his office chair considering his lunch options, which meant it was a good time to call.

I punched in the number, and he answered on the third ring.

"Hi, Frank," I said. Before I could say more, he interrupted.

"Oh no, Feldstein. Don't tell me there's another body in that town of yours with the name that sounds like a candy bar." It was true that when I had called him in the past, it was to get advice about a death — well, a murder in town, to be exact.

"No, no, Frank. No dead bodies this time. All the citizens of Cadbury by the Sea are alive — as far as I know. I wanted to ask your advice on something else."

"Okay, Feldstein. I get it. You've got boy trouble again. Shoot."

I laughed. I'd never called him about boy trouble, as he called it, nor would I ever do so. "It's something else," I began. "Do you remember I told you I had some information that would shake up the town? Well, now I have even more. I know who it is —"

"Who what is, Feldstein? You're going to have to bring me up to speed if you want my advice. You do know I have a life here that has nothing to do with that town you're living in, right?"

I was hoping that I wouldn't have to start from scratch, but I could see his point. What was going on in Cadbury was hardly of earthshaking importance to him. I began by telling him about the Delacorte family, who were the local royalty. The family had owned a cannery and a fleet of fishing boats and still owned lots of property around town. Vista Del Mar, the hotel and conference center across the street from my house, where I held the yarn retreats, had belonged solely to Edmund Delacorte.

When Edmund had died, it had been very specific in his will that Vista Del Mar was to go to his children. His only son had died in an accident a year or so after Edmund's death, and since it seemed there were no other children, the hotel and conference center had gone back into the family estate. All that was left of the Delacortes now were Edmund's two sisters, Cora and Madeleine. I explained all of this to Frank.

"It only *seemed* there were no other children," I said. I debated with myself whether I should go into the whole story of how I'd come to the conclusion that Edmund had a love child. Frank only had limited patience, and I was afraid it would run out if I went through telling him I'd found an envelope of photos that was marked *Our Baby* in a dresser that had belonged to Edmund. The baby was clearly a girl, and as far as everyone knew, he had only had a son. I didn't know if Frank remembered that he had helped me figure out that Edmund had made money drops to the mother through them both accessing a safety-deposit box, but I didn't bring it up and got right to the point. "I found out that Edmund had a love child, but I didn't know her identity, not until I found some evidence that made it clear who the baby is. Well, she's not a baby anymore. All I have to do is tell her who she is, and then she can get a DNA test. I have samples of both Edmund's and the baby's mother's DNA."

"Details, Feldstein. What kind of samples?"

I didn't have to look through the rest of the contents in the large manila envelope to know there was a sample of Edmund's hair with the roots I'd gotten from an old hairbrush. It was amazing — you could be dead for years, but hair stuck in an old hairbrush survived. The mother had licked an envelope, and I had that. I listed the details off to Frank with a certain amount of pride in my detective skills.

"Okay," he said. "Now what evidence led you to the baby's identity?"

"A teddy bear in the photos," I said, imagining his expression as I said it. He didn't disappoint. I heard him choking on whatever he was drinking as we talked.

"A teddy bear," he repeated in an incredulous tone. "I got to hear this one. How did a teddy bear give the kid's identity away?"

Frank didn't know anything about needle craft. Actually, I hadn't known much either, until recently. I struggled, trying to find a way to explain it so he would understand. "There was a one-of-a-kind handmade teddy bear in the pictures next to the baby girl. The style is distinctive, like a fingerprint. I know who made it, and I'm sure the woman will recognize it."

"Now it's coming back to me," Frank said. "I think I asked you before what was in it for you?"

"Nothing," I said.

"Then I recommend you sit on it. Those Delacorte sisters aren't going to be happy with someone trying to claim part of their estate. From the way you describe that town, I don't know that anybody would be happy with you for sharing your information."

"I bet Edmund's daughter would like to know who she is, and I happen to know that an inheritance would certainly help her out."

"Don't be so sure, Feldstein. My advice is to keep quiet awhile longer. Once the cat is out of the bag, you can't put it back." There was silence on my end, and after a moment Frank said, "Is there something else?" His mention of a bag had brought me right back to my problem, but I was pretty sure he wouldn't be any help there.

"That's it," I said finally.

"Then I've got to go. The delivery guy is here with my sub sandwich." I heard a click, and he was gone.

There was one thing he was definitely right about: the whole cat in the bag thing. I left the envelope where it was. There was always tomorrow.

The red tote bag banged against my leg as I walked, and I had to stop more than once to pick up a loom that tumbled out and force it back in as I went to my yellow Mini Cooper, which was parked in the driveway.

My house was the edge of Cadbury. The look was wilder here, with more trees, no sidewalks and of course Vista Del Mar across the street. I glanced toward the hotel and conference center as I pulled onto the street. Something large and cumbersome was being pulled down the driveway. It was impossible to see what it was, as it was covered in blue tarps. This was the beginning of the biggest week of the year here in Cadbury, and I had a feeling it was connected.

Cadbury by the Sea's real claim to fame was not the moody scenery, but the tens of thousands of striking orange and black butterflies that arrived in October to overwinter in a stand of trees behind a pink motel. There was even a statue of a monarch butterfly near the lighthouse. Tomorrow was the kickoff of Butterfly Week in Cadbury. There were going to be events each day, ending with a parade and the coronation of the Butterfly Queen.

I might live on the edge of Cadbury, but

it was still a small town, and it only took five minutes or so to get downtown. There was an authentic feeling to the place. No "ye olde" anythings — if anything was old here, it was because it had been around for a long time. The buildings were a mixture of Victorians that were built when that was the current style and some more streamlined mid-century-style structures that looked plain in comparison.

Grand Street was the main drag in town. The two directions of traffic were divided by a parklike strip of grass and trees, with some benches thrown in. I found an angled parking spot near my destination.

There was more than the usual Saturday morning activity on the street. Several people on ladders were putting up banners on the light posts, and the shops along the street were decorating their windows. The theme to all of it was the monarch butterfly.

I lugged the bag out of the car, somehow managing to keep everything inside it as I threaded past all the activity and turned onto a side street that sloped down toward the water. I was so used to being able to see the Pacific from just about everywhere that it almost didn't register. I'd also gotten used to the constant hint of moisture in the air and the background sound of the rhythm of the waves. Of course, I chuckled to myself — today there was a parking spot right in front of my destination, Cadbury Yarn.

The store was actually located in a small bungalow-style house. As I crossed the front porch, I noticed they had added a banner covered with butterflies that flapped in the ever-present breeze. Inside, the store seemed busier than usual. The table in what had once been a dining room was filled with a group of women chatting while they worked on their yarn projects.

Gwen Selwyn, the shop's owner, was ringing up a sale at the glass counter in the center of what had been the living room. She looked up as I came in and offered me a welcoming wave. It was strange to realize she had no idea that she was the love child of Edmund Delacorte. I went over what I knew about her. It was obvious from her appearance that she was more interested in serviceable than stylish. She was somewhere in her fifties, and I would have laid down money that the nubby brown sweater she was wearing was her own creation. Making something like that was still only a dream to me, but Gwen was one of those people who could knit without even looking at her work. I was sure that any color in her cheeks came from the cool damp air. She was not likely to wear makeup any more so than she was to do anything about the streaks of gray that had begun to show up in her short chestnut hair. Even though she was widowed, I'd also bet that she would never be caught hanging out in the local wine bar looking for a hookup. As far as I could tell, all her energy went into trying to keep the yarn store and her family afloat.

Today I noticed there seemed to be an extra furrow to her brow, and for a moment I considered ignoring Frank's advice and pulling her into the storage room and blurting out that she was the secret Delacorte heir. But the place was busy, and that's not the kind of news to just dump on someone between ringing up skeins of hand-dyed yarn.

"We're over here," Crystal Smith called to me, waving from a room off to the side. A table sat in front of a window that looked out into the strip of space between the house and its neighbor. Three captain-style chairs were around it. Crystal was Gwen's daughter, though any resemblance was well hidden. Gwen leaned toward neutrals, while her daughter was all about splashes of color. Her dark hair fell into tight ringlets, and she had a thing for wearing pieces that didn't match. I couldn't remember ever seeing her in a matched set of earrings or a pair of socks that were the same. She managed to wear all kinds of eye makeup and have it work. The one time I'd tried to emulate it, I came out looking like a sad raccoon.

It was just the two of us for now, and Crystal offered me a chair. "I hope Wanda shows up soon. I have to leave for the football game so I can cheer on my son. Go Monarchs!" Crystal said, shaking her fist in a supportive gesture. "It was very nice of you to bring the corn muffins last night," she said.

"It was my attempt at showing town spirit," I said. As soon as I'd heard about the tradition of a chili dinner the night before the team's homecoming game, I'd decided to make a contribution. The event was held in the multipurpose room of the natural history museum. Long tables had been set up and the walls decorated with pennants for the Monarchs. I had just gone into the kitchen and dropped off the muffins.

"Too bad you didn't stay for the dinner," Crystal said. "The boys were all excited being served by their parents and the coach. There was lots of cheering and 'We're going to win this year' kind of stuff."

"The woman making the chili didn't seem that happy with my donation or my presence," I said. "Besides, I had things to do."

"That would be Rosalie Hardcastle, and I'm not surprised she wasn't gracious," Crystal said. "She's very possessive of the dinner. She started the tradition and cooks the chili from her recipe. If it's any consolation, the boys really scarfed down those muffins."

"Well, that's history now anyway, so on to the present. We've got a problem," I said, hoisting the bag onto the table. Wanda Krug came in just as the bag flopped over on its side and all the long looms fell out and hit the floor.

Though Wanda was a golf pro at a local resort, which made her an athlete, somehow whenever I saw her all I could think of was "The Teapot Song." She was short and stout as the lyrics proclaimed, and she had a habit of putting one hand on her hip and gesturing with the other. The funny thing was that with her bland style of dress — polo shirts and comfortable loose slacks — it seemed like she should be Gwen's daughter.

Crystal and Wanda had become my regular workshop leaders for the yarn retreats. They were both much better with yarn craft than I was and never agreed on anything.

Somehow I'd thought that would balance things out.

I retrieved the long looms, thinking how much they resembled something you'd put on the wall to hang coats on. I left the bag on its side and shoved them back in. "And that's without any yarn. There's no way I can give bags out with all this." I mentioned that I'd planned to pick up the boxes of looms and stuff the bags later today.

The loom idea had been Crystal's, and she had given me a quick demonstration on how to use them, making a point of telling me that knowing how to knit wasn't necessary. I had trusted her to come up with a plan for the workshops. Apparently, she hadn't thought about the logistics of how to handle the looms.

I regretted that I had waited so long for the three of us to meet about the upcoming retreat. Wanda tried to lift the bag. She had good upper body strength and had no problem holding it.

"You're right. You'll get somebody complaining they got a muscle strain from carrying this around." She set it back down. "I guess Crystal didn't think about that." There was a tiny bit of triumph in Wanda's voice.

Crystal ignored the comment as well as

the bag problem. "We should really talk about the plan for the workshops." She had a plastic bin and began to take out knitted items and lay them on the table. I looked at the array of hats, scarves and shawls.

"These were all made with the looms?" I asked. In my basic lesson I had just made a swatch using part of a circular loom. I was going to be almost on the same level of my retreaters when it came to skill with the device.

Crystal nodded and encouraged me to handle the pieces. I was surprised how thick and soft some of the scarves were.

"But what's the plan?" Wanda said. "I know how to use the looms, but if I'm going to be instructing and helping, I have to know with what."

Crystal shrugged. "I thought we'd just offer them patterns that went with the different kinds of looms and let them pick what they want."

Wanda assumed her teapot pose. "Obviously you aren't a teacher. You have to have structure, a plan for how you're going to direct the workshop. We should tell them what to make." Crystal blanched at the criticism.

I wasn't an expert with the looms or really any yarn craft, but I had spent time as a substitute teacher, and I knew what Wanda was saying was true, but I didn't want to alienate Crystal.

"Isn't the point of the workshops to teach the group how to use the looms and then guide them through their projects?" I said. The two of them agreed. "I know one of the reasons the looms seemed like a good idea is that it's quick to make projects, which means the group ought to be able to make a number of them during the retreat. What about this for a plan: after you teach them the basics of how to use the looms, have everybody make one of these using the circular looms." I picked up a plain navy blue beanie. "Then have them make something like this." I draped a thick scarf over my arm. "And after that they can make whatever they choose."

I think because I suggested it rather than Wanda, Crystal saw the point of telling the group what to make and having them all doing the same thing at the same time. "Okay," she said, "but we have to give them some freedom of choice. Who wants to see them all making their hats in the same color? It'll look like a factory instead of an expression of their creativity. I'll go along with having the whole group make the same first two projects, but we have to let them be able to pick their own yarn."

I looked to Wanda to see if she would agree. "It's your retreat, so if that's what you want," Wanda said with a shrug.

"It seems like a compromise," I said. "I'm not very good at imposing my will, and I'd rather we all agree. I do better when I get everyone on my side. That's what I did when I was a teacher."

"All right," Wanda said finally. "And as for the tote bags — I would suggest stuffing them with the folders like you have in the past. They can get a schedule, basic instructions for the looms and probably something about Butterfly Week this time. Maybe put in some yarn. Then we'll hand out the looms at the first workshop. They can just carry around the one they're working on and leave the rest in the meeting room. At the end of the retreat, they can take their whole set with them. By then it will be their problem, not yours."

I looked to Crystal, who rocked her head back and forth in a semblance of agreement.

"We'll deal with the people who fuss about using the looms when we get to it," Wanda added.

"What?" I said. I had expected the group to love the whole idea of using the looms.

"Knitting purists might not be so happy,"

Wanda said. "It doesn't have the same grace as knitting with needles. And the novices still have to learn how to do something."

Crystal didn't seem happy with the comment. "Wanda, you'll see. It will be fine."

With that settled, we started to talk about Butterfly Week. This time I had planned a longer retreat and had arranged for my retreaters to take part in all the town's activities.

"Did I tell you that Marcy is in the running for Butterfly Queen?" Crystal asked. Marcy was her daughter, and I still had a hard time realizing that the free spirit had teenage kids. She went on for a few minutes about how she'd been in the Princess Court one year. "It was pointless," Crystal said. "I knew there was a committee, but that woman ran the show, and I'm sure she really picked who she wanted to be queen. What is she doing here now?"

Both Wanda and I followed Crystal's gaze into the main room to see who she was talking about. I recognized the woman from the chili dinner as she went by.

"Rosalie Hardcastle," Wanda said. "She likes to think she's a big mover and shaker in town. My sister is in the Princess Court, too. I better go and say hello to Rosalie. Then it's off to the football game with the rest of the town. Go Monarchs." Crystal and I watched as Wanda went up to the woman and really laid it on thick.

"If she thinks that's going to help her sister, she's crazy," Crystal said, clearly perturbed — maybe because she hadn't come up with the idea first. Rosalie gave Wanda a haughty smile in response to her greeting, then Wanda sailed out the door.

I noticed that Gwen's brow seemed even more furrowed as Rosalie pulled her aside, taking her away from the customer she was helping.

"What does she want with my mother?" Crystal said. I was surprised at her tone. Crystal always seemed like a free spirit type who kind of rolled with the punches. But then, I supposed she was protective of her mother. I knew that Crystal had come back to town with her two kids when her rock musician husband had taken off with a younger woman and left her stranded. Gwen had taken them in with no question, even though her house was small and money was tight.

"It doesn't seem like good news," I said as I got a better look at Gwen's expression. Rosalie was a pretty woman, probably somewhere in her late forties. But by now her personality was catching up with her looks, and I noticed a harshness about her expression. "But maybe that's just the way she always looks," I said. "That's pretty much the expression she had when she said thank you for the muffins."

"She appeared a little softer when she came out of the kitchen last night so the team could thank her," Crystal said. "Kory is such a good kid. He's the one who said they should give her a 'Hip hip hooray' for the chili."

I thought of the dark-haired gangly boy. "I just can't get used to the idea that you have a sixteen-year-old son who is taller than you."

Crystal smiled. "I got an early start. I would say it was a big mistake running off with a musician, but I wouldn't trade my kids for anything. Rixx doesn't know what he's missing." Every time I heard her ex's name all I could think was how pretentious it was.

"You probably don't know this, but Rosalie has an inflated view of herself," Crystal continued. "She's really a piece of work. She was Butterfly Queen three times and even tried to get the town council to make it a permanent position for her." Crystal rolled her eyes. "She made the chili dinner a tradition when her kids were in high school and her son was on the team. Some-one suggested changing it to maybe a spaghetti dinner or having someone else make the chili, but no, it has to be her secret recipe, and she always has to make it the morning of, in the community room, with no one around." Crystal laughed. "It's no wonder she didn't appreciate your corn muffins. She acted like they were some kind of invaders. I'm sure she would have conveniently managed to drop them into the trash and not served them, except I showed them off to the other parents before she had a chance. We put them out on the tables."

Rosalie finally left, and Crystal looked at the wall clock. "The game is about to start. I have to go."

"Go Monarchs," I called after her.

By the time I went outside, the street was much quieter. It seemed the whole town was going to the game, except me. I could only make my town spirit go so far, and I had bags to put together.

A police cruiser pulled up behind my car, and an officer got out as things began to topple out of the tote bag again. "Need some help?"

Before I could say yes, Dane Mangano stuck his foot in a round loom that had started to roll down the street. He hopped

30

on one foot as he reached forward to pick it up. Dane was my neighbor and a Cadbury PD officer. Really he was more, though I kept trying to fight the feeling. There was definitely a spark between us, which he seemed anxious to pursue, but I had put the brakes on. I didn't have a good track record of sticking with places or people, and even though I seemed to be settling into Cadbury and my aunt's business, I couldn't predict the future. So why start something? And if I were to stay, it could turn out even worse. What if we dated and broke up? I was still an outsider, and he was a town hero.

"Why aren't you going to the game?" I said as he took the bag from me and managed to fit the loom pieces all back in. He set it down on the floor of the front seat and waited until it settled.

"Somebody has to protect the streets of Cadbury," he said with less than his usual enthusiasm. I knew the truth was that Dane had gotten in trouble with his superiors because he'd helped me in the past, and as a result was now working every holiday and the worst shifts the rest of the time.

"I'm sorry," I said. Dane shrugged and gave my shoulder a quick squeeze. "It was worth it. But you've got to give me another chance."

He was referring to our attempts at a date. There had been two, and neither had turned out well. The first time, we'd gotten the business from the locals sitting around us. I blushed thinking of all their comments about what a cute couple we were and how when we got married would I make my own wedding cake. The next time we tried going to a tourist trap out of town, where we were sure not to meet anyone who knew us. That part of it had worked out, but someone had choked on a hunk of chicken. Dane had jumped into action and gotten the chicken piece out. I won't go into gory details, but it was a lot more messy than the typical Heimlich maneuver. The guy's wife fainted, a bunch of EMTs showed up and the restaurant was closing, so we ended up getting our dinner to go and eating in his truck. So much for a romantic evening.

Dane was much more than a pretty face. He practically oozed character. When his father had disappeared, leaving him and his sister with an alcoholic mother, Dane had taken care of the family. I'd heard he did a good job pretending to be a bad boy, but he was also the one who took his sister shopping for her first bra.

Growing up that way could have left him

angry and bitter, but instead he really did want to keep the streets of Cadbury safe. He knew bored teenagers were likely to get into trouble, so he converted his garage into a karate studio and gave the kids lessons and let them hang out. On top of that, he fed them copious amounts of spaghetti with sauce so delicious my mouth watered at the thought of it. He fed me, too.

While I might excel at dessert, I sucked when it came to regular food and mostly ate frozen entrées. But the relationship wasn't all take on my part. I left him muffins and cookies a lot of the time.

It was probably because he was such a great guy that I held back even more. I had tried to explain my hesitation to him, and his answer floored me. He actually said he'd gladly have his heart broken if it meant he'd be able to spend time with me. Was he sure he was talking about me?

I apologized again. I knew some of the kids who hung out at his place were on the football team, and I was sure he wanted to cheer them on.

"It's okay," he said, not sounding too convincing. "I have more things on my mind." He looked up and down the street. There didn't seem to be any need of his services, and he continued. "Chloe lost that job at the diner in Gilroy and everything that went with it — including her own place."

"So she's back staying with you?" I asked. He nodded.

Chloe was Dane's sister and kind of a wild child, the type of woman my mother would have described as hard. She dressed to show off as much skin as possible and had hair that looked like she used crayons to color it, and though Dane had never said anything about it, I had the feeling she wasn't too picky about who she went home with. I didn't mean to be judgmental, but she was somebody I couldn't understand at all.

"If only that was all there was," he said. "She's decided that she wants to be Butterfly Queen. She's in the Princess Court."

"Then she made it into the finals?" I said, surprised.

"It doesn't work that way. Anyone can get into the Princess Court. All they need is a sponsor. I wish she had talked to me first." He sounded dejected. "She went straight to the owner of the beauty supply store. Apparently, she's a big customer." Dane rolled his eyes as he gestured toward his hair. "I guess it's nice that she got something out of buying all that hair dye." Dane rested his hands on his equipment belt as he checked the street again for criminal activity, but there was just an old man walking a beagle. I guess the only chance he'd do something requiring Dane's attention was if he didn't pick up after his dog.

"She's really into this princess thing. She told me she thinks it's going to open some doors for her. She won't listen to me. Maybe you could help her pick out something to wear that looks like a princess for the event tomorrow night?"

"You're kidding, right?" I said, and he let out a weary sigh. I'm sure he knew that Chloe wouldn't listen to me, either.

"I just hope there isn't any trouble," he said.

2

Sunday morning I awoke to the phone ringing. Julius jumped off the bed at the sound.
Did he know it was the dreaded Sunday
morning call from my mother? It was all
her doing, but she had decided that instead
of her random phone calls during the week,
we should make it every Sunday instead.
My mother was a cardiologist, but somehow
she couldn't seem to understand the time
difference between her in Chicago and me
on the tip of the Monterey Peninsula in
California. Or maybe it was just her way of
trying to force me to get up earlier.

I didn't really mind the early wake-up
today, because the first of my retreaters were
arriving this morning. Scott, Bree and Olivia
had been with me from my first retreat and
had come to every one since. By now they
felt more like friends, particularly since they
were always looking to help me out. They
had started coming a day or so early to have

their own pre-retreat, and I'd come to call them the early birds.

I got the phone on the fifth ring. "Hello, Mother," I said, trying to banish the sleepy sound from my voice.

"I didn't wake you, did I?" she asked. She always said that, and I always denied it. Why, I don't know. What was wrong with being asleep on a Sunday morning at eight o'clock? I knew what was coming next. It was to my mother's great disappointment that I wasn't a professional something. To her, that meant having some kind of degree or certificate. So it didn't matter that I was being paid to bake desserts at the Blue Door and my muffins were sold at a number of coffee spots around town, or that I had successfully resolved some local murders without some piece of paper to prove I was proficient.

She had offered to send me to cooking school in Paris, and actually had the whole thing still set up, just waiting for me to agree. My mother was sure she knew me better than I knew myself, and she thought that the whole Cadbury experiment, as she called it, would never last.

"There's a new term starting," my mother said in a cajoling voice. "The City of Lights, cafés, the Eiffel Tower — and you'd have a certificate from the finest French cooking school!" She went right from there to the Private Investigator Institute in Los Angeles and how the application she had put in for me was still active. "They give me a call about once a week and say they're looking forward to you starting the program. Wouldn't it be nice to have a real license?"

I decided to take a new tack, simply not responding to what she said. I'd change the subject to talk about what I wanted just like politicians did.

"The retreat I'm putting on this week is going to be different than the others. I'm including all the events going on in town. It's the biggest week of the year here, with the return of the monarch butterflies." I could almost hear my mother groan.

"You mean like the swallows' return to Capistrano?" she said in an unimpressed voice.

"I don't know what they do for the swallows, but the return of the butterflies is a big deal here. There are events all week and then a parade on Sunday when the Butterfly Queen is announced."

"How quaint and small town," my mother said. "Casey, you're wasting your talents staying there. I know you think you're honoring your father's sister's memory by going on with these retreats, but really, you should be thinking of the future."

I figured I could distract her by bringing up some kind of conflict, and so I mentioned Rosalie Hardcastle and how I'd heard she'd wanted to make being Butterfly Queen a lifetime position — well, for her, anyway — and that now she was one of the judges. I mentioned that Dane's sister was in the running, knowing my mother had seen her primary-color hair when my parents made their surprise visit to Cadbury. I waited, expecting some kind of firecracker response, at least about Dane's sister and her suitability to be queen.

But my mother pulled the same trick I did and simply ignored what I said and changed the subject. By then I was tuning out what she was saying, and all I heard was something about giving her regards to someone.

It was only after we hung up that I realized she hadn't offered me her usual line about being a doctor, a wife and a mother when she was my age. By the way, I think my mother would have given up the offers of cooking school and the detective academy if I'd added Mrs. to my name. Well, maybe not Mrs. Just Anybody. I think she was still hoping I'd somehow resume my relationship with Dr. Sammy, but that was a whole other story.

A short time later I was dressed in comfortable black jeans and a black-and-white-striped sweater under a red fleece jacket and on my way out the door, as Julius watched from the kitchen counter. I wished he would stay inside and not go wandering across to Vista Del Mar, where he was a very unwelcome guest, but I think he knew he annoyed the manager and got some kind of perverse cat pleasure out of it. Julius had made it clear he was his own cat and it was useless to try to restrict him.

As soon as I crossed the street and started down the driveway of the hotel and conference center, the scenery changed. My street was on the edge of town and pretty rustic — no sidewalks, streetlights or well-manicured front lawns. The front yards around me had either ivy or native plants, which was the politically correct term for weeds.

But Vista Del Mar took wild to a whole new level. The hotel and conference center were spread over about one hundred acres of gentle slopes with narrow roadways running through them. The grounds were allowed to grow completely as they willed. If one of the lanky Monterey pines fell down, it was left where it was to decompose. It was rumored that the same was true if a deer or raccoon bit the dust on the grounds. As a result, I never looked into the brush grasses too closely.

The color of the tall grasses ranged from a brownish green to a full-out golden toast. The only spot of real green was an area appropriately called the grass circle. The buildings were mostly over one hundred years old and, with their weathered wood shingles, had a moody look. Vista Del Mar had started out as a camp and was a run-down resort when Edmund Delacorte had bought it. He'd restored the place to its original state with great care.

This was not a place with fluffy towels and sheets with high thread counts, or any of those kinds of luxuries. The guest rooms were spartan to say the least. We're talking narrow beds that were almost like cots, bathrooms so tiny you could barely turn around in them and no phones or TV. The only amenity was a clock radio. The rooms were in two-story buildings that were spread around the grounds, and each had a cozy lobby with comfy chairs and a fireplace. Single-story buildings with the meeting rooms I used for my retreats were spread around the grounds as well.

I walked down the driveway to what I considered the heart of Vista Del Mar. The Lodge was located in the center of the grounds, and the building was like a huge hotel lobby. Meals came with the rooms and were served in the Sea Foam dining hall, just down the way from the Lodge. A small chapel was set off to the side, near the entrance to the sand dunes. Finally, there was Hummingbird Hall, which could be set up as an auditorium or a ballroom.

I was sure Edmund Delacorte would be smiling if he could see the condition of his beloved property. His sisters Cora and Madeleine owned it now, but it was run by Kevin St. John. His title was manager, but to me he seemed more like the lord of the place.

Edmund would definitely approve of the refurbishing that had been done, as everything was kept to the original style. So in a certain way, walking into Vista Del Mar was like stepping back in time. What made it seem even more so was Kevin St. John's decision to go unplugged, meaning there was no Wi-Fi, cell reception or even TV. Communication was limited to landline phones housed in vintage phone booths at the front of the Lodge and a big message board outside the gift shop.

It was going to be less of an issue for my retreaters this time, as we were going to be leaving the grounds for activities in town. They would be able to get cell phone reception in town, and some of the coffee places had Wi-Fi. I supposed my retreaters would be happier this way, though I'd noticed that by the end of the past retreats, my group had realized the benefits of being unplugged.

All the moisture in the air seemed to absorb noise, and I barely heard the waves though the beach was close by. I saw a group of guests gathered for a nature hike move toward the entrance of the sand dunes.

As I passed one of the small parking areas, I noticed that most of it was taken up by something covered with a tarp, which I assumed was what I had seen being pulled in the previous day. Parking was at a premium because Vista Del Mar had been built without cars in mind. Curious what it was, I stopped and lifted the blue plastic to see what could be so important that it was allowed to take up so much space. It seemed to be a platform with a bunch of stuff piled up in the middle. The sides were painted white with something sparkly mixed in, and there were some decorations stuck to the sides. When I lifted the tarp high enough to let more light in, I saw the decorations were paper monarch butterflies that looked like they needed some refurbishing. And then I got it. I knew one of the big events during the coming week was the choosing of the Butterfly Queen, and this must be her float for the big parade on Sunday.

I covered it up carefully and continued on my way to the Lodge. I had arranged to meet Liz Buckley there. She was the local travel agent, and she had gotten me two new people for this retreat. It was the first time she'd sent any business my way.

I heard the echo of voices when I walked into the Lodge. I would call the cavernous room inviting, but it was hardly cozy with its high ceiling and open framework. Someone was shooting pool in the back of the room. The door to the gift shop was open, and there were several customers. At the other end, the door to the Cora and Madeleine Delacorte Café was open, and the smell of fresh-brewed coffee spilled out.

Kevin St. John was standing with Liz Buckley near the massive wooden registration counter. He wore his usual dark suit, white shirt and conservative tie, which made him look more like an undertaker than the manager of this rustic resort. Even though it was Sunday, Liz was in her usual business attire of dark slacks, white shirt and a blazer. Today's was camel colored. I couldn't make out their conversation, as they were speaking in low tones. They heard my footsteps on the polished wood floor and looked up.

"Good morning," I said in my best upbeat voice. Kevin, who never seemed particularly pleased to see me, grunted a greeting.

"Hey, Casey," Liz said with a friendly smile. "Ready to take care of business?"

The arrangement for Liz's people was a little different than for my other retreaters. She had been helping a foreign travel agent with arrangements for two of their clients, who were looking for a different experience. "I really hope this works out. It could be beneficial to both of us." She handed me a manila envelope. "This has their information, and the check is in there, too."

"On my end, I have rooms lined up for them and everything they'll need for the retreat." I avoided looking at Kevin as I spoke. Personally, I would have preferred to handle the transaction in her office in downtown Cadbury, away from the manager's critical eye, but she had wanted to do it this way.

I noticed that her smile faded, and it was like she was suddenly under a dark cloud. I assumed she was worried about the two re-treaters.

"Don't worry, your people are going to have a unique experience," I said, trying to reassure her.

"I hope you're right. The last thing I want to hear is anybody asking for refunds."

"You and me both," I said.

"Well, I better go. We have a lot of setting up to do." When I seemed perplexed, she continued. "The Butterfly Week committee is having their kickoff event here tonight."

"Then you're on the committee who picks the Butterfly Queen?" I said.

She shook her head. "No, we're responsible for all the events of the week. The Butterfly Queen committee is separate. I wouldn't want to be on it, since Rosalie Hardcastle has basically taken it over. Somebody needs to remind her that it's just a small-town event and we're not crowning somebody who is going to run a country." Liz let out a sigh. "Well, I have things to do. We'll be in touch."

She'd barely reached the door when Kevin St. John started castigating me.

"Ms. Feldstein, I can't believe your insensitivity. All you care about is your retreats. You could have at least offered her your sympathy before she started going on about your business." He went back and forth between calling me Casey and Ms. Feldstein. When he used my last name, it was usually for some kind of rebuke, like now. I had tried calling him Kevin once, and he'd made it clear that was never acceptable. So, now even in my mind he was Kevin St. John. I didn't mean to sound like a victim, but the man didn't like me.

All I could say was, "Huh?"

"The game," he said, as if he was trying to jog my memory. Apparently, he read my blank expression. "Then you didn't go." He shook his head in disapproval. "I see. You didn't even have enough town spirit to go to the most important game of the year. Or even to find out the outcome."

"I don't know what you mean about not having town spirit. I brought muffins for the chili dinner the night before. But from your comment, I'm guessing that the game didn't go well," I said.

"It was a crushing loss for the team. The two star players came down with something the morning of the game and couldn't play. Maybe it was from the muffins you brought," he said.

I wasn't going to waste time defending my muffins when I knew there was no way they would have made anyone sick, but I was still a little baffled by why he thought I should offer my sympathy to Liz. "I didn't know that Liz was such a fan."

Kevin made a tsk-ing sound of disbelief. "You really are out of the loop. Her husband is the coach of the team."

I had always heard of him referred to as only Coach Gary and had never wondered about his last name. "Now it makes sense why she seemed upset." I glanced toward the window that looked out on the wood deck. Liz had already picked up a box that seemed to have decorations and was heading down the stairs. I considered going after her to offer my condolences about the game, but it felt fake to me. The whole importance of the football game escaped me. In fact, the importance of *sports* escaped me.

"I suppose you have an opinion about Rosalie Hardcastle?" I said. It was only since the chili dinner that she had been on my radar.

I heard Kevin choke on a laugh, as if I'd just said the most ridiculous thing. "You won't get any gossip from me. Except I bet she thinks it was your muffins, too."

I was relieved when he finally walked away and went out the door. I saw his golf cart drive off and figured he was probably doing surveillance of the grounds. My fingers were crossed that he would not find Julius wandering around. The cat was not a welcome visitor to the resort. I opened the envelope Liz had given me. As she had said, there was an information sheet for each of the women. I noticed that they were Danish and seemed to like yarn. The check was in another envelope. I looked at the amount and let out a sigh. Both travel agents had taken a commission, and what was left was just enough to cover the women's rooms and the retreat materials. There was nothing left for my profit. I'd have to figure something out if Liz continued to feed me retreaters. I went up to the desk to talk to the young woman behind it. I was over at Vista Del Mar all the time and knew all the clerks. I wasn't great with names though, so I usually knew them by an identifying feature. This woman always wore her hair in elaborate braids.

"This check is made out to me, but it's for two of my retreaters," I told her. "Could I sign it over to Vista Del Mar and have you deduct the cost of their rooms and give me in the difference in cash?"

"We don't usually do things like that, but I'm sure it would be okay this once." She took the check and handed me some cash.

"It looks like some of your people are here," she said, gesturing toward the window that faced the driveway. The airport shuttle was just pulling in.

I'd barely reached the door when it flew open and my three early birds burst into the Lodge. Scott Lipton, Bree Meyers and Olivia Golden had come to my very first retreat and the ones after. Not only had we become friends, but they were helpers besides. Bree rushed to give me a hug. She still looked very much the busy mom. She had a fluff of blond hair that didn't seem to require much attention. Her soft blue jeans and hoodie sweatshirt seemed like they were probably her daily uniform. The adjustment of going unplugged had been hardest on her. She was accustomed to texting, talking, e-mailing and updating her Facebook status constantly. But she had adjusted and eventually even seen the benefit, and she helped when other retreaters went through electronic withdrawal. Scott looked every bit the clean-cut business type, and if he hadn't had some yarn and needles sticking out of his soft-sided briefcase, I doubt anyone would have guessed he was a knitter. He'd told me that the retreats had been the first time he'd felt free to knit in public, and now he helped anyone who showed an interest in the craft. And I was so happy to see Olivia, whose almond-shaped face had a glow of happiness. She'd come a long way from the angry person who'd attended the first retreat.

She was bubbling over, wanting to tell me about the new chapter she'd started in her life. I only heard enough to gather that she had met someone new.

The four of us went back to the massive registration desk. I was glad that Kevin St. John was still making his rounds. The clerk with the braids had no problem letting them check into their rooms early.

Once they had their keys, they left their bags in the corner of the Lodge and we headed toward the Cora and Madeleine Delacorte Café. It had been opened recently and was a great addition to the place. It mirrored the gift shop on the other end of the Lodge, and its walls were mostly windows looking out onto the grounds.

It was early in the day, and they were still putting out stock.

"Hey, Casey," a young man's voice said. All I saw was some curly black hair above the top of a box. A moment later, he looked around the side, and I saw that it was Kory Smith, Crystal's son.

"What are you doing here?" I asked. He

51

set the box down on the counter and began to take out small bags of potato chips and attach them to a metal thing with clips.

"I'm working here now." He glanced toward the wall of windows and out to the grounds. "I love this place."

Crystal was the kind of mother who was friends with her kids, and as a result neither Kory nor his sister Marcy seemed to have that teen idea that adults were the enemy.

I'd made my mistake about the game with Liz, and I wasn't going to repeat it with Kory. "You're on the football team, aren't you?" I said, getting ready to tell him how sorry I was about the loss.

"Yes, I'm a proud Monarch, even if yesterday was a disaster." He finished with the potato chips and began to flatten the box.

"I'm so sorry about the loss," I said. I might have overdone the somber tone, because he gave me a strange look. I thought about what Kevin had said. "I heard a couple of the players got sick."

He nodded. "They spent the whole day locked in the bathroom."

"You don't happen to know why?" I asked.

He shrugged it off. "Somebody said maybe it was something they ate. I don't know about that — I was sitting right next to them, and the coach brought chili to all of us." The man behind the counter gave Kory a look, and the teen snapped to attention. "I'd love to chat, but there are apples and bananas to be put in a basket."

He sounded so genuinely happy to be working at Vista Del Mar, it made me smile. Considering what I had figured out — that Edmund Delacorte was his real great grandfather — it made sense. I so wished I could tell him. But if I decided to ignore Frank's advice, I had to tell Kory's grandmother, Gwen Selwyn, first, since it all really started with her.

3

"What's going on?" Bree said, looking around the Sea Foam dining hall as the three early birds and I walked in. They had spent the afternoon enjoying the surroundings, and we'd agreed to meet for dinner. The large space was usually filled with sizable round tables available to all the guests, but this time a portion of it near the massive stone fireplace had been set aside. A banner announcing Butterfly Week hung across the fireplace, and a podium was set up in front of it. All the tables had centerpieces of big bobbing orange and black monarchs.

I looked around, hoping to find a table far away from the proceedings, but the other side of the room had been closed off, since Sunday night was the slowest night for guests at Vista Del Mar. The weekend people had checked out, and those coming for the week generally arrived on Monday.

I finally steered our group toward a table near the windows, but I quickly realized there was no way not to be part of what was going on. Kevin St. John was at the microphone, tapping it to see if it was working, while others were filing in and taking their seats at the round tables in the special section.

I suggested to the group that it might be a good time to get our food, before the line was flooded with the special guests. I let the three of them go first and then followed them to the back of the room. The food was served cafeteria-style through an open space from the kitchen. It wasn't haute cuisine but was always tasty and filling. There were some trays of appetizers sitting on the counter. The woman from the kitchen saw me checking them out. "Those are for the special event," she said, rolling her eyes. I moved down and looked over the counter to the trays of hot food. The early birds had gotten their plates and were already heading back to our table. There was no line yet, so I took my time choosing between the options. Did I want stuffed chicken breast, mashed potatoes and mixed vegetables, or did I want the slices of beef with roasted potatoes and mixed vegetables? Really what I would have liked was some of Dane's spaghetti. I was thinking about the garlicky sauce and wondered if there was any chance he would have left a plate of it at my door.

"I found something that explains what happened," a woman's voice said behind me. I snapped out of my daydream, realizing I wasn't alone in the line anymore and that I'd better get moving.

"What do you want?" a man asked. She must have been having the same dilemma I was, because she said she'd have to think about it. I quickly told the server that I'd take the chicken. When I looked back, I saw Rosalie Hardcastle in line with a man with light hair. I had heard nothing but bad stuff about her lately, so I took my food and left the area quickly.

When I got back to the table, Kevin St. John was speaking. It hadn't occurred to me until then, but he was obviously on the Butterfly Week committee. I mostly tuned out what he said. It seemed to be about how the yearly celebration always started with a dinner at Vista Del Mar, and then he suggested that everyone get their food before the program began.

"I'm glad we beat the rush," I said to Bree, Olivia and Scott. A moment later Lucinda Thornkill came up to the table and pulled out a chair.

"I'm sorry I'm late," she said. "Even with the Blue Door closed tonight there was just so much to do." She poured herself a glass of iced tea. "Tag dropped me off." She gestured toward the back of the room as Tag walked away from the kitchen area. It was hard to miss his thick brown hair — it didn't quite go with a man of his age. "I don't know what's bothering him. I've asked him if he's worried about something, and he keeps saying no."

Tag was Lucinda's husband, and together they owned the Blue Door restaurant. I suppose you could say they were my bosses, since I baked the restaurant's desserts. Even though they were both in their fifties, they were almost newlyweds. The back of the Blue Door's menu chronicled the romantic story of their relationship: how they'd been high school sweethearts who'd gone separate ways, and then years later, when he was a widower and she was divorced, had reconnected and gotten their chance at happily ever after and fulfilling their dream of moving to a small town and owning a restaurant. The only fly in the ointment was that Tag had changed a bit since high school. He'd gotten a lot fussier about details.

But Lucinda took it all in her stride, at least most of the time. She was grateful to get away for a few days with the yarn retreats, even if it was only by a few miles.

Maybe because we were both considered outsiders by the locals, we'd become friends. Our ages and style differences were no problem. She was always perfectly put together — I was sure she put on lipstick before she got the mail. Her clothes were strictly designer, with classic lines that never went out of style, like her Ralph Lauren coat that reminded me of a Native American blanket, which she had hung on the back of her chair.

Lucinda looked at the long line for food and said she'd wait.

I'd brought a tote bag with a small round and a small long loom, the tools that went with them and some yarn. I set them on the table for the early birds and Lucinda to look at. I was wishing I was better able to explain how to use them.

"Look, there's Crystal," Lucinda said. "And Wanda, too." I saw the two women carrying plates of food and waved them over.

After all the hellos, my two teachers noticed the looms on the table. Crystal set down her plate and picked up the small round loom. The three early birds and Lucinda seemed a little dubious. "What hap-

pened to good old-fashioned knitting?"
Olivia said.

"You'll love it once you get the hang of
it," Crystal said, beginning to wind yarn
around the pegs. "This is the basic way you
cast on. I love the specialty looms for socks."
She stopped and lifted her pants legs, showing off her handmade socks, which of course
didn't match.

Not one to be left out, Wanda picked up
the long loom and demonstrated a different
kind of casting on. "The looms will be use-
ful for the non-knitters."

"Are you two here for the festivities?" Lucinda asked.

"I came because the yarn store is part of
the celebration. We're hosting butterfly
crocheting," Crystal said. "And my daughter, Marcy, is in the Princess Court."

I mentioned seeing her son, Kory, and
how much he seemed to like his job at Vista
Del Mar. I was still trying to get used to the
fact that she was the mother of such old
children when she looked so young herself.

"My sister, Angelina, is one of the Butterfly Princesses, and I came to see her get her
crown," Wanda said. Wanda's sister was
much younger than she was, and though
they had similar features, they had somehow
come out differently on Angelina. Wanda on

her best day was handsome, but her sister was a beauty all the time.

"Who picks the princesses?" Bree asked.

"They pick themselves. That's why there are so many of them," Wanda said, pointing at the large table where the princesses were sitting. "All they need to do is get a sponsor."

"Cadbury Yarn is sponsoring Marcy." Crystal smiled. As if there would have been any doubt.

"I got the resort where I work to sponsor Angelina," Wanda said. "All they had to do was give her a piece of paper saying they were her sponsor and make a contribution."

A tapping on the microphone got my attention. Kevin St. John was back at his spot, talking again. He droned on, introducing the assorted committees. I mostly tuned him out until he got to the Butterfly Queen committee. He introduced Cora and Madeleine Delacorte as the heads of the committee, and they waved at the crowd, but Rosalie Hardcastle popped out of her seat and took a bow.

She was on her way to the podium with a box she'd grabbed off her table before Kevin could even point to where the princesses were sitting. I noticed that she wore a crown that had jeweled butterflies along the top. She did have a regal way of carrying herself. Or maybe that was the only way she could keep the crown from falling off.

"Kevin, I'll take over now," Rosalie said. "We really need to get on with things." I'm not sure he would have relinquished the microphone if she hadn't simply taken it and moved it closer to her. He stood there for a moment as if he didn't know what to do, then he finally returned to his seat. I had never seen him bested before, and it was pretty clear he didn't like it.

"Before I introduce the court and give them their princess crowns, I want to talk about the kind of person the committee wants as queen. As a three-time former queen myself, I know the importance of the job. One of you will be the guardian of the butterflies." Rosalie began to tell stories about her time as Butterfly Queen and how she had made appearances at the history museum for a whole year, teaching school children about the butterfly's life cycle.

She segued from there into talking about her family. "Hank and I are finally stepping into the prominent place in town where we belong," she said with a haughty expression.

"What's that about?" Wanda said.

Crystal shrugged. "I heard they made a

donation to the natural history museum. She's always envied the Delacortes' position in town, so maybe she supposes having a Hardcastle Pavilion at the museum will make her just as important."

"Pavilion?" I asked, thinking of the small museum.

"She calls it a Pavilion; the rest of us call it an exhibit."

At the podium, Rosalie was finally wrapping things up. "I'm sorry to have gotten off the subject, but you all must know how much I care for Cadbury by the Sea. Now, to give the princesses their crowns." She held a tiara up.

"Your chili lost us the game," someone shouted out. Rosalie's head shot up, and she seemed annoyed.

A man from the table in front rushed up and took over the microphone. "That's just wrong. As coach of the Monarchs, I'm as upset as the next guy that we lost the game, maybe more upset, but there is no point looking for a scapegoat. I'm sure Rosalie's chili was just fine. The boys probably just caught a stomach bug."

I leaned over to Crystal. "Is that Coach Gary?" I whispered, and she nodded. I'd heard the name before but never had a face to connect it to. With his angular face, strong jaw and powerful build, he looked just like what I'd expect a football coach to look like. He was very good-looking, with sparkling blue eyes and strawberry blond hair cut in a traditional neatly trimmed style.

"In my first official duty as Lord of the Butterflies," Coach Gary said, "I'm urging you all to let go of the loss and focus on the upcoming week."

He pushed the microphone back in Rosalie's direction. "I agree with Coach Gary about moving on, and I am sure, without a doubt, that it was not my chili. Of course, I can't be that sure about the corn muffins that were brought in," she said.

There was a rumble of conversation, and I saw a number of people looking my way. Once I got over my shock at what she'd said, I wanted to get up and defend myself, but Lucinda was faster. She rushed up to the podium, flashed her eyes at the former Butterfly Queen and pulled the microphone over. "That's ridiculous. Casey Feldstein makes all our desserts at the Blue Door, and they are just fine."

Another familiar face came out of the crowd and joined Lucinda at the microphone. "In case any of you don't know, I'm Maggie, owner of the Coffee Shop. We sell Casey's muffins, and they're always delicious." She looked over at me and gave me a thumbs-up.

"We'll see about that," Rosalie said, returning to her position at center stage. "Now if we can get back to the business at hand, I'd like to distribute the crowns."

Lucinda had returned to our table, and I leaned in close and thanked her for defending me. I noticed that her brow was furrowed.

"I might have acted too quickly. I hope I didn't make it worse." The introductions had begun. Rosalie had put on a pair of glasses and was reading from a list. "We have Marcy Smith, sponsored of course by Cadbury Yarn." Crystal's daughter went up to the podium, and Rosalie placed a tiara on her dark hair. She had not gone the way of her mother and was dressed in a demure pink dress. There was a round of applause for her, and I saw that her grandmother, Gwen, was clapping loudly near the door. But when I looked again, she'd gone.

Wanda's sister, Angelina, wore a similar-style dress in lavender linen and smiled when she got the tiara. Something about the whole princess thing seemed like a throwback in time. Rosalie kept announcing names and placing crowns on heads, and then finally she said, "Chloe Mangano?"

She looked around the room.

At the sound of her name, Chloe stood and started to walk to the podium. A gasp went through the crowd. I think it was the electric blue hair. Personally, I thought it was better than the cherry red shade it used to be. There was no demure sheath dress for Chloe. I'm sure her brother, Dane, would be cringing if he was here. She wore a micro miniskirt made out of leather and a midriff-baring top. Her lips were done in a dark wine red, and she'd gone heavy on the eye makeup. The most ridiculous part of the outfit was the leather gloves.

"Who sponsored you?" Rosalie said in an accusing voice.

"Cadbury Beauty Supply," Chloe answered, then turned to the crowd. "They appreciate my business for hair dye." A chuckle went through the crowd, but Rosalie seemed aghast.

"This isn't some kind of joke. The Butterfly Queen is a serious job, and frankly, you look all wrong for it. What do you even know about monarchs?"

Chloe pulled the neckline of her shirt down and exposed her shoulder, showing it off to Rosalie and the crowd.

"She's got a monarch tattoo," Lucinda said with a giggle. "That girl really knows how to stir this bunch up."

I glanced toward the door to see if Dane had stopped by to see his sister's big moment. He hadn't, but then he'd been pretty clear to me that he didn't approve.

He wasn't alone in that. Rosalie shook her head in disgust at the tattoo. "I'm afraid you simply aren't right to even be in the Princess Court," she said.

"That's nonsense," Chloe countered. "There is no such rule. You're just some old stodgy woman who needs to move with the times." At that, Chloe took the tiara out of Rosalie's hand and plunked it on her head.

"You have no authority to crown yourself," Rosalie said, taking it back. "As head of the Butterfly Queen committee, I say you are disqualified. And now, if you will please just leave."

I wasn't sure what Chloe was going to do. She looked like she was going to explode. Finally, she stormed off, looking back when she got to the door. She yelled something, but I couldn't quite make it out. It was either "You better watch your back" or "You bet I'll be back."

All I could think was, thank heavens Dane wasn't here.

4

"Aren't you going to the blessing of the butterflies service?" Crystal asked. Once Chloe had left, Rosalie had acted like nothing had happened and finished with her crowning, and then everybody began to leave. The early birds, Lucinda, Wanda, Crystal and I walked outside together. I said we hadn't decided and my two teachers went on ahead.

After the bright light inside, it seemed dark and mysterious out on the grounds. I looked to the group.

"We thought we'd hang out in the Lodge and play with these," Bree said, holding up the small round loom.

"You can go to the service if you want to," Lucinda said to me. "We can certainly entertain ourselves." She held up a tote bag from a past retreat and pulled out her work. "I'm making another worry doll. With the way Tag has been acting, he needs his own."

I looked to Bree, Olivia and Scott. "If you are sure you don't mind, I would like to see what it's all about."

"We'll be fine," Bree said. "The loom is kind of like something I had when I was a kid. It'll be fun to play with."

Olivia was holding the long loom. "I want to try what Wanda showed us."

"It's fine with me if you go, but I'll be sticking with my needles," Scott said, giving a disparaging glance at the loom in Olivia's hand. "I've had a hard enough time dealing with being seen with knitting needles, let alone carrying around one of those things."

When we reached the Lodge, they went in and I continued on, following the trail of people. The chapel was tucked in the corner of the main part of the grounds, almost where the sand dunes began. Like the other buildings, it was built in the Arts and Crafts style and had stones on the outside. Light streamed out through the windows and the open front and back doors. Inside, it had the same kind of open framework as the Lodge, which made the small building seem larger.

I took a seat in the back where I could see everything that was going on. The princesses were in the front row. I couldn't help but notice the one empty seat on the center aisle, probably meant for Chloe. All the committees for the upcoming week sat in the first couple of rows. Madeleine Delacorte turned around in her seat to look over the crowd. She waved when she saw me.

The doors were left open even when everybody was inside, filling the space with cool night air that was tinged with the smell of wood burning from all the fireplaces.

Liz Buckley came up to the front of the chapel and welcomed everyone. "I can't believe another year has gone by," she said, and the crowd murmured back with similar sentiments. "But here we are again, about to celebrate the wonder that the monarchs have chosen our lovely town to spend the winter. It's especially amazing because these particular butterflies have never been here before. It was their great-grandparents who left here last February, and then somehow, one generation of offspring to another, passed along a mysterious genetic code for the monarchs to find their way back to Cadbury by the Sea."

She was joined at the front by a man and woman with guitars. They began to sing. I couldn't quite make out all the words, but it seemed to be a song declaring gratitude that the monarchs chose Cadbury. After that, an assortment of clergymen stood in the front, and each offered a blessing to the returning butterflies. When they had finished, they filed out the front door and came into the back and sat in the row with me. Then the lights went off, and Liz acted as narrator, talking about the journey of the monarchs. Someone had begun to play the piano in the front. The music was supposed to reflect the butterflies' journey and grew loud and thunderous as Liz said that neither rain nor storms could deter them from their destination.

"Sounds like they're postal workers," the woman next to me said. There was a lot of shifting around going on, and I sensed people moving around the chapel.

The music got more dramatic, and Liz spoke over it. "Could there be a king or queen butterfly who leads the way? Or maybe a lord?" I heard someone come in the back door, and then something made a fluttering noise.

"Ooh look, they added LED lights to the Lord of the Butterflies," the woman next to me cooed. I saw giant butterfly wings outlined in tiny white lights. The wings fluttered, and the audience began to clap as the butterfly moved down the center aisle in the dark. The music reached a crescendo as he arrived at the front of the chapel, and the lights flicked on. By now I had figured out that Coach Gary was in the costume, although not by looking at the giant insect costume — his head and body were completely clothed in black, and he was topped with black antennas. He'd made reference to being Lord of the Butterflies at the dinner. In the front of the room, the princesses were standing up, holding cardboard trees and dancing around. Rosalie was sitting on a high stool, dressed as the sun.

The pianist played happy music, and the giant butterfly moved among the trees.

The music stopped, and everyone froze, as if waiting for something, but nothing happened.

"And now," the butterfly said as if prompting a line. Still, nothing happened, and the princesses and butterfly couldn't hold their poses anymore and began to move.

"Rosalie, did you forget your line?" the butterfly said, breaking character. The whole chapel turned toward Rosalie. She seemed to be clutching the big cardboard orange circle attached to the front of the costume. Coach Gary approached her, and I heard a gasp go through the people in the front. I stood to see what they were reacting to just as Rosalie fell off the chair. The light

71

reflected off the knife sticking out of her back.

5

Everyone reached for their cell phones, apparently having forgotten that there was no cell service anywhere on the Vista Del Mar grounds. A rumble of discontent went through the crowd, and at that moment, I think Kevin St. John regretted his decision to go unplugged. He was already on his feet, telling everyone to stay put and that he would go to the office and call for help.

The princess group was in the front. They were so stunned by what had happened, they looked like they'd gone back into freeze-frame mode.

Coach Gary slipped off his wings and bent over Rosalie to assess the situation. It only took a few minutes for the place to be overrun with sirens and flashing lights. The paramedics rushed to Rosalie and within moments had her loaded on a gurney and were taking her to the waiting rescue ambulance. A group of uniformed officers and a familiar figure in a rumpled tweed jacket were gathered at the front of the chapel. Lieutenant Borgnine took one look at me and shook his head with dismay. He said something to the others and came toward me. He gave just the slightest wince as his right hand went to his temple, like he had the beginning of a headache. I had a pretty good idea it was related to seeing me.

This wasn't my first go-round with the gruff-looking man in the rumpled sport jacket. For a long time I'd imagined that he had a whole wardrobe of jackets that looked the same, but I'd finally come to believe he had just the one. "Well, Ms. Feldstein," he said as he got close. "So once again you seemed to be connected to a crime scene."

I was still processing what had happened. It hadn't hit me until just that moment that there was no question that foul play was involved. Of course, there was no way for someone to accidentally get stabbed in the back.

"Let's not waste time. Just tell me what you know. I'm sure you must have to go off and bake your cookies."

I didn't bother to correct him. He knew very well that I baked muffins and desserts, and he'd enjoyed both.

"I was just here for the Blessing of the

Butterflies, like the rest of the crowd," I said.

I saw Dane, in uniform, out of the corner of my eye. He saw me talking to Lieutenant Borgnine and gave me a sympathetic nod. Neither Dane nor I were on the lieutenant's list of favorite people. Like most cops, Lieutenant Borgnine thought he had an extra sense that pointed to the bad guy, so when I'd found the real bad guy more than once and proven his instincts wrong, he hadn't taken it well. And Dane had gotten bad marks for helping me.

I saw Dane looking over the crowd, and I realized he was looking for Chloe. He didn't know she had never made it to the service.

Lieutenant Borgnine pulled my attention back to him. "Ms. Feldstein, if you could focus, we can get done with this. Tell me what you saw."

"The lights went off," I said with a shrug. I was thinking back to being in the darkness. "There was some dramatic music, and then the Lord of the Butterflies came down the aisle." I hadn't really noticed much more.

"What about when the lights came on?" he asked.

"I don't know. I guess I saw the princesses at the front. And then everything stopped." I shrugged again. "I stood up and saw the woman dressed as the sun fall over with a knife sticking out of her back." He didn't seem happy with my answer, and he scribbled something down. I had told him what he asked for — what I had seen, not what I thought about what I'd seen or what I knew about the victim.

"You're thinking about something," Lieutenant Borgnine said, eyeing me warily. "Out with it." It was more an order than a request.

"I've told you all I know for certain," I said, without a twinge of a guilty conscience that I was holding back information from the police. It was all I knew for sure.

The lieutenant and I seemed to be on the same page about talking to each other. It was a necessary evil, and we both wanted it over with. "Well, I think we're done for now," he said. "But, Ms. Feldstein, if you have any thoughts about anything, bring them to me. No investigating on your own, right?"

I laughed off the last part. "Investigating on my own? With all I have to do this week? I don't think so."

He looked dubious, but I actually meant it. As far as I could tell, there was no reason for me to get involved.

I beat a hasty exit and headed for the

Lodge. Inside, Lucinda, Olivia, Scott and Bree were hanging by the window, trying to see what was going on.

"What happened?" Bree said, her face drawn in worry.

"I hope Tag is all right," Lucinda said, glancing around as if she expected her husband to make a sudden appearance.

I assured Lucinda that Tag had nothing to do with what had happened, and then I gave them the details. They listened with rapt attention and then all started talking at once.

"Was Rosalie the woman at the podium?" Olivia asked. "She certainly wasn't very nice to the princess with the blue hair."

"Weren't they trying to blame her for the football team's loss?" Bree said. "My boys just started T-ball, and it's shocking how upset the parents get when the kids mess up. I suppose it's even worse when it's high school."

"You don't really think someone would try to kill her over that?" Olivia said.

"You don't understand how people are about sports," Scott said. "It was a homecoming game, and they lost to their arch rival." Scott looked at all of us to see if we understood.

"Geez, I sure hope that nobody believed her when she said my corn muffins were the problem," I said. "I could be next on somebody's hit list. And what if word spreads around town that my muffins were suspect? There goes my business."

"I'm sure you have nothing to worry about," Lucinda said, trying to reassure me. "Still, it would be good to know what made those kids sick, so the issue is settled."

Scott picked up his needles and began to knit. Since he'd come out in the open about his knitting, his skills had taken off. He was making a scarf with an intricate design of squares on an angle. He saw me admiring it and explained it was something called entrelac and offered to give me a lesson.

"Too much on my mind right now," I said, giving it a pass.

I reassured the group that everything was under control and they ought to enjoy their get-together. Even so, Lucinda went off to use one of the landlines to contact her husband.

I watched Bree use the tool that came with the looms to lift the loops over the top loop and off the peg. She had a nice rhythm going and made her way around the circle no time. She had started to wrap the next row when Lucinda returned with a relieved expression. "Tag just got home." The relief faded, and she appeared worried again.

"Something's going on with him. He barely seemed concerned when I told him what happened to Rosalie Hardcastle."

"Why don't you just ask him?" Olivia said.

"I did," Lucinda said. "And all he said was that everything is fine."

Just then, Kevin St. John began making the rounds of the room, stopping to talk to the guests that were playing table tennis, pool and board games. Finally, he got to us.

"I suppose Ms. Feldstein has already filled you in on what happened. The best thing you can do is just to carry on with your plans." His moon-shaped face appeared calm, but I had a feeling it was all a front. I asked him about Rosalie's condition. "She's in intensive care," he said, but his expression didn't look hopeful, and I guessed that he knew more.

Lucinda knew I had to go and assured me that they would be fine. I noticed they had all taken out projects they'd brought with them, and I heard the soft click of their needles as I walked away.

All this and I still had baking to do.

6

The Blue Door restaurant was located on Grand Street, in the center of Cadbury by the Sea. The streets were always quiet this late, but on a Sunday night they were deathly quiet. Banners hung from the light posts, proclaiming Butterfly Week, but there were no passersby to see them. The only place open was Cadbury Drugs & Sundries. It had a relatively new owner and had gotten special permission from the town council to stay open twenty-four hours.

The Blue Door was closed on Sunday, so I didn't have to deal with any lingering diners or the cook acting territorial about the kitchen. I unlocked the door and flipped on the lights. Like the yarn shop, the restaurant had originally been a house, and the main dining area was made up of the former living room, dining room and sunporch. The tables were all set for the next day.

The deal I had with Tag and Lucinda was

that I would make the desserts for the restaurant first, and then I was free to use the kitchen to bake the muffins I sold to the coffee places around town. I carried two recycled plastic bags holding everything for the muffins into the kitchen, put on some soft jazz and started to lay out the ingredients for carrot cakes. Since the upcoming week was all about the monarchs, I was sticking with desserts and muffins with a similar color scheme. In no time I was busy grating carrots and measuring cinnamon, lost in the sweet scents, until a rap at the door startled me.

It wasn't the first time I'd had visitors while I was baking. Everybody knew where to find me most nights. I went back through the dining area, wondering who it was this time. The door had glass on top, but since the lights were off on the long porch that ran along the building, I couldn't see anything but darkness until I was actually at the glass.

"It's me," Dane said, gesturing toward the handle with an impatient motion. I opened the door quickly and let him in. I was surprised that he was in uniform, which meant he was still on duty. After what had happened earlier, I instantly panicked, particularly when I got a good look at him.

He usually greeted me with a teasing smile. This was the first time I'd seen him look undone.

"What's the matter?" I asked, wondering if I should hug him. The uniform, with its equipment, made it seem off-limits.

"I can't stay long. Lieutenant Borgnine can't see me here, though I don't know how much worse he can make my schedule." He led me into the kitchen, where no one could see him from the street, and started to talk quickly. "Rosalie Hardcastle died, and Borgnine got an earful about some kind of fuss my sister had with Rosalie. He's declared her a person of interest, which is basically saying he thinks she did it and is just waiting to get enough evidence to arrest her. Of course, I was taken off the case." He stopped and closed his eyes and let out a sigh.

"Can you tell me what happened?" he asked. When I described the fuss Rosalie made about Chloe being in the Princess Court and that Rosalie had basically banished her, he groaned and shook his head with dismay.

"I told her it wasn't a good idea, but she wouldn't listen." He leaned against the counter. I tried to reassure him that she hadn't gone to the Blessing of the Butterflies service. But as I said it, I knew that it didn't mean anything.

Dane looked into my eyes. "My sister is a lot of things, but she's not a killer. My hands are tied, but yours aren't. You've proved Borgnine wrong before. Do you think you could find out who killed Rosalie?"

My knowledge of Rosalie was minimal at best. The only time I'd spoken to her was when I'd dropped off the muffins at the chili dinner. I got the message loud and clear. She viewed me as an outsider intruding on her territory.

"Wow. This is the first time someone's asked me to be a detective, and it's coming from a cop, no less," I said. I could see the life come back into his face, and the tilt of his head and the way he was looking at me out of the corner of his eye signaled he was back to his usual teasing manner. I was all set for a smart reply, but before he could say it, there was another rap at the door.

Dane looked stricken. It was useless to consider ignoring it — it seemed everyone in Cadbury knew I was there at night to bake.

"I'll get rid of them," I said. I walked to the door, expecting to see the bulldog-like lieutenant, and was already preparing my speech when I saw I was wrong.

83

"Sammy?" I said, opening the door. Sammy was Dr. Sammy Glickner, my ex who had relocated to Monterey. He insisted it had nothing to do with my living in the area and everything to do with his desire to further his magic career. He was also known as the Amazing Dr. Sammy. But no matter what he said, it was obvious he still had hopes for us. I think the phrase is "wears his heart on his sleeve." He was a tall teddy bear of a man, goofy and warm, and I cared for him, just not in *that way.*

"You have to help me, Case," he said frantically. He was the only one who'd ever given me that nickname, which I thought was funny since it was just dropping one letter.

Dane must have been listening from the kitchen and realized it was not Borgnine. He stepped out of the kitchen, obviously curious as to what was going on.

"It's my parents," Sammy said, pointing behind him. "I can't tell you everything now, but they're staying at the Butterfly Inn and they think we're together — living together." He had a pleading look in his eyes as I heard footsteps on the wooden porch.

"Why did you rush ahead so quickly?" Estelle Glickner said, coming into the restaurant. She seemed faintly out of breath and was followed by Dr. Bernard Glickner. He looked like an older version of Sammy, but without the fun. Both men had coarse black hair that only worked in a very short style. Sammy had let it get longer once, and it had reminded me of one of those magnet toys where you put the hair made out of iron filings on the guy's head and it stuck out. Bernard's was tinged with gray. I could see a Hawaiian shirt with white orchids on a black background under his fleece jacket, which bore the North Face logo. Estelle was a tiny woman with short fluffy graying hair who had no problem making her presence felt — kind of like a Chihuahua. She was wearing a matching women's Hawaiian shirt and similar fleece jacket. I guessed it was their vacation wear.

"See, here's Casey," Sammy said, putting on a bright smile and throwing his arm around me. "My folks want to see our place," he said. Meanwhile, they'd noticed Dane.

I must have had a deer in the headlights look. Who wouldn't under the circumstances?

"Case, I forgot my key," Sammy said, watching as his mother gave Dane the once-over.

Dane stepped forward and introduced

himself. "I live down the street from —" He faltered for a second before adding "them." He lightened the moment by smiling and saying he'd stopped by to see if I had any muffins ready. "You know us cops, always on the prowl for something sweet."

There was an awkward moment, and then Dane went to the door. "Have to keep the streets of Cadbury safe!" He caught my eye and held it for a moment before he left.

"Your mother said to say hello," Estelle said, and I wanted to groan. Now I understood my mother's comment. I'd only been half listening to her by then, and she'd said something about giving her greetings to someone. Of course, she knew Sammy's parents were coming. And I bet my mother knew what they thought was going on with Sammy and me.

I fished out the key from my purse and handed it to Sammy. He mouthed a thank-you out of his parents' sight, then made a big fuss of telling me not to work too late and that he'd be waiting up for me. He also took the opportunity to give me a warm hug and a good-bye kiss.

I heard his mother grumbling about my working so late as the three of them went to the door. "Good night, dear," she said, turning back to me. "I'm sure we'll be seeing lots of you while we're here. Sammy's dad and I want to talk to you two about something."

Sammy threw me a hopeless glance as he escorted them out the door.

I would lay down money that his parents wanted to talk wedding plans. Great, just what I needed — another complication.

Hours later, a row of carrot cakes sat iced and ready for the next day's patrons. The muffins were packed up and ready to be dropped off at the various coffee spots in town. The only life on the street was around the drugstore, and even that was quiet, with just one car parked in front of it. My footsteps echoed on the sidewalk as I made my rounds.

I dropped off the last batch of muffins at the cafe at Vista Del Mar. The Lodge stayed open all the time, and a sleepy clerk was leaning on the massive wooden registration counter. The cops seemed to have given up for the night. The chapel was cordoned off, and I imagined a tired officer was making sure no one disturbed it.

I was about to get in my car and drive across the street, and then I thought about Dane and felt bad that he'd been cut off when he was telling me about his sister and asking for my help.

I walked up the Vista Del Mar driveway and looked down the street. His lights were still on. I could see lights on at my place as well. I would deal with whatever was going on there later. Here on the edge of town, there were no streetlights, and I needed my flashlight to see my way.

Once I got outside the Vista Del Mar grounds, there was cell reception, so I called ahead to tell Dane I was coming. He had the door open before I reached the few steps up to his small porch.

He was wearing a pair of sweats and a T-shirt. "So, this is what it takes to get you to come over," he said, back to his teasing ways. We had been circling each other for a while. There was no doubt I felt attracted to him and he to me. In any case, once we'd changed our status from just friends to — well, I'm not sure what to call it — I'd avoided going to his house. It wasn't so much him I was worried about. It was me. Dane was hot on all fronts, and I was afraid I'd forget all my reasons why I thought dating was a bad idea and get in over my head.

But tonight was different. This wasn't really a social call, though I was glad to see he was back to himself.

"I'm sorry about the way things went at the Blue Door," I said. "Sammy totally

88

blindsided me. I had no idea his parents were in town and no idea that he'd told them we were living together."

"Sammy wove a real web of deceit," Dane joked. Even though Dane could have considered Sammy competition, he actually liked him. Everybody liked him. The idea of Sammy being deceitful or spinning a web of intrigue seemed funny.

"You know I would be glad to help with Chloe," I said, getting to why I'd come over. We were standing in his living room, and the couch looked very inviting after the hours of standing while I baked.

"Maybe she'll talk to you," he said. Chloe came out of the back. She was wearing the same outfit from earlier and had a defiant expression.

"Chloe, this isn't a joke," Dane said. "That woman is dead, and Lieutenant Borgnine has his sights set on you."

"That's crazy. How could anybody think I killed that old bag?" she said. She nodded a greeting at me. With all of us there, it felt okay to sit down on the couch. There was no concern there'd be any kind of cuddling.

"Go on, Casey, ask her whatever," Dane said, clearly frustrated.

"The obvious question is, where were you when Rosalie got stabbed?" I asked, hoping

89

she had a great alibi.

"I was too bummed to go anywhere," Chloe said. "I went for a walk on the beach to cool off."

"You never went anywhere near the chapel?" I asked, and her eyes flashed.

"No, I just told you. I wasn't there when she was stabbed."

"That might have come out wrong," I said. "I wasn't implying that you weren't telling me the truth. I just wondered if you might have seen something or someone."

Chloe chewed on the inside of her mouth. "Okay, maybe I did watch the whole thing from a distance for a while. I was supposed to be in there, playing a tree with the rest of the princesses."

I saw Dane do a double take. The idea of his sister doing something as hokey as playing a tree surprised him.

Chloe flopped in a chair and put her feet up on the coffee table, and I could see Dane wasn't happy with it. Since he'd brought her up, he felt responsible for any lapse in her manners. I thought she just liked to bug him, like kids do to their parents.

"I was thinking of going to the service anyway," Chloe said. "I was going to tell that Rosalie woman she had no right to throw me out. The rule is that as long as you have a sponsor you can be a princess." She wore a defiant expression. "But I changed my mind. I just watched until the princesses took their seats. I could see the empty one that was supposed to be mine through the open door in the front." Chloe's face brightened, and she sat forward. "No more fussing from that old queen. Now that she's out of the way, I'm back in the game." She pulled a tiara out of her bag and put it on her head. "I bought my own. No butterflies on it, but it will do the trick until I get back my real one."

She adjusted her feet, giving her brother a look that said she knew that what she was doing bugged him. "I should have figured that all those other goody-goody types couldn't wait to tell the cops about the argument I had with that woman."

"So then you're sure that you didn't stab her?" I said.

Chloe let out a snorty kind of laugh. "Of course not. Why would I do that?"

When I heard Dane let out his breath in relief, I realized he hadn't asked her if she'd done it. I think he was afraid of the answer. Dane stepped in. "Chloe, I told you if you insisted on going through with the princess nonsense, there was going to be trouble. If you wanted to do it, you should have changed your appearance."

"I did," Chloe said with a smile, jutting her shoulder out so we could see her monarch tattoo.

Dane shook his head in frustration. "This is serious. Do you understand that at any moment the cops can come in here and arrest you? There is nothing I can do to help you. I've been ordered to stay away from the case."

"Maybe I should head for Brazil," she said. Dane's eyes flared with anger, and she quickly added that she was just joking. "You said Casey is kind of a detective. She'll figure out a way to get me off the hook. Won't you?" She looked at me, and I nodded and said I'd do my best. "Well, there you go," she said, as if my saying it was a done deal.

"You really shouldn't try to get back in the Princess Court," Dane said.

She stood up and put her hand on her hip and looked down at her brother. "No way. I'm in it to the end." She didn't wait to see his reaction and left the room.

Dane sat shaking his head for a few moments. "She doesn't get it. It's like she's poking the town in the eye with her attitude and those clothes." He put his head in his hands. "Where did I go wrong?"

I knew he'd done the best he could and imagined how tough it must have been on both of them when he'd had to deal with all her girl stuff. I knew from both of them that he'd done embarrassing things for her. Having an alcoholic mother and an absent father can't have been easy.

I was going to try to say something reassuring, but Dane's composure changed suddenly. He sat upright and seemed to notice for the first time that we were sitting next to each other on the couch.

His lips curved into a mischievous grin. "Is this what it took to get you to finally come over and sit next to me?"

I gave him a playful punch on the arm, my way of saying I thought it was a ridiculous comment. But even so, I moved farther toward the side of the couch.

This time he laughed. "What kind of maniac do you think I am? One touch on the arm and I jump all over you?"

I didn't say anything, and his eyes lit up with a new possibility. "Maybe I'm not the problem," he said teasingly. "Maybe you're afraid that one brush against my arm and you'll be all over me."

"Nobody is going to be all over anybody," I said, getting up. "I have to go home."

"About that," Dane said. "What's going

on with Sammy and his parents? Are they all there waiting for you?"

"You heard as much as I did. Who knows what surprises are waiting for me at home."

"Maybe you need a police escort," he joked.

I passed on his offer and headed for home, not sure what to expect.

7

I drove my car from the Vista Del Mar parking lot across the street and up my driveway, where I pulled next to Sammy's BMW. I took a deep breath and headed to the back door. Julius was sitting outside waiting for me. I know it was probably my imagination, but it seemed like his yellow eyes were asking me what was going on.

I took the spare key out from under the rock near the back door. As I walked into the kitchen, Sammy came in from the other part of the house.

I looked around him, trying to size up the situation.

"It's okay, they're not here," he said. "I'm sorry, Case. They completely surprised me. They were at some medical meeting in San Francisco and decided it would be 'fun' to show up unannounced."

I took off my beige fleece jacket and then pulled out a chair. "I think you have some 'splaining to do." It was a pretty lame impression of Ricky Ricardo talking to Lucy in the old *I Love Lucy* shows, but Sammy got it and laughed.

There was a puppy dog look about his eyes when he looked at me, and I figured something big was coming.

"You know what my parents, particularly my father, think of me doing magic," he began. "I couldn't tell them I was staying in Cadbury because I was finally getting to do my act."

"It's not like you gave up your urology career," I said, and he winced.

"The practice I had in Chicago was much more prestigious than what I'm doing here. I'm just filling in for a guy who took a year off. They knew there had to be more to it than I just wanted a change, so I told them I was here with you. That we were together — living together, you know, in one house."

"I get it," I said. "And of course they shared the news with my parents."

"Just recently. I told them it was a secret, but they blabbed anyway."

I shrugged it off. "Fine. I won't say anything while they're here. How long can they be staying?"

"There's another problem," he said. "When they called me, they were already

96

checked into the Butterfly Inn. It was too weird. They were in the parlor having a glass of wine, and I answered my cell in my room just a short distance away."

Even though Sammy had been staying in Cadbury for a while, he was still living at the Butterfly Inn. The B and B had given him a large room on the main floor, which must have been a library or study in the days when the imposing Victorian was a personal residence.

"I had to arrange to meet them somewhere just so I could sneak out of the place and tell the owners not to tell them that I was living there." Sammy put his head down in worry. "You see the problem. I can't go home while they're here."

This was all getting a little intense, and I'd had a long night. I offered to make us some cocoa. I used the instant packet kind but added milk instead of water.

"Thanks," he said when I handed him a steaming mug. "By the way, my folks really liked your place."

"They did not," I said. I knew them better than he thought. "How much did you let them look around?" I thought of my bedroom and the unmade bed. Then I considered the absurdity of being upset if his mother thought I was a bad housekeeper.

"Okay, maybe what they said was it would be nice as a getaway place for a weekend. And don't worry, I kept them away from the bedroom."

There was an *and* coming, and I knew what it was. "Let's just cut to the chase. You want to know if you can stay here while your parents are in town, right?"

His whole demeanor brightened, and he reached over and hugged me. "Case, like I always say, you're the only one who gets me. See, you know what I want before I even ask."

"But it will have to be in the guest house," I said.

"Fine, great, no problem," he said, seeming seriously relieved. "They won't stay long. Probably just a day or so. They can't stay the whole week." He seemed suddenly worried again.

"I'm sure they'll be gone before the weekend," I reassured him. "And before they find out you're working as a professional magician."

"That sounds so good when you say it." His face lit up, and he hugged me again. "Case, you really are the only one who understands. If there is ever anything I can do for you . . ." He looked hopeful. "You don't even have to ask — the answer would always be yes."

I drained the cocoa and was about to suggest he go to the guest quarters when I realized he had no idea what had happened at Vista Del Mar.

I filled him in quickly, including the fact that some people were blaming Rosalie's chili for the loss of the football game. Sammy knew all about that. He was already deeply entrenched in the town and had gone to the game.

"Wow, everyone was sure bummed when those two players got sick," he said. "But stabbing Rosalie Hardcastle over it seems a little extreme. Still, small towns go crazy about their local teams."

"But could they have gotten food poisoning from her chili, or from something else they ate?" Sammy's specialty was urology, but he had to know about other medical stuff as well.

"It possibly could have been the chili if it was left out for a long time, or if some of the meat wasn't cooked enough, but most likely it would have come from some kind of contamination after it was made." He started to go through the different kinds of bacteria that could cause a problem, and I tuned out. The really troubling question was, could my muffins have been the source?

I interrupted him.

"Someone yelled out it was the corn muffins I brought."

"Oh," Sammy said. "Well, if the eggs had salmonella and the muffins weren't cooked enough that could have been it."

"They were cooked enough," I said quickly. I was upset with his answer. I wanted him to say it was impossible for the muffins to be the problem.

"Case, you know it might not have been food poisoning at all. They could have just picked up a norovirus."

"But is there a way to prove what it was?" I asked, and Sammy thought for a minute.

"If there was anything left over from the food, they could send samples to a lab." Suddenly Sammy got why I was asking. "You think someone is going to come after you next?" He adjusted himself so he was sitting taller. "Maybe it's good I'll be staying here. I'll be like your bodyguard." He glanced around. "If it would make you feel safer, I can stay in here with you."

8

It was funny — I could feel the different vibe of Monday morning even before I got out of bed. It was almost like I could hear all the shops in town opening. By now I had gotten used to the weather here. October or June — what was really the difference, other than the length of the days? It was always cool and mostly cloudy, but not the gloomy kind of clouds that showed up before it rained. In fact, for all the moisture in the air here, we got amazingly little rain. This morning the sky was a bright white, like the sky had been spread with an even layer of clouds.

I mentally started going through the things I had to do, for the moment forgetting all about Rosalie Hardcastle. Not for long though — Tag called on the landline before I'd even gotten out of bed.

"Rosalie Hardcastle is dead," he said in a nervous voice. "It's all over town. I wanted to tell Lucinda, but with all that unplugged stuff, her phone won't work, and it's not the kind of message I want her to see on that board."

I sat up and put my feet on the cold floor as I let the information sink in. Julius had taken to sleeping on my pillow, and he joined me, sitting close.

"Tag, you need to take a breath," I said. I knew that Tag had all kinds of issues about orderliness and things being in their correct place, but he still seemed to be overreacting.

"You don't have to worry. Lucinda is safe." I realized I shouldn't have said that since actually I could only vouch for her safety from the night before. Of course, he caught me on it.

"Then you've seen her this morning?" he said.

"Not exactly, but I'm right across the street. If anything happened, I'd know about it."

"Now the cops are going to step up their game. They're going to be looking for anyone who had a problem with that woman, aren't they?" he said.

"Are you trying to say you had a problem with her?" I asked.

"No," he said, too quickly.

"Did you hang around Vista Del Mar after you dropped Lucinda off?"

I heard him take a gulp of air. "I didn't see anything. I don't know anything. I really have to go. Just please tell Lucinda to call me."

Under the circumstances, he would usually just go to Vista Del Mar and check on her himself. Something was off.

I found some fuzzy slippers and went toward the kitchen. I needed some coffee to clear my head. I heard someone rustling around. Both Julius and I stopped short while I assessed the situation. The only weapons available were some very long knitting needles sitting in a jar.

Julius kept pace with me as we went to the kitchen. I ran in, holding the long needles out like a fencing sword.

"Geez, a little overreaction, don't you think? Maybe you're the one who stabbed her," Chloe said, using her hand to push the needle away. "I couldn't take any more of my brother's lectures. You really shouldn't leave your door unlocked." A chair was pulled out, and a half-drunk glass of orange juice was on the table.

"Thank you again for last night. I was going to bring you breakfast in bed," Sammy said, coming in the door. He held up a container with two cups of coffee and a bag that smelled of egg sandwiches. Then he saw Chloe. "Hi, I didn't realize you had company."

Chloe looked from Sammy to me and shook her head. "And I thought you were different." She went out the door.

Sammy had never met Chloe. Actually, until the whole Butterfly Princess thing, she had kept a low profile in the small town, mostly hanging out in the tough areas of Seaside. He was surprised to find out she was Dane's sister. "And the chief suspect," I said.

Sammy was confused, as he still thought Rosalie had been murdered because of the football game, and I had to explain that Chloe was one of the Butterfly Princesses and Rosalie had very publicly kicked her out of the competition.

He looked at the glass of juice. "I came in to tell you about breakfast, but you were still asleep. I thought it would be okay to leave the door unlocked since I was coming right back. I didn't expect to have a Goldilocks show up."

I shrugged it off, and Sammy put down the coffee and sandwiches. He took the glass to the sink. He pulled out a chair for me. "Let's eat while it's hot." He pointed to one of the cups of coffee. "I got you a cappuccino and an egg and half-Swiss, half-cheddar sandwich." It was exactly what I would have asked for, if he'd consulted me. I saw a little triumphant smile on his lips. I think he was hoping that I would say something about how he really *got* me, too. No matter what he said about being in Cadbury to pursue his magic career, I knew he hoped the real magic would be that we got back together. I did everything I could not to give him false hope.

He ate quickly as he reeled off his morning schedule. He was still a doctor and a surgeon, and was headed into the office. "I'll pick up some of my things later. I got my parents to go whale watching, so I won't have to worry about running into them at the B and B." He pretended to be very interested in his breakfast suddenly. "My parents are insisting on spending more time with us, both of us. I know this is asking a lot, but could you manage something with us — even a cup of coffee?"

I couldn't say no to Sammy, so I said I would try. He started to gather up the paper cup and wrapping of his sandwich. "I know they're going to want to come by here again. Do you mind if I spread some of my stuff around? If you think you're a detective, it's nothing compared to my mother." He added a laugh at the end as if it was a joke, but I knew he was one hundred percent serious.

Weren't Sammy and I a pair? Both in our mid-thirties and still so wound up with our parents.

As soon as he left, I got dressed and headed across to Vista Del Mar. The rest of my retreaters would be coming later in the morning, and I had to set up. I saw a couple of cop cars, almost hidden by trees, in the service parking lot at the back edge of the property. A white van was pulled up in front of the chapel, blocking the view. Now that Rosalie had died, the investigation had changed to homicide, which had stepped everything up. I was sure Kevin St. John was doing everything he could to keep it invisible to the guests. The Lodge was still quiet, with only a few people in the seating area and one guy shooting pool by himself. Nothing was set up, and I had to get the clerk to find someone to round up a table and some chairs for my registration.

At least when I checked on the rooms for my people, all was well. Finally, my table and chairs were set up under the window. I just had to add the tote bags. What a relief that we'd worked it out that the looms weren't going in them. I imagined trying to get the overstuffed tote bags across the street. Visions of rolling round looms danced through my head.

Sammy's coffee had helped me feel alert, but I needed another dose, so I headed for the café. There were a few people at the tables. As usual, I checked the basket to see that my muffins had been put out, though by this time of the morning, a lot of them were usually gone.

I was stunned to see the basket was still almost full. The clerk behind the counter saw me checking them out and suddenly looked uncomfortable. I didn't have to wonder what was going on — it was obvious. People had believed what Rosalie said about the corn muffins making the football players sick and now clearly thought there was something wrong with everything I made. I saw my baking career going down the tubes right before my eyes.

I abandoned my plans and rushed back home. The kitchen still smelled of the breakfast that Sammy had brought. Julius was parading in front of the refrigerator like it was some kind of protest march.

"Your stink fish," I said, feeling a pang of guilt that I'd forgotten to give him his morning spoonful. "It's not like you're going to starve," I said, pointing at the special bowl I'd gotten him with his name on it that was filled with kitty crunchies. Julius swished his tail in response, which I took as his way of saying, "Don't be ridiculous."

I held my breath as I took the open can out of the plastic bag and then went through the triple layers of plastic wrap and doled out a generous spoonful under his watchful eye. He was on it before I even moved away.

I headed right to the phone after that. I had the number on auto dial now, so with a push of a button, I heard the distant phone begin to ring.

I tried to keep the panic out of my voice as my old boss answered. "Good morning, Frank."

"Oh no, Feldstein. What's wrong? You never say good morning, and your voice sounds shaky."

"Frank, I'm in trouble. It's a disaster," I said, trying to pull myself together.

"I thought you said that nobody had died in that candy bar town of yours when you called before."

"What a difference a couple of days make," I said. "Okay, somebody was stabbed in the back at the Blessing of the Butterflies service last night, and the person of interest is my cop friend's sister. And he did ask me

108

to see what I could find out. But there's another death I'm worried about. My career."

"Feldstein, how do you manage to get so much on your plate in such a short time? You better tell me everything." I heard the squeak of his reclining office chair, as he made himself comfortable while he listened. Frank was always pushing that chair to its limit. I had this image that one day the chair would revolt and fling him out of it like it was a catapult.

I had to start at the beginning, with the chili dinner, the football team's loss and how the whole town was upset, before I got to how it affected me. "You know how rumors work. One minute someone is making a comment that my muffins might have been the cause, and then it gets changed into a certainty. Then all my muffins are suspect. There are never as many muffins left at this time of the morning," I said.

"Any chance it was the muffins?" Frank asked. When I objected, he said he had to know the truth if he was going to help.

"Of course not. I use all the rules of safe food handling."

"That's good news, Feldstein. It sounds to me as if that woman was trying to get the heat off her chili by blaming your muffins.

But suppose somebody still thought it was her chili that made those players sick. So they stabbed her as revenge for the team's loss." Frank let it sink in for a moment. "You just have to hope that the killer doesn't decide to take out anyone else who made food that night. Do you see where I'm going, Feldstein?"

I swallowed so hard it sounded like something out of a cartoon.

"I'm telling you, you really ought to be carrying," Frank said.

"Carrying?" I said.

"A gun, Feldstein. With all the trouble you get into, you ought to have protection."

"I'd probably shoot myself in the foot," I said. "Besides, I do sort of have protection."

"That cop down the street?"

"No, more like the Amazing Dr. Sammy." I told Frank about the situation with his parents and that he was staying with me.

Frank laughed a loud belly laugh. "Feldstein, you do lead a complicated life. What's he going to do if somebody comes after you, make a bunch of scarves come out of their ear?" Frank's tone changed from amused to impatient. "Got to go. I have a client coming in. We have a new specialty — personal background checks of people you meet online. The stories I could tell. But not now.

Keep me posted." I heard a click, and he was gone.

Usually, talking to Frank made me feel better. Not this time. It wasn't a happy thought that someone might want to murder me over my muffins. I pushed the thought onto the back shelf of my mind. It was time to concentrate on the retreat.

Julius was checking his bowl for any missed crumbs of stink fish as I went out the kitchen door. I pulled my bin on wheels to the guest house. It was perfectly neat inside and almost didn't even look as if someone had slept there. Sammy had made the bed and folded it back into the wall. The row of tote bags was just as I had left it on the counter after I'd filled them. I loaded them up and headed back across the street.

By now things were starting to stir on the Vista Del Mar grounds. The housekeeping golf cart drove past me, loaded with linens and towels. A delivery van was parked in the driveway. A couple pulled their suitcases into the Lodge. I caught a whiff of the breakfast smells coming from the dining hall and imagined the early birds and Lucinda sitting together.

I dragged the bin inside the Lodge and began setting everything out on the registration table. As soon as I was done, I went back into the café. I told myself it was to get the coffee I'd wanted earlier, but I knew it was really to check on the muffins. My heart fell when I saw that they'd only sold one since I'd been there. Normally by now, there would be just one left. I made a hasty decision and took a deep breath before I asked the counter guy to take away the sign in front of the basket that announced they were Casey's Muffins. "Just let them be generic for now," I said.

"It doesn't matter," he said. "Everyone knows who made them."

9

By midday, the Lodge was bustling with activity. The van from the airport was making regular trips, dropping off guests. There seemed to be an extra buzz of excitement in the air due to the coming week's activities. The early birds and Lucinda had joined me at the registration table before any of my retreaters showed up, and I shared the news about Rosalie. Olivia, Scott and Bree were concerned because they had seen her in the dining hall, but it was Lucinda who was most upset, particularly after I told her about Tag's call to me that morning.

She was about to rush off to the phone booths to call him when I stopped her. "There's something else." I told her about the muffin situation and my concern about rumors flying around town. "I think you should tell Tag to take my name off the desserts for now. Just until I get to the bottom of things."

Lucinda nodded in agreement. "I know there was nothing wrong with the muffins, but you know Tag. He's so meticulous, if there is even a hint of any problem, he takes it over the top. I'll just tell him that we're doing a test to see if having your name on them makes us sell more desserts." She turned back before she left. "And of course, I'll help you figure this all out any way I can."

A group of women came in and stopped in the entrance, looking around. Kevin St. John was circulating around the Lodge doing his host thing. He went over to them and then pointed them in our direction.

"Here they come," I said to my helpers. Bree, Olivia and Scott assumed their positions. Olivia took half the registration list and Bree the other half. Scott was ready to assist with their rooms. Having their help made it so there was never a line for long, and everyone got a more personal welcome.

When I saw Liz Buckley come in the door with two dark-haired women, I said I'd take care of them. I was sure these were the two people that the travel agent had brought to me. I wanted to do everything to make their stay successful so that Liz would push more business my way.

Liz handled the introductions and gave

me their names. I smiled and nodded, but I knew I'd never remember them. They were from Copenhagen, and their English was a little awkward. I had learned during the first retreat I'd done that I couldn't possibly remember all the retreaters' names. It was much easier to hook on to some identifying feature. The two women became simply the two Danish women.

I personally handed them their tote bags, and Scott made sure they got their room keys and directions to the building.

When all twenty-five retreaters had checked in and were set up for lunch and some free time to look around Vista Del Mar before the first workshop, I went home. Julius was parading in front of the back door when I got there. He followed me inside and stuck close as I walked through the house. It was obvious Sammy had returned while I was gone. He'd gone all out. His shaving stuff was in the bathroom, and his robe hung on the back of the door. He'd left a pair of shoes with socks stuck in them, which was really very unlike Sammy. He wasn't a throw-your-socks-on-the-floor kind of guy. He'd left a stack of American Association of Urologists newsletters in the living room on the coffee table. The only thing he hadn't left was any hint of his passion for magic.

"It's just for show," I said to Julius, who had jumped on the pile of newsletters and seemed intent on knocking them to the floor. The black cat didn't seem to believe me, and I decided to give him an extra serving of stink fish to pacify him. I'm sure that was probably bad cat training, but it worked. Julius did figure eights around my ankles in happy anticipation of his treat.

After I'd fed him, I turned on the oven to preheat and took out some logs of butter cookie dough. I sliced them, sprinkled on some slivered almonds and popped them in the oven. The sweet buttery scent filled the air as they baked. Presentation is everything, so once they were cool, I put a doily in the bottom of a round tin and arranged the cookies before putting on the lid.

I also did a little fix-up on my appearance. I'd settled on practically a uniform for the retreats of black jeans and black turtlenecks, with some of my aunt's knitted and crocheted creations to add some color. There were so many pieces to choose from. Today I picked a loose cowl made out of a nubby yarn in shades of turquoise. I redid my makeup and added some lipstick. As I looked at my reflection, I wondered how Crystal managed all that eye liner and blush and didn't look overdone. On me, even simple red lipstick seemed blindingly bright.

The best outerwear for the area was fleece, and I had a whole wardrobe of different colors and styles of the cuddly material. I decided to go all the way for bright and picked out a red fleece that was designed to look like a shirt.

As I went across the street once again, I noticed that the air was a nice kind of cool — bracing, but not like a slap on my skin. Thanks to all the fireplaces in the Vista Del Mar buildings, the air always had a hint of wood smoke, mixed with the scent of the ocean. There was lots of activity now that lunch had ended and the newly arrived guests were checking out their surroundings. I'd included a map along with the schedule in the folders, so I felt confident my group would find our meeting room.

The meeting rooms were in single-story buildings sprinkled around Vista Del Mar. Some took up the whole building and some just half. All the buildings in Vista Del Mar had names. I'd chosen Sea View for our group. It was located on the top of a slope and, as its name implied, had a vantage point through the dunes to the water. The inside seemed cheerful and cozy after the flat light of outside. A fire was going in the fireplace, and coffee and tea service had been set up on the counter near a small sink. I put the tin of cookies next to the stack of white ceramic mugs.

Two long tables had been set up parallel to each other. I checked through the stack of boxes against the wall. They were filled with sets of long and round looms. There were also plastic bins filled with an assortment of yarns. I was just considering how to distribute everything when Wanda and Crystal arrived. I was always struck by the difference in their styles. Crystal, with all her unmatched everythings and layers of colorful shirts and bouncing ringlets of black hair, made Wanda, in her comfortable beige slacks and pale yellow floral top, seem so bland.

We greeted one another, but they both seemed a little done in. I had successfully put everything about the previous night out of my mind, but seeing them brought it all back. I figured it was best to deal with it now, before the retreaters arrived.

"I suppose you know about Rosalie," I said. They both nodded.

"It still doesn't seem real," Crystal said. "It's almost as if it was somehow part of the service. I wasn't a fan of Rosalie's, but still."

Wanda seemed to want to get on with the

matter at hand and started looking through the boxes of supplies. "I'll put a set of looms at each place," she said. She pulled out some marker pens. "They can mark the boxes with their names, take out the round loom we're going to use first and store the rest back in the big boxes."

Crystal didn't object, and we all started taking out the sets of looms and distributing them around the table.

I knew it was best to find out what they knew while it was still fresh in their minds, but I didn't want to come across as grilling them. At the same time, I had to get to it, because our group would be arriving soon.

"Was there anything different about the service this year?" I asked.

Wanda stopped what she was doing. "No, it was the exact same program. So much the same that you could set your watch by what the pianist was playing."

"So then everyone knew when the lights would be off," I said. "Did either of you notice anything when it was dark?"

"There was just a lot of shifting around," Crystal said. "The princesses all had to go out the front door and grab their cardboard trees and assume their positions. I was trying to look for my daughter, but with the music and the narration it was hard to focus on anything."

"I wonder where Liz Buckley was when all that was going on," I said.

Wanda put a set of the looms on the table. "She uses one of those cordless mikes, so she could have been anywhere."

We'd finished setting the looms out, and the two of them began to distribute samples they'd made using the looms on their respective tables. There was no doubt as to which samples belonged to whom. Wanda's were all rather utilitarian, done in basic blues and tan, while Crystal's had mixtures of orange and purple and hot pink, usually paired with something with sparkle.

"Rosalie mentioned someone named Hank during her spiel at the podium," I said. "Who is he?"

Wanda was quick to answer, which figured since she always liked to give an impression of superior knowledge about everything. "He's her husband. And he wasn't there, if that was going to be your next question. He's nothing like her, except in that they're both native Cadburians." Wanda put her hand on her hip. "She was so into the importance of the Butterfly Queen. You know how she was queen herself three times and tried to get the town council to make her the permanent queen? When that didn't

120

work, she tried to get it for ten years, then five years, but they threw out the whole idea of anything more than a year."

Crystal added that they were rarely seen together, something about him working odd hours. Wanda nodded in agreement, and I realized I was running out of time. The re-treaters would start arriving at any moment.

I got to the point. "Do either of you have any idea who stabbed her?"

It was getting too weird to see them both in agreement, but in unison they said, "It was the girl with the blue hair."

I wanted to ask more, but Lucinda came through the door, followed by the other re-treaters.

"Showtime," I said. It was silly, but I could feel my heart rate kick up and my breathing get shallow. The early birds and Lucinda spread themselves equally between the tables, and the rest of the group followed suit.

When they'd all filed inside, I noticed that Liz Buckley had walked with the two Danish women and was standing outside, watching through the window. I knew the travel agent wanted to make sure that nothing would go wrong, but I thought she was taking it too far.

I let my two workshop leaders do the

welcoming of the group and stepped outside to hopefully reassure Liz.

"They're going to be fine," I said as I reached her.

"I suppose I am overreacting. I think I'm still unnerved over what happened last night. It was supposed to be a happy time."

"Then you know Rosalie died," I said. Liz's eyes opened wide, and she sucked in her breath in surprise. Apparently, she'd missed the news. Then she did something odd. I noticed just a hint of what seemed like a hopeful smile.

"That might change everything," she said, and abruptly walked away.

I went back inside and walked straight into chaos. Wanda had gotten right into things and had clearly told them all to take out the correct round loom for their first project of a hat. As I watched, she gave them directions to mark their boxes and then get them out of the way. There were already grumblings from several of the women that loom knitting wasn't really knitting. But things really seemed to have hit the fan when Crystal told them to pick the yarn they wanted to use. Go figure. After Crystal's whole fuss about having different yarns so they could express their creativity while still doing the same project, they all wanted the navy blue yarn.

I stepped to the front of the room and put up my hands. I remembered dealing with an unruly group when I'd been a substitute teacher. I'd always found distracting the kids worked, especially if it was with something pleasant.

"Let's all take a break," I said. "There's tea and coffee, and I brought homemade cookies." None of them knew there was any question about my baking, and they swarmed the tin.

I told the women who objected to the looms that they could use needles, then I told Crystal to go to the Lodge and call her mother. I assured the group we'd have more navy blue yarn in no time.

The group was still sipping drinks, munching cookies and socializing when Gwen Selwyn came in, wheeling a stack of bins. She was a little breathless and I thanked her for rushing over. We set up in the corner, and I worked with her to hand out the navy blue yarn, while taking back the other colors. When she finished, she turned to the group.

"Ladies, and Scott," she said, smiling at the male early bird. "I dropped off a supply of yarn and notions at the gift shop last night. I'm looking forward to seeing you all when you come into Cadbury Yarn later in the week. I know you are all going to love learning how to crochet a monarch butterfly."

With her mission accomplished, she snapped the lids on the bins and went outside. I followed, wanting to thank her again for all her help. And in the back of my mind, I wondered if this was the time to tell her about the proof I had that she was Edmund Delacorte's daughter.

"I'm happy to do it." She stopped on the path to respond to my thanks. "I was very fond of your aunt, and I'm pleased that you took over the retreats. They're a real boost for our business. Not only do you get a lot of supplies through us, but when the other guests see your people working with needles, they want to knit, too, and they buy the yarn we supply to the gift shop." She gathered herself up, and I sensed she was going to go.

"There's something else I want to talk to you about," I said.

"It's about what happened last night, isn't it?" Gwen said. "What a thing to happen here. I think everyone is trying to put on a good front and just carry on despite it." She adjusted the lid of a bin that had come loose. I realized right then that this was definitely not the time to bring up her real identity. However, it might be a good time to ask her a few questions, as I remembered that she had been on the grounds the night before.

"I noticed you said you came by last night to drop off the yarn. Didn't I see you come in the dining hall when Rosalie Hardcastle introduced the Princess Court? I suppose you wanted to see your granddaughter get her crown. Marcy must have been very excited. Did you stay for the Blessing of the Butterflies?"

Gwen had started to walk now, and I was following her down the path. "I have to get back to the store. I did look into the dining hall when Marcy got her crown, but the Blessing of the Butterflies seems like stupid theatrics to me. I heard a bunch of commotion coming from there as I was leaving, which made me even gladder that I didn't go."

"When did you hear what happened?" I asked, struggling to keep up with her fast pace.

"Last night, when Crystal and Marcy got home. My daughter was upset that the police insisted on talking to Marcy. The one with the rumpled jacket came by this morning to talk to her again and ask her if she saw anything. She told him that she didn't.

How could she have seen anything if the lights were off?"

"Then she has no idea who stabbed Rosalie?" I asked.

"It was the girl with the blue hair," Gwen said. "After what Rosalie did to her, who could blame her?"

I stopped in my tracks, but Gwen went on, the wheels of the carrier making a squeaking noise as she went down the path. It was clear I wasn't going to get any more out of her, so I turned and headed back to the meeting room.

Now that everybody had the same yarn and the same round loom, Wanda gave them instructions how to cast on using an e-wrap. Crystal didn't object — I think she had accepted that Wanda was best at giving instructions.

"Aren't you going to join us?" Wanda asked me. I actually liked being part of the workshops. When I'd started doing the retreats I'd had no skills with yarn, but I was getting there. I grabbed one of the round looms and some extra yarn Gwen had left and took a seat. By the end of the workshop, all of us had mastered the e-wrap cast on and had begun our hats. The funny thing was that the knitters who had been so insistent on sticking with needles saw the rest of us working with the looms and felt left out. They ended up joining us, saying they wanted to have the loom experience, too.

When the workshop ended, they all headed off for free time before dinner and our evening event. As had happened with my previous retreats, a few groups arranged their own smaller gatherings to knit together before dinner. Some of them went to the living rooms of the buildings their guest rooms were in, and some went to the Lodge.

Lucinda caught up with me. "You did a great job at straightening things out. Who would have figured they'd all want to use the same color?" Like the others, she'd taken her work with her and took out the loom to examine the rows of stitches hanging off it. "This looks like a way I can make something quickly and easily. Just my style." She smiled and then noticed that I seemed quiet. "What's the matter?"

I let out a mirthless laugh at her question and told her what Dane had put in my lap. "And Wanda, Crystal and Gwen all said they thought it was Chloe who stabbed Rosalie, as if it was a given."

Lucinda didn't say anything for a minute. "I don't like to have to say this, but if you consider the facts, it could be true. There was that whole fuss between Rosalie and Chloe in the dining hall. I don't really know Chloe, other than what you've said about her, but she doesn't seem like someone who would go away quietly." Lucinda's last comment was certainly diplomatic.

"It just can't be true," I said. "I haven't gotten any exact details yet, but I am getting the vibe that Rosalie wasn't well liked. And Chloe may have some edges, but I just don't buy that she would stab someone."

We'd reached the center of Vista Del Mar, and there were people walking toward the Lodge. "She's lucky to have you on her side," Lucinda said. "If anybody can help her, it's you."

I appreciated her belief in me. "There's more," I said. Lucinda stopped walking and turned to me. I told her about Sammy and his parents, and her expression lightened.

"Good, something for comic relief. He's a grown man — why can't he just tell his parents that he loves magic and he actually has a career here? Maybe if they saw him in action, doing table magic at Vista Del Mar, they'd see how much it means to him. And how much the crowd likes it, too. Tag and I even talked about having him do his act at the Blue Door on one of our slow nights, but there doesn't seem to be enough space."

"If you met his parents, you'd understand. Actually, you probably will meet them. They want to do things with 'the happy couple' while they're here."

"You know that I'm here if you need any help," my friend said. We started to walk again, heading into the Lodge. There was a lot of activity going on. A group was gathering for a nature walk, and the pool table and table tennis were both in use. The seating area was filled. I saw that some of my group had taken over a table and were putting out their knitting things. As always, there was a line for the old-fashioned phone booths. It was a hard adjustment for people to go without cell phones and Internet when they were so used to being instantly connected.

"I have to call Tag," Lucinda said, looking toward the line. I offered to let her use my place, but she said she wanted to stay on the grounds and keep the illusion that she was away on vacation somewhere going as long as possible.

I was about to leave when the clerk behind the massive registration counter waved me over.

"I wanted to tell you about this directly," she said. "So you can take care of it before Mr. St. John finds out." It was common

knowledge among the staff that he was looking for a way to push me out of the retreats.
Luckily, I got along with the workers and
they were on my side. The clerk handed me
a check, and it was stamped Returned for
insufficient funds. I started to panic until I
saw that it wasn't my check, but rather the
one Liz Buckley had given me for the two
Danish women's retreat costs. I'd merely
signed it over to Vista Del Mar to cover their
rooms, but the clerk reminded me that I'd
gotten cash for the difference. Just what I
needed: another problem.

10

While my group enjoyed their free time before dinner and the evening's activity, which was something called the Beckoning of the Butterflies, I went into town. It was late in the day, and I hoped that Liz was still in her office. I was sure that the problem with the check was some kind of mistake, and I just wanted to take care of it quickly, so Kevin St. John didn't find out.

The street was unusually busy. Cadbury got tourists from all over the world, but this week there were even more. It was very festive with all the banners hanging from the light poles. They fluttered in the wind, and it almost looked like the monarchs were flapping their wings.

Cadbury Travel was located in one of the bland-looking modern buildings on Grand Street. I thought the Victorian-style storefronts were so much more interesting, with their bright colors and fish-scale siding.

A bell rang on the door when I walked in, and Liz looked up from her desk. She was on the phone and held up a finger to let me know she'd be with me in a minute. I took a seat and glanced at the posters of the Manhattan skyline and a cruise ship going through the Panama Canal. I checked out the rack with brochures on river cruises.

When she hung up, she waved me over to the desk and offered me a seat. "Is there a problem with the Danish women?" she said with a worried look.

I assured her that everything was fine with them. I took the check out of my bag and laid on the desk, turning it so she could see the red words stamped on it. "I'm sure this was just some kind of mistake," I said.

The color drained from Liz's face, and she swallowed loudly when she saw that I had signed it over to Vista Del Mar. She took out her checkbook and looked at the register.

"The bank must have made some kind of error. I'm sure there's money in the account," she said with a forced smile. "Let me give you a new check."

She seemed to be trying to hide her embarrassment as she handed me the new check. "I guess since you gave the check to Vista Del Mar there isn't any way to keep

132

this quiet."

I told her only the one clerk knew and I wasn't going to spread the word. When I looked up she was leaning on the desk. "Thank you so much," she said, almost in tears. I had been considering asking her about the Blessing of the Butterflies, but it didn't seem like the right time.

The whole episode with Liz left me unnerved. She had always seemed businesslike and in control of things, especially compared to me, as I tended to be all over the place.

Instead of heading back to my yellow Mini Cooper, I went down the street to the Coffee Shop. That was actually the real name of it. People in Cadbury shunned anything that smacked of cuteness and preferred to go for the clear meaning. I had started out calling my muffins clever names like 40 Carrots and Merry Berry, but I'd quickly gotten the message to simply call them what they were. So while my blueberry muffins would forever be The Blues in my mind, when I made them for the town coffee spots they were simply called blueberry muffins.

And in my mind the Coffee Shop was known as Maggie's. The smell of freshly ground coffee permeated the small shop on the corner. Maggie was behind the counter, dispensing drinks. There was a line, and I was glad to see that she had help. Maggie always wore something red. It was her trademark of sorts. I'd heard she'd adopted it as a way to keep herself cheerful after she'd lost her husband and daughter. Lately, she'd simplified and usually just wore a tomato red apron and a matching head scarf.

I waited until the line went down to wave her a greeting. Before I could say a word, she said, "One cappuccino coming up." Maggie's personality was as warm as her color of choice. She'd been the first person to sell my muffins and make me feel welcome in town. Maggie also knew everything about everyone in town.

I took a tiny table in the corner, and a moment later Maggie brought my drink over, along with one for herself. She slipped into the seat across from me. "It's been crazy all day. I need an excuse for a break."

"Thank you for standing up for me last night," I said. I took a sip of the hot drink, which, as usual, was made with just the right balance of steamed milk and espresso.

"Nonsense. I was just speaking the truth. I'd say something about how lousy I thought Rosalie's behavior was, but under the circumstances it seems like very bad taste."

I wanted to tell her about my dealings with Liz Buckley, but I'd given my word to keep it quiet, and Maggie *was* like information central. Besides, Rosalie Hardcastle was the hot topic. "What a shock," I said, before explaining I'd been there when it happened.

Maggie gave my shoulder a reassuring pat. "I was there for the dinner and the scene with the princesses, but then I left. There are only so many times I can watch the Blessing of the Butterflies," she said.

"I heard it was always the same." I drank some more of the cappuccino, enjoying the boost it gave me. It had been a long day, and it was far from over.

"That's an understatement." She checked the counter to make sure her helper was managing. What she'd said had made me think of something.

"If it was always the same, then it would have been easy to figure when Rosalie would be sitting with her back to the open door." Maggie nodded and I continued. "Someone just had to come at the appropriate time with a knife."

"I'm afraid that doesn't narrow it down. I think everybody in town knows the program by heart. It really was a perfect setup for murder — the lights off, loud music with lots of people moving around and Rosalie in the perfect position to get stabbed in the back."

"Poor Rosalie was a sitting duck," I said. I expected Maggie to say something about how terrible it was, but she surprised me.

"This might be in bad taste, but it's also the truth: she wasn't a very nice person." Maggie's tone was surprisingly harsh. "Unlike her husband. Have you ever met him?"

"No. I just heard that everybody seems to like him."

"Yes, Hank is a great guy and was easy pickings for Rosalie. I don't know if you've seen him, but he's kind of plain. She made a play for him when she was Butterfly Queen for the first time, so she was like a town celebrity. He's an easy-going person and was flattered by all her attention. He didn't get it. It wasn't Hank she wanted as much as being a Hardcastle. Rosalie wanted to be a big deal in town, like the Delacortes, and the closest she was going to get was being a Hardcastle. They weren't close to the Delacortes in terms of a fortune, but Hank's family owned a lot of property around town." Maggie chuckled. "Rosalie never liked it that Hank's parents were low-key like he is, and she never got to play the wealthy matron." Maggie played with her cup and seemed to be thinking about something. "But now everything has changed, and for Hank as well." It almost seemed like she was talking to herself.

"It seems strange that he wasn't at the event the other night," I said.

"He was probably working," Maggie said. I wanted to get more details, but there was a sudden rush of customers. "Break time is over," Maggie sighed, picking up her cup.

I took a moment to finish my drink before I got up to leave. I glanced toward the counter and felt my breath stop when I saw the basket Maggie kept my muffins in. It was still half full. Maggie saw me looking.

"It doesn't mean anything," she said. "Everything is off because of Butterfly Week."

No matter what she said, I knew the truth, I thought as I left the Coffee Shop. My muffins were definitely under a cloud of suspicion.

I remember what Sammy had said about testing samples of the food. Could there be anything left from the chili dinner to test? On the chance, I took a detour and walked down a side street to the Cadbury Natural History Museum. A banner announcing Butterfly Week was draped across the statute of a whale in front of the Spanish-style building. It was tiny compared to the Field

Museum I'd gone to in Chicago, but it dated from the late 1800s and served as a community center.

I went into the entrance hall. One whole side of the museum was devoted to the monarchs and their travels and life cycles. There was even a model of the local area that had become known as the Sanctuary in a glass case, complete with tiny butterflies hanging on the trees.

The entrance to the multipurpose room was at the back. A bunch of kids were making papier-mâché butterflies, and no one even looked up when I went through. The large room looked a lot different from the night of the chili dinner. Then, there had been long tables with checkered tablecloths set up for the team and their families. The walls had been decorated with the high school team's pennants.

A swinging door led to the kitchen. It was deserted at the moment, but I saw a bunch of things packed in a box marked *Chili Dinner.* I started to take everything out in the hopes of finding a leftover muffin. It would be rock hard by now but could still be tested. The pennants were on top, and some large pans were underneath. I assumed the pans must have been Rosalie's. I took everything out and didn't find even a crumb of a muffin, so I started to pack everything back in. A strip of paper fluttered down. I picked it up and saw it was some kind of receipt. It seemed to have been tucked between the pans, so I put it back. I finished by putting the pennants across the top.

I checked the refrigerator to see if there was any of the chili left. If I got it tested and it was the culprit, my muffins would be off the hook. But all that was in there were several brown bags with names on them. I assumed they were staff members' lunches.

I was on my way out when I remembered that the Hardcastles had donated an exhibit to the museum. Actually, I think Rosalie had called it a pavilion, which implied an addition or a big space. I asked about it at the front desk and was directed to the main room. Everyone was flocking to the butter-fly exhibit, so I had the room to myself. That is, if you didn't count all the displays of animals specimens, which was a nice way of saying dead stuffed animals. Was it my imagination or did they seem to all be star-ing at me with those shiny glass eyes? It was supposed to be educational to be able to see all the wildlife up close, but it was also creepy, particularly in the deliberately low light. I liked to think that all they had all died naturally before they ended up being stuffed and put on display.

I noticed some little brass plates in front of the glass cases and saw they explained that the exhibit was a gift from someone. There was clearly no pavilion, and I began to think it was more likely a glass case. I didn't feel like making the rounds of the whole room to find the Hardcastle exhibit and was about to go back to the front and ask the docent to be more specific about its location, but it turned out I didn't have to. As I took a step back, I felt something behind me, and when I turned I found myself almost in the embrace of a seven-foot grizzly bear, his long claws next to my face. When I looked up at his black eyes, I almost thought they were moving, but then I realized that it was just a reflection in the glass eyes from outside. I knew the bear wasn't alive, but it definitely made me uncomfortable, and I quickly stepped away from his clutches. As I moved, I noticed a large brass plaque that said the bear was a gift of Rosalie and Hank Hardcastle.

It was definitely the biggest animal on display, and from what I was learning about Rosalie lately, it made sense. It certainly stood out from the rest of the room.

When I got outside and looked at my watch, I was shocked to see the time. I had to get back to my retreaters.

I made a quick stop at home first and was surprised to see I had seven phone messages. When I checked, they were all from the coffee places that sold my muffins, asking me for just half the usual order. Only Maggie hadn't called to change her order. Of all the things I'd considered happening to make me leave Cadbury, it had never occurred to me that there would be a problem with my baking business. Without it, I could never afford to stay. Julius must have sensed trouble, because he was practically glued to my ankle and for once wasn't trying to get me to serve up some stink fish.

"Don't worry, wherever I go, you're coming, too," I told him. The way I looked at it, Julius and I had found each other. I still wasn't sure which of us was the pet, but then, he was the first animal companion I'd ever had. "I'm sure they sell stink fish everywhere."

Julius watched me from the kitchen counter as I went out the door and back across the street. When I'd first seen him wandering the grounds of Vista Del Mar, it seemed like he'd been abandoned. I hoped he realized that wasn't going to happen again.

I tried to put a positive spin on my troubles by telling myself that at least I wouldn't have to do as much baking. With everything else I had going on, that was actually a good thing. The dinner bell had already rung, and just a few stragglers were on the path as I made my way to the dining hall. With all of Lucinda's restaurant experience, she naturally acted as host, so I didn't have to worry about getting to meals on time. I made a stop in the Lodge and gave Liz Buckley's new check to the clerk. She seemed a little hesitant to take it.

"I'm sure this one will be fine," I said.

"At least I know where to find you if there's a problem," she joked.

I went on to the dining hall, and as I'd expected, Lucinda had gotten three of the round tables for our group. She was circulating with iced tea and coffee and making sure everyone was happy with the meal. She pointed out an empty seat, and I went to the table. Since running the workshops was work for Crystal and Wanda, they had gone home for the day. It always made me laugh to see how our tables were littered with yarn. I was relieved that everyone seemed happy. Two of the early birds clustered around me to share their news. Bree had found somebody who seemed a little lost and was having a hard time adjusting to the lack of electronics. She'd been through both experiences but had eventually realized that there was something to be said about not spending all your time with your face in a phone.

Olivia was holding a small long loom. "This would be perfect to make squares on." Olivia's passion had become getting knitters and crocheters to make eight-inch squares that she sewed into blankets and then passed on to assorted charities. Now whenever she came, she was always looking to have the group make squares during one of the impromptu gatherings. "It will be so much faster," she added.

Scott had moved to another table and was talking to a family. I noticed the father was knitting as they talked. Scott had found a kindred spirit.

I joined the retreaters for the meal, once again realizing I'd been too busy to eat. When dinner ended, I gathered up the group and told them to head over to the Lodge, where everyone was meeting ahead of that night's monarch event, the Beckoning of the Butterflies.

When we got there, I spotted the Delacorte sisters and went over to greet them. Cora had on an overcoat and scarf. Her puff of brown hair seemed recently styled, and she was holding her purse on her arm just the way Queen Elizabeth did. She threw a disdainful glance at her older sister. Madeleine had always been the more timid of the two and up until recently had been so quiet that I'd actually wondered if she was able to talk. But all that had changed — she claimed because of me. She'd joined my last retreat, and the ensuing adventure had caused her to come out of her shell. She seemed to be making up for lost time.

"Check out these jeans," she said proudly, kicking out her leg. I heard Cora groan with irritation. She couldn't understand why it was such a big deal that her seventy-something sister had just started wearing the denim pants.

Madeleine might have gone a little over-board — I noticed her pants were distressed with a fashionable tear at the knee — but she seemed so happy with them that all I could do was smile and tell her they looked great.

"With Rosalie gone," Madeleine said, "we're back in charge of the Butterfly Queen committee. That woman took it upon herself to be the head of the committee." She glanced at Chloe, who was sitting across the room. "She just showed up and said she was back on the Princess Court. I suppose there's nothing we can do — Rosalie was totally wrong about putting her out because she didn't like the way she was dressed — but it still seems like bad form, all things considered. Everyone says she's the one who stabbed Rosalie."

"I have it on good authority that she didn't do it," I said. Cora was listening and joined the conversation.

"Who's the good authority?" the more formal sister asked.

"She told me she didn't do it."

Cora's mascaraed eyelashes fluttered. "As if she would tell you the truth. But I know you're innocent until proven guilty, so we'll let her stay in the court." Cora glanced around at the growing crowd. "I hope we can get through this evening without any problems." She pulled out some leather gloves and held them in her hand.

I heard someone calling my name and saw that Sammy had just come in, along with his mother. They made their way over to me. Sammy seemed subdued and his mother annoyed. "I don't know where your father went," she was saying. "After the whale watching I went to take a nap, and when I got up, he and the car were both gone." She looked around at the crowd.

"Sammy said there's some special event tonight. I was hoping we could sit down someplace and talk about your future," his mother continued.

Just then, Crystal's son, Kory, came through the crowd and saw Sammy. He went up to him and pulled on his ear, while Sammy's mother watched. "Aren't you going to make a quarter app—" Before he could say the rest of "appear," I took Kory's arm and led him aside. I told him the truth, that Sammy's mother didn't know about his magic act. "Not everybody's mother is as cool as yours," I said.

"Poor guy," Kory said.

Sammy's mother glanced around impatiently. "What are we waiting for?" she said.

"It's who," Kevin St. John said, overhearing her. I was surprised to see that he'd added a fleece jacket over his suit. "And here he is, the Lord of the Butterflies." Coach Gary had just walked in, with Liz at his side. She seemed to have recovered from our afternoon encounter. Gary wore the large wings over his leather jacket. Kevin St. John seemed unusually animated and leaned in to speak to Sammy's mother. "You'll see it was worth the wait. It's going to be truly magical." Sammy winced at the word.

Coach Gary walked across the Lodge and opened the door that led out onto the deck. He waved for the princesses to come first, and then for the rest of us to follow.

The crowd spilled out onto the deck and then went down the stairs and moved en masse to the boardwalk that led through the dunes. All our feet clattered on the walkway as we followed along, and I felt bad for any deer that were wandering in the dunes. We reached the edge of the Vista Del Mar grounds and the street. The usually empty street was lined with cars, and more people joined the crowd as we crossed the street. There was no traffic, and we all crossed in a constant stream. It was easy to see the white sand, even in the dark. Walking became a little more difficult when we reached the sand, but we continued on to almost the water's edge, then everyone spread out.

"We call this the Beckoning of the Butterflies," Coach Gary said. "We thank them for coming here and admire the magic that draws them here, following in the footsteps of their ancestors even though these particular butterflies have never been here before."

The breeze whipped through the crowd, and the waves made a rhythmic sound as Coach Gary and the princesses gathered together. There was a large bin near the water. The princesses each took a cylinder from the container. I saw someone with the kind of lighter used for fireplaces going from princess to princess. The flame was applied to the bottom of the cylinder, and then the princess held up the glowing cylinder and let it go. The sky lanterns floated up and out over the water, carrying their beckoning lights.

For the moment, I forgot all about my troubles and my worries regarding Chloe. It was absolutely beautiful as more and more of the cylinders took off into the night sky. I felt someone link arms with me. I looked over and could just barely make out Dane's angular face.

"Chloe banished me from all of this princess stuff, but I didn't want to miss this. It's really something, isn't it?" More of the lights sailed out over the water. "Even if it's just ceremonial. I heard the butterflies had already started arriving days ago," Dane teased.

I gave him a playful poke in the arm. "Aren't you Mr. Bust the Perfect Moment."

"Give me a chance and I'll create a perfect moment." I couldn't see his eyes, but I bet they were dancing. The last of the lanterns went up, and everyone applauded. "That's my cue. I've got to go." I'd felt the brush of his equipment belt and realized he was in uniform, which meant he was on duty. He touched my arm and then walked off in the sand.

In the darkness it was impossible to see who was who, and I followed the crowd as everyone headed back to the street. Some people began to splinter off and head to their cars, and others continued through the Vista Del Mar gate onto the boardwalk, through the dunes.

Sammy must have had some kind of radar, because even in the dark, with all those people, he found me as I was walking on the boardwalk. "Case, the good news is that my father finally showed up. The bad news is that they are insisting we spend some time with them — both of us."

Back to reality and the pile of problems facing me. "When?" I asked.

"They were talking about now," he said. "I'm really sorry, but the sooner we do it, the sooner they'll leave."

I saw his point and thought over what I still had to do. "I suppose I could do it for a half an hour. Just let me see my retreaters first."

Sammy gave me a bear hug. "Case, you're the best. I'll tell them we'll meet them in the café." He moved on ahead to find them and give them the good news.

The boardwalk ended, and the crowd

spread out even more. As I went up the stairs to the deck outside the Lodge, I caught up with the two Danish women. They were all smiles and told me in hesitant English how much they were enjoying the retreat. I looked around for Liz Buckley, knowing it would reassure the travel agent, but I didn't see her.

We walked into the cavernous building together. I was glad to see Lucinda, Bree, Scott and Olivia gathered by the window looking out over the deck, and I brought the Danish women over.

Bree's fluff of blond curls bounced as she talked. "Next year, I'm bringing my boys. This whole thing about the butterflies is magical. Imagine that somehow they know just where to come, when they've never been here before, but their great-grandparents have. Or maybe it's great-great-grandparents."

Lucinda smiled at Bree's excitement. "It certainly brings a lot of attention to Cadbury."

Scott usually had the buttoned-down look of a businessman, but for once his face was beaming. Olivia was the only one who wasn't gushing over what we'd just witnessed and seemed almost glum.

"Sorry, but the whole event reminded me

of my ex. I heard that he and the new wife took off in a hot air balloon after they said their vows," she said. She'd come so far in moving on with her life that I hated to see her take a step back. Thinking about her ex's marriage, particularly the fact that her children had gone to the wedding, stirred up all kinds of upset for her. I hoped changing the subject would make her forget about it. "Remember, you were going to try using a loom to make squares," I said. The idea of collecting knitted and crocheted squares that she could sew together into blankets and donate had become almost an obsession with Olivia, and she immediately brightened.

"What a great idea." She looked at the group. "Why not have a session right now?" She went over to the retreaters and suggested they move to the living room–like lobby of the building their guest rooms were in. She made sure to let the Danish women know they were included.

"Are you coming?" Lucinda asked, hanging back as the others moved toward the door.

"I wish." I told her about having to meet Sammy's parents. "I hope they say whatever they have to and then leave. I have too many things going on to be able to keep up with the masquerade of being his girlfriend." Lucinda gave me a sympathetic hug and then went on to catch up with the others.

The Beckoning of the Butterflies seemed to have left a lot of people anxious for a treat. As I crossed the large space, I saw that the line for the Cora and Madeleine Delacorte Café was spilling out the door into the main area of the Lodge. As I got closer, I saw that Sammy's parents were already in line, in a position near the door. Coach Gary squeezed past the line as he exited the café with a cup of something hot. He'd removed the monarch wings and had his leather jacket unzipped. He was all smiles and seemed almost to glow from the success of his Lord of the Butterfly duties. I saw several people speak to him and assumed by the humble bow of his head and big smile that he was collecting compliments.

As he passed Sammy's parents, Sammy's dad stopped him. No smile and bowed head this time — Coach Gary's expression darkened instead. I suppose Dr. Bernard Glickner was probably telling him something about the sky lanterns being dangerous. Sammy's father must have realized he'd said the wrong thing, because the next thing he did was pat Coach Gary on the shoulder.

The only way I could describe the move was that it looked like they were in solidarity about something.

I tried to thread my way through the line to join them but kept getting dirty looks, like I was trying to cut in front. I'd almost reached them when a tall woman who looked like the stereotype of an old maid librarian blocked my path and gave me a scathing look.

"Missy, there's a line," she said, holding her arms out. I was going to point out Sammy's parents but decided it wasn't worth the battle. I'd just wait until they saw me. Maybe I had another motive as well — I was now close enough to hear what they were saying. I hoped they would spill whatever they planned to "discuss" with me and Sammy. Better to be prepared.

Satisfied that I wasn't going to try to pass her, the librarian turned away from me, and I was able to get in even better hearing range of Sammy's parents.

"I know where you went," Estelle said. "Bernard, you have a problem."

"I do not," he countered. "Just because I'm bored with a butterfly festival and went looking for something else to do doesn't mean I have a problem." They moved into the doorway of the café. "This detour was your idea anyway."

"You should have used that time to talk to your son." Estelle seemed to move her head a lot as she spoke. "There's something he's not telling us. She's working a couple of jobs. His mind seems to be on something other than his medical career. That house is tiny. Did you see Sammy's socks on the floor? He never does that."

"Aren't you Mrs. Detective," he said. "But I agree, he's hiding something. He's never had any sense where Casey was concerned."

They said something after that, but it was drowned out by the conversation going on behind me. I wondered what his parents had up their sleeves.

Sammy came barreling through the line. He grabbed my arm and prepared to move around the librarian. She started to block him, but Sammy's parents turned and saw us.

"There you two are," Estelle said. The librarian made a disgruntled noise and then let us pass.

We found a table in the corner and spent a few minutes settling in with our drinks and making small talk about Vista Del Mar. Poor Sammy kept looking around nervously, probably afraid someone who knew about his magic show was going to suddenly appear and say something.

And then they got down to it. "It looks like the two of you are having lots of fun here playing house," Bernard said. "But Sammy you need to come back to Chicago so you can pick up your career again before it is too late and you lose your spot in the practice."

I was listening and watching the dynamics of the room at the same time. I saw Lieutenant Borgnine use his badge to push through the line and come inside. The bulldog-shaped man squinted his eyes as he looked from table to table. I tried to will myself invisible, but it didn't work, and his gaze rested on me.

Estelle was talking to me about the advantages available for Sammy in Chicago. "You wouldn't want to be responsible for holding him back, would —" Just then the lieutenant reached the table and interrupted her.

He ignored everyone but me. "I know what you're doing, helping that boyfriend of yours. He's off the case and so are you."

I'm not sure what upset Sammy's mother more, being cut off or what Lieutenant Borgnine had said. Sammy leaned back in his chair as his eyes went skyward in hopelessness. Bernard scowled at his son.

I took the chicken's way out. "Thanks for

the drinks and suggestions, but I have to get to the restaurant to do my baking," I said, quickly pushing back my chair. As I walked toward the door, I glanced back and saw that both the elder Glickners were leaning close to their son and seemed to be lecturing. I knew the topic was me.

11

I took a few minutes to refresh myself as I drove to downtown Cadbury and parked the yellow Mini Cooper in front of the Blue Door. There were more people on the street than was usual for this time. Butterfly Week or not, all the stores except for the drugstore were closed, and the restaurants that had been persuaded to stay open all week during their usual extended weekend hours were in the process of closing.

The Blue Door's waitstaff had finished clearing up and was setting up for the next day. Tag was by the front, taking care of the last diner's check. My eye immediately went to the spot where my desserts were displayed. I had such a reputation that people often ordered their dessert to be set aside even before they ordered their dinner, so they'd be sure to get it. The usual sign that read DESSERTS BY CASEY was missing, and there was a half of one of the cakes left.

Tag saw me looking. "See what happens when we don't put your name on them," he said. "Lucinda made me promise not to tell you'd baked them, either. I was just told to say that we were trying something new if anyone asked." As an afterthought he added, "You probably should bake one less cake."

I wasn't happy with the suggestion, but I didn't say anything. Obviously, Lucinda hadn't told him why I didn't want my name associated with the desserts. His manner made me think that either he hadn't heard any rumors about my muffins being suspicious or he'd ignored them.

He seemed even more fidgety than usual and kept looking out the window. I went to take my supplies into the kitchen. The wait-staff had just finished up and were heading out the door. I took my supplies back to the kitchen and saw the chef slinging his back-pack on his shoulder. "It's all yours," he said. The words were friendly enough, but his tone sounded begrudging. There was always this awkward switch-over, since we both seemed rather territorial about the cooking space.

As I was putting the muffin supplies out of the way, Tag stuck his head in. He seemed nervous and preoccupied. "I'm not leaving quite yet. Just go on about your baking and don't pay any attention to me," he said. He was acting so strange I wondered if I should try to contact Lucinda, but then I remembered she'd told me that he seemed worried about something and was being secretive.

Since it was obvious I had a lot less baking to do, instead of beginning to set out the ingredients for the cakes I was going to bake, I hung by the door to the dining room to see what was going to happen.

I heard a soft knock on the glass door and then Tag's voice talking to someone. I waited to see if the person would come inside, but instead Tag went out onto the porch that ran along the side of the converted house. There was another door in the kitchen that led to the same porch, but it was solid wood. I opened it a crack and looked out into the darkness. A little light came off the street lamps along Grand Street, but it only illuminated the area enough for me to see Tag was talking to another man. They were keeping their voices low, and I couldn't make out any words, although I could pick up a little of their body language.

They weren't adversarial — if anything the other man seemed apologetic. Their conversation ended abruptly, and the other man turned to go. As he got to the stairs, the light illuminated him, though I only saw him from the back. He didn't seem familiar to me. All I could see of his clothing was a jacket that seemed like a Windbreaker, and when the streetlight hit his footwear, I saw that he was wearing boots. The shine on them made me think they were rubber.

Tag never looked in my direction, and I slipped the door shut as he went back inside. I made up an excuse to come into the main part of the restaurant. He was standing looking out the window as if he wasn't seeing what was there at all. He muttered something to himself that sounded like "Thank you."

I cleared my throat to announce my presence. "Everything okay?" I asked.

It took him an extra moment to react. "Why are you asking?" he said, seeming nervous again. He straightened a few knives the waitstaff had left slightly off-kilter and then, without waiting for me to answer, said he was going home.

When he'd gone, I went back to the kitchen, wondering what I should say to Lucinda about Tag's behavior. I really didn't want to be in the middle of something, and yet she was such a good friend to me, I felt an obligation to tell her what I'd seen.

I turned on some soft jazz and tried to set

a better mood for my baking. I had decided on a basic chocolate layer cake and sweet potato muffins. I was taking out the baking chocolate when I heard a knock at the door.

I peered into the darkness of the front porch to check who my visitor was before unlocking the door. Dane bobbed his head closer to the glass pane and smiled.

I opened the door and invited him in. "I couldn't talk before," he said. "I was on duty, and there were too many ears around."

He was definitely not on duty now. His faded blue jeans hugged his body, and he wore a thick hoodie on top. With all the karate and running, his body was in perfect shape and always seemed to be full of potential energy. He had an angular face with a stubborn jaw.

He sniffed the air. "You're getting a late start," he said. "There's usually something baking by now."

So far I hadn't told him anything about my worries, and I debated whether to bring it up now. It seemed like he had enough on his plate with his sister. Dane followed me into the kitchen, took off the hoodie and offered to help. He saw the baking chocolate on the counter. "Do you need this chopped?" he asked.

It didn't really need to be. But it would

melt faster and more evenly if the chocolate was in smaller pieces. I handed him a chopping blade, and he set to work.

"So, Chloe isn't giving up on being a princess," I said. Dane stopped what he was doing and turned to me with a confused shake of his head.

"I don't get it. Chloe has never wanted to be part of anything around Cadbury until this. Of all the things to choose. She's my sister, but I don't think she has a chance to become Butterfly Queen, even with Rosalie Hardcastle gone."

"I'm sorry I really don't have anything to report on her killer yet," I said. I certainly didn't want to tell him that everyone I'd talked to seemed sure that Chloe was the killer. "You probably know more than I do."

"Yes, nobody is supposed to tell me anything, but I'm just so lovable they can't help themselves," he teased. "I know that the cause of death was the stabbing and her body has been released. Because of all the hoopla around here all week, I heard the town council talked her husband into waiting for the wake and funeral. They won't happen until the monarchs have all been welcomed and the queen crowned."

"What about the knife?" I asked.

"This is actually a good place to ask about

it," he said. He looked around the kitchen and started opening drawers.

"If you're looking for the chef's knives, he takes them with him. I don't know if it's because the chef is worried I might use them and do something bad or he isn't sure if he's coming back and wants to be certain he has his belongings." I pulled out a drawer. "This is what's here for me to use."

Dane looked through the drawer and pulled out a paring knife. "It was something like this, and it had a label that said *Vista Del Mar Kitchen* on it." He handed it to me, and I looked it over.

Before I could ask who had access to the resort's kitchen, Dane was already telling me that the butterfly group had ordered special food. "They had a cheese plate, and there was a knife with it. It seems most likely that's where it came from. So, anybody who helped themselves to a hunk of cheese could have taken the knife as well."

"What about fingerprints?"

"There were a lot of different fingerprints all over the handle. But somebody finally got the bright idea that you hold a knife differently to cut cheese than to stab someone."

"For someone who's off the case, you seem to know an awful lot," I said.

"It's all my charm," he teased. "I just wink and everyone falls at my feet, except you. Anyway, they found some smudged prints, but it doesn't matter, because Chloe, in her own confused style sense, had gloves on."

I remembered her outfit, and it did seem odd that she'd chosen to cover her hands when she'd left so much of the rest of herself exposed.

"Lieutenant Borgnine caught up with me earlier. He seemed to know that I was helping you." I put down the knife. "And he told me to back off."

"I wonder how he found out?" Dane said. He put his hands up in innocence. "It couldn't have been anything I said. It's probably just his cop instinct, which this time happens to be right."

"It was really awkward, too. I was sitting with Sammy and his parents in the café, and he talked about my boyfriend, and it was obvious he didn't mean Sammy."

Dane leaned against the counter, and a cloud passed over his expression. "Have you found out why they're here?"

"They want Sammy to go back to Chicago. His mother was starting to work on me. They didn't say it exactly, but I think they're willing to do whatever it takes."

Dane grew thoughtful. "You mean like

getting you to go back with him, probably with a ring on your finger?"

"Something like that, but remember, they think he's here because of me, that we're a couple. I wish he'd just tell them about the magic and let them explode and leave."

"Sounds like a good plan to me," Dane said, seeming relieved.

I let out a heavy sigh, and Dane studied my face. All the stuff he'd gone through with his family and then all the work he'd done with the local kids had made him very perceptive to people. Without me saying a word, he knew there was something else wrong.

He took my hand and led me to the small sunporch, where the tables sat all ready for the next day. He pulled out a chair and urged me to sit, and then he took a chair for himself. "Okay, let it all go. Whatever it is, I'm sure I've heard worse."

I hung my head. "It's about my baking." I told him about Rosalie's comment about the corn muffins. "She was trying to get the heat off her chili and put it on me."

He started to say I should let it go, but I interrupted him. "I'm not upset about that. I'm worried that now people will think — are thinking — there's something wrong with my desserts and muffins." He scoffed at the idea, but I continued. "It's real. Sales are down. Everybody but Maggie called up and asked me to halve their order. Even here." I made a vague gesture toward the front of the restaurant, where the dessert counter was. "I had them take my name off the carrot cake. Tag seems to think we're doing some kind of test."

"Just relax," Dane said, putting his hand on mine. "Everyone will forget about the football game in a few weeks. It turns out it wasn't just local pride. I heard there was some illegal betting going on, and some people were angry that they lost." He shook his head at the absurdness of it. "They even bet on what day the first butterflies would actually arrive."

"You think they're betting on who gets to be Butterfly Queen?" I was joking, but only halfway. What if that was true?

"If they are, Chloe is definitely the long shot." He got up and took me back in the kitchen. "Lieutenant Borgnine gave me the early morning shift downtown, and I probably should be home sleeping, but I'm not leaving you stuck like this. Chop-chop. Time to get back to work," he said with a wave toward the empty bowl on the table. "Go cream that butter and add the sugar. We've got goodies to make."

12

I woke up groggy Tuesday morning. I probably would have overslept, but Julius was standing on my chest, licking my forehead with his sandpaper tongue. I'd fallen into bed with my clothes on, and I suspected that some muffin batter had gotten stuck to my hair.

"Not as good as stink fish, huh?" I said when the cat tired of it and stepped off me onto the bed. I lay on my side for a moment, thinking about the night before and the day ahead. Dane had stayed with me until the two chocolate cakes were frosted and set on their pedestal dishes and the smaller orders of muffins had been taken around town. He even walked with me onto the grounds of Vista Del Mar when I dropped off their supply.

"May they all speed out of those baskets," he said, waving his hand as if it was a magic wand.

"I think that's Sammy's domain," I said. And, out of nowhere, as we were going back down the driveway, he put his arm around me and kissed me.

"I don't know why you're still so skittish about our relationship. Why not just throw caution to the wind and admit what everybody else knows? We have a thing for each other."

I knew what he was saying was right. We did have a thing for each other, but I was still too worried about what would happen when it didn't work out. I hadn't said anything to him, but if my baking career died, there was a good chance I'd have to leave Cadbury. All of this was getting uncomfortable, and I struggled to change the subject. I brought up Tag and how he'd been acting.

"He snuck out on the porch to meet up with some guy in a Windbreaker and weird rubber boots," I said.

"Not so weird around here," Dane said. "He sounds like a fisherman. Probably for squid. They go out late."

"But why would Tag be meeting a squid fisherman?"

Dane glanced around the restaurant. "You're the detective. Why do you think?" Of course, the answer was obvious.

"He wants to add it to the menu and was arranging to get it directly from the fisherman," I said and Dane nodded in approval.

"Though I imagine Tag will call it calamari. Sounds more appetizing than a plate of squid."

I took another minute to lay there thinking about the night before. I winced remembering how Sammy had opened the guest house door when Dane and I were walking up my driveway. It was so awkward. Sammy had told us both that his parents had taken off the gloves after I'd left and laid into him that he was wasting his time in Cadbury.

Julius interrupted my thoughts by stepping onto my hip and looking down at my face as his tail swished. He wasn't going to leave me alone until he got his morning snack. I went barefoot into the kitchen.

The phone rang while I was trying to wake myself up with a cup of coffee. I'd finally moved from instant to using a filter in a ceramic holder and brewing it a cup at a time. I considered not answering the phone for a moment. I didn't have to look at the screen to see who was calling. There was only one person who called this early.

"Hello, Mother," I said, trying to sound more awake.

"I just thought I'd check in and see how

things are going," she said. I saw right through it. She wanted to find out how it was going with Sammy's parents.

"You knew they were coming, didn't you?" I said. "And you knew they thought Sammy and I were back together."

"Estelle might have mentioned they were considering stopping by to see Sammy after the medical conference. And that they were hoping to convince Sammy to leave Cadbury. She tried to enlist my help in convincing you two to get married. I told her that I wasn't the kind of parent who interfered in her children's lives."

I was having trouble holding back a laugh. Not interfere, ha! My mother finished talking, and there was a silence I was supposed to fill with how things were going. When I started to talk about something else, she got impatient.

"Casey, just tell me what happened."

I had too much on my mind to play around anymore, so I just spilled it all, about Sammy pretending to be living at my place and that he was just giving lip service to his parents and had no intention of leaving Cadbury.

"He's staying at your place?" my mother said, with an uplift in her voice.

"In the guest house," I said. I wanted to

get off the phone quickly. My mother could read my voice too well, and I was afraid I'd let on that something was wrong. Then she'd work at me until I spilled it all. My worry about losing my baking business would only fuel her efforts to get me to take her up on cooking school in Paris, or even better, throw in the towel on the whole thing and move back to Chicago.

"Got to go," I said. "A big day ahead of me." Then before she could question me any more, I hung up.

Julius and I both heard a key in the lock and turned as Sammy came in. He was freshly dressed, and his eyes went right to my coffee. It was then that I remembered I was still wearing the black jeans and turtleneck from the day before, and I could only imagine what a mess my hair was. I expected some kind of revulsion to show in his expression, but I might as well have been Cinderella after the fairy godmother did her work, by the way his face looked.

Sammy was so unshakable — he was one of those people who didn't seem to get down. He reminded me of those toys that just bounced back up again when you knocked them over. He seemed unaffected by the grilling his parents had given him. I wished he could give me a lesson in that.

Even though I'd been in control of the call with my mother, she still always got to me. I offered to make him a cup of coffee and gave him his choice of the yogurt in the refrigerator.

"I cleared my calendar," he said. "I'm spending the whole day with my parents. I'm hoping I can talk them into going home. Then life can go back to normal."

"Good luck with your mission," I said, setting the mug in front of him and pouring the boiling water into the filter. I left him with the fresh coffee dripping into his mug.

It took a couple of soapings to get the hardened cake and muffin batter out of my hair. I added a peacock blue cowl over the fresh black turtleneck and grabbed an olive green fleece. When I came through the kitchen, Sammy was gone. He'd washed both our mugs and put them in the drainer.

It felt good to be outside in the cool damp air. The sky was a pale apricot as the sun tried to make a showing. I rushed down the driveway and passed the Lodge without stopping, heading directly to the Sea Foam dining hall.

There was a buzz of conversation and the clatter of dishes and silverware. I took in the breakfast scents of pancakes and maple syrup, mixed with the pungent aroma of bacon, and my hunger surged. I went directly to the food line and loaded a plate with a little bit of everything. Then I went in search of a seat.

"Sit by me," Lucinda said, waving me over as I passed her table. I set down my plate in the adjacent spot and pulled off my jacket. As I sat down I looked over at the other tables with my retreaters. I saw that everyone had brought along their loom and was working on it — including Scott.

"So, they really did give up," I said, discreetly indicating the needle enthusiasts who were sitting together.

"I don't think they wanted to be left out." Lucinda held up hers, and I was impressed at how much knitted material was hanging through the center.

"Where's your loom?" she asked.

"I've had a few things on my mind," I said — an understatement. "I left everything in the meeting room."

Lucinda put down the loom and picked up her coffee cup.

"How did it go last night?" Lucinda asked. "Was Tag okay?"

I knew she was asking because she'd mentioned that he'd been acting strange lately, like he was worried about something, and when she had asked about it, he'd insisted everything was fine.

I considered how to answer. With all that Dane and I had figured out about Tag's meeting with the fisherman, it seemed likely that the worry Lucinda had noticed might be tied to him arranging for the squid, though why he wouldn't have told her was beyond me. But then I didn't understand a lot of what Tag did.

"He should be fine now. I think he worked it out so that you'll be getting the freshest squ— I mean, calamari," I said, explaining what I had witnessed.

"What?" Lucinda said, snapping to attention. "There's no calamari on the menu. He's adding something without discussing it with me."

"Maybe he was planning to surprise you when he got it all together," I offered. *Which I had now ruined.* It was useless to suggest she forget what I'd said.

Her eyes were flashing and she wanted to rush off to the Lodge and call him. *What had I done?* I convinced her to wait to talk to him in person when we went downtown later, figuring she would be more rational by then. I needed to do something to get her to calm down.

I borrowed from what I'd learned during my teaching days. When dealing with an

174

unruly student, I'd found that getting them to help me with something calmed them right down. I pushed the loom toward her.

"I am still having trouble wrapping the yarn around the pegs. Could you show me how you do it?" It worked like a charm. Lucinda's expression relaxed as she picked up the loom and began to work with the yarn.

She was completely back to herself as she joined the others when breakfast ended. Meanwhile I went to the Lodge to make sure the transportation was set to get everybody into town that afternoon for a Butterfly Week event. I passed the chapel on my way. Kevin St. John had put up a temporary fence with a covering to block the view of the building, so that the guests had no idea the small structure was still surrounded in yellow tape. As I looked at the fence, Lieutenant Borgnine came from behind the screen and surveyed the area before noticing me.

I expected him to immediately get the pained expression that my presence tended to inspire and head in the other direction, but instead he walked directly toward me and called my name.

"As long as you're here," he said, when he'd reached me, "it's come to my attention that you had an altercation with the victim."

"Altercation?" I said. A silent standoff followed my question. He didn't want to give more details, and I didn't know what he was talking about, except that he was trying to say that I might have a motive to kill Rosalie. I knew I was kind of a thorn in his side, but was he so desperate to get rid of me that he was pointing the light of suspicion on me? Kevin St. John came by in his golf cart and stopped it next to us.

"I was just asking Ms. Feldstein about her altercation with Rosalie Hardcastle, but she seems to have amnesia," the lieutenant said.

"Maybe I can help refresh her memory," the Vista Del Mar manager said. "Rosalie said it was your muffins that made the two players get sick, which caused the football team to lose the biggest game of the year. And you seemed very upset, as you insisted it couldn't have been your muffins."

Now I knew what they were talking about. "I'd hardly call that an altercation. She was trying to get the blame off her chili and said it could have been something else, like my corn muffins." I looked the rumpled cop in the eye. "Actually, it was Maggie who defended the muffins. Not me."

The two men traded satisfied nods. "Whatever, Ms. Feldstein," Lieutenant

176

Borgnine said. "But we know a good part of your livelihood is dependent on your baking. If someone put the quality of something you baked in question, you might have gotten angry, very angry."

"You have to be kidding." I started to pull away.

"We'll be in touch," the lieutenant said.

The morning workshop was uneventful, and the group went right to lunch from the meeting room. I stayed with them, enjoying the grilled cheese sandwiches and tomato soup. After lunch, the retreaters gathered in front of the Lodge and loaded into the small bus to go to the main part of Cadbury. I had pushed the whole episode with Lieutenant Borgnine and Kevin St. John out of my mind. It was too ridiculous to even consider, and we had a full afternoon ahead of us.

When I first got the idea of including the Butterfly Week activities in the retreat schedule, I was told I had to include a trip to the Monarch Sanctuary. It made perfect sense, since the actual butterflies were what all the hoopla was about.

The stop to see the butterflies proved to be very popular. When the bus turned onto the side street, I was surprised to see it clogged with traffic. The driver had trouble finding a place to park, but eventually, the group filed out, and I led the way.

The word *sanctuary* made it sound a lot grander than it was. There was just a small sign at the end of a driveway that looked like it had originally been an alley. The road went past a local motel to a stand of tall trees. It had been pointed out to me that the butterflies had chosen the trees first, and after the fact, the area around them had become considered a sanctuary.

A number of docents were standing near a kiosk that had butterfly information. They were easy to pick out, because they were dressed in monarch orange, with bobbing black antennas on their heads. Throngs of people were walking around the small area, looking up at the trees. The sun had burned through the clouds and was filtering through the greenery — or what at first appeared to be greenery. As I looked up, I began to see movement, and the trees became alive with fluttering wings. The trees were literally covered with butterflies hanging from the foliage. Every so often, bunches of them would leave their roost and flutter around, which brought out aahs from the crowd.

One of the docents had stopped next to me and was speaking to the gathered group. "Warm air makes the monarchs more active," she explained.

There was no need for me to babysit my group here, and I began to look around at the flow of people coming down the driveway. It was impossible to miss Cora and Madeleine Delacorte. Cora didn't know the meaning of casual and wore a suit under a coat and low heels. As always, she carried her handbag Queen Elizabeth–style. Madeleine made an odd contrast. Up until recently, she'd dressed just like her younger sister, down to the green eye shadow. But then she'd gone rogue and fallen in love with jeans. I'm sure Cora was horrified by her sister's black jeans and fleece jacket. When I looked down and saw I had on a similar outfit, I realized I might have been the inspiration.

When I noticed Cora and Madeleine had the rest of the Butterfly Queen committee with them, I understood they were there on official duty. The Princess Court followed the two women like a line of ducklings. I surveyed the group as they reached the center of the Sanctuary. Chloe had done another hair color change — underneath her tiara, her dark hair now had an orange tint. I wondered if she thought the very fitted black tracksuit with *hot* written across the back of the pants was more appropriate than her previous midriff-baring outfit.

The committee and the princesses gathered around a docent while some of the other volunteers brought out a couple of lawn chairs and a large covered bucket and set them up near the group. Cora stepped forward and began to speak to the crowd.

"Butterfly Queen is more than a ceremonial title. Our queen has to be a monarch of the monarchs. All week, the Princess Court will be led through the paces of the queen's jobs, so the committee can evaluate who truly should have the title."

The docent came forward and explained how they tracked the butterflies and the need to mark them. She sat in one of the lawn chairs and reached in the bucket to demonstrate. I was surprised to see her hand come out holding a monarch by the wings. She examined the butterfly's wings first and determined it hadn't been marked, then used a marker to make an X mark on the wing. She looked to the line of princesses. "Not only will the queen be a regular docent here at the Sanctuary, it will be her job to help mark and keep track of the butterflies during their stay."

I heard someone calling my name — well, a shortened version of it. Sammy was the only one who called me Case.

"There she is," he said. I saw his parents walking behind him. "I told you we'd run into her."

I smiled at his parents, who looked like they wished they were anywhere but there. It made me chuckle inside to see that they both wore beige fleece jackets with *Cadbury by the Sea* embossed on them.

Sammy came over and gave me a big hug and kiss. I knew it was for his parents' benefit, but he was also taking advantage of the moment. I thought that moment had gone unnoticed by anyone other than his parents, but when Sammy let go, Chloe, in all her orange-haired glory, was standing near me. "Does my brother know about this?" She pointed an accusing finger at me and Sammy. She seemed about to say more, but then she made an exasperated sound and went back to her place at the end of the line.

"What did she mean?" Estelle said, glaring at me.

Sammy stepped in and tried to smooth things over, saying it was just a misunderstanding. His father chimed in a moment later. "It didn't look like a misunderstanding to me."

Time to make a getaway. I pretended that Lucinda had waved for me to join her. "I'm sure Sammy told you that I'm here with my group and they need me." Before I escaped in the crowd, I gave them each an awkward hug and said how glad I was to have seen them. When I did join Lucinda and looked back to where they'd been standing, I saw that they were gone.

The group had seen their share of monarchs and heard enough of their story and seemed ready to move on. The docents had begun to have the princesses try their hand at examining and marking the monarchs. Chloe had positioned herself at the end of the line of princesses. I wondered if she would make a run for it before it was her turn. I couldn't help it; I wanted to see what Chloe would do, so I stalled them.

One by one they took their turns: Crystal's daughter, Marcy; Wanda's sister; and the other young women. They were all awkward at the job, and most of the monarchs escaped their grasp. Chloe kept moving up in line, and her mouth was locked in a defiant slash.

I heard some muttering in the crowd when her turn came. I wasn't sure if it had to do with her being the chief person of interest in Rosalie's death or just that she was so out of sync with the rest of the court. She stepped up and looked over at the crowd, not letting go of the tough expression. She dipped her hand in the bucket and came up with a butterfly. The docent started telling her what to do next.

"I got it covered," Chloe said. She held on to the butterfly and examined its wings. Then she took the marker and made a mark before letting the butterfly go. "Nailed it," she said, holding her arms up in a triumphant manner.

"Maybe she did," Lucinda said, standing next to me. "But I don't think it won her any points."

I waved the group over, and we headed back to the bus. "Next stop, Grand Street," I said, taking my seat in the front. Lucinda was sitting next to me as we began the short drive to the main street in Cadbury.

"I don't know what to say to Tag," she said. "Why would he go behind my back and add calamari to the menu and while I was gone meet up with a fisherman to arrange for his catch?" I was relieved she sounded less upset than before and suggested that maybe she ought to just let it be until after the retreat. She didn't give any indication if she agreed.

After a very short ride, the bus let us off. Each day Grand Street seemed busier with all the added tourists. Cadbury had strict rules about what stores they would and wouldn't allow. There were no big-box stores or even chains. As a result, the downtown area was reminiscent of the past, which made it very appealing.

The group followed me down the side street that sloped toward the water. When they saw the bungalow-style house with Cadbury Yarn sign, I heard a number of people comment on how charming it was. They eagerly trooped inside.

"This was such a good idea," Lucinda said, stopping next to me as we reached the main room. "That must be what we're going to be making," she said, pointing out the crocheted monarchs that were hanging all over the store. A table in the front was stacked with kits and a sign that said MAKE AND TAKE.

Like in the rest of the town, there was more business than usual in the yarn store. Small groupings of chairs were spread among the cubbies of yarn, and most of them were full of people working on making butterflies.

When Gwen had first suggested I bring the group in to learn how to crochet a butterfly, it seemed like the perfect activity, since it had both yarn and butterflies in it. There had been some grumbling when the retreaters first saw it on the schedule, though. Most of them didn't know how to crochet and seemed baffled by it. The Danish women were the only ones who were really proficient. I reminded the group that I put on yarn retreats, not just knitting retreats. I remembered from my substitute teaching days how the kids had balked at anything new. I figured it had something to do with the fear of not being able to do it, but Gwen had assured me she'd be able to teach them.

Crystal came into the main room and greeted the group before taking us back to what was once the dining room. It looked out on a tiny yard, which was filled with native plants, or at least that was how the townspeople always described them. It was certainly nicer than calling them weeds. They were green, and they thrived.

"Everyone find a seat," Crystal said, indicating the folding chairs that had been set up in the bright room. "You'll find a kit on your chair."

There was a buzz of conversation as they all started looking through the small shopping bags. Gwen had given me a pre-lesson, so I knew the bags had a couple of crochet hooks, small hanks of yarn in the monarch colors of orange and black, a tapestry needle and some written instructions.

I looked around, expecting Gwen to come in and start the lesson. "I don't know what's keeping my mother," Crystal said. "I can start, but this is really her thing."

It was easy for Crystal to get their attention. She had on several layers of shirts in deep pink, orange and purple, with the bottoms showing over one another. Different-shaped earrings dangled from her ears, and as usual, she'd pulled off wearing heavy eye makeup without looking like a clown.

Lucinda was listening along with everyone else as Crystal had them take out some yarn and make a slip knot, but she still looked distracted. I knew she was probably ruminating about the calamari and I wished I had said nothing. I had thought she would be relieved that his inner turmoil was about seafood. I was certainly wrong.

I glanced back toward the main part of the store. Gwen had hired extra help for the week, and a woman I didn't know was ringing up sales. Marcy was helping with customers, too. She was wearing her princess crown — she must have come to the store when she'd finished with her Butterfly Princess duties. It was amazing what a big deal this week was in Cadbury. The kids even had it off from school.

I finally returned to the front and asked Marcy about her grandmother's whereabouts. "She's in the storage room," Marcy said, pointing to a door. I pushed it open and went in, expecting to see Gwen gathering up some extra stock. Instead, she was standing very close to a man, and they seemed in such deep conversation that she didn't notice my presence.

I got a side view of him, so all I could really see was that he had shaggy dark hair and wore faded jeans with a work shirt tucked in. I finally cleared my throat to announce my presence. Gwen's head shot up with a worried expression.

"The lesson!" she said, seeming to suddenly remember. "Go on back in the store. I'll be with you in a moment." She had moved to further block my view of the man with her.

I followed her order and stood outside the door to the back room, expecting them both to exit. I was totally surprised to see only her come out.

"Where's your friend?" I blurted out, trying to see back into the room before the door slid shut.

Gwen was so different than her daughter. There was an impassive quality about her, and her face showed no emotional response to my question. "I don't know what you mean."

I knew that I wasn't crazy and that there had been someone in there with her. I pushed the door back open and looked inside. The storage room was empty, but I noticed there was another door.

Why was Gwen being so secretive? Was he a secret boyfriend? It made me wonder what a date would be like for someone her age. It was kind of like imagining my mother on a date. Did flirting change when you got older? The whole image was unsettling, and I gladly pushed it out of my mind.

Gwen didn't say a word, and I followed her back to the group. Crystal had taught them the stitches they needed for the monarchs but gladly stepped aside for her mother to take over.

Lucinda seemed to be distracted and was just holding her crochet hook and staring off in space. Finally, she laid down her work and came over to where I was standing.

"I can't take it. I have to confront Tag about the calamari." She pulled on her Ralph Lauren jacket and headed for the door. Lucinda had helped me out of some difficult situations before, so I rushed after her, hoping to help her this time.

Over at the Blue Door, lunch was just

finishing up. Sammy and his parents were at a table by the window. He waved wildly when I came in and went to pull out a chair. "Case, you made it for lunch," he said, as if we'd had some plan. I snagged Lucinda's arm to keep her from rushing up to Tag alone. We stopped at their table, and I introduced her as my boss.

"Remember, Case makes all the desserts," Sammy said proudly. He went on about how they sold out all the time. His father glanced toward the counter, where the chocolate cakes were on display. Only one piece was missing.

"I don't know what's going on," his father began. "But your mother and I know you're keeping something from us. She's working two jobs; you seem to have time on your hands. And that tiny little house. Is she supporting you? Are you even working in a urology practice?"

Lucinda pulled free. "I have to talk to Tag."

I left Sammy to tell his parents whatever he could come up with as I followed along behind Lucinda. "It's only a menu addition," I said.

"That's where it starts. Who knows what he'll do next? He is so different than the boy I knew in high school."

Tag was talking to one of the waitstaff when Lucinda rushed up to him.

I still questioned if all that hair was really his. The thick brown mop looked almost like a wig.

"You can't go adding calamari to the menu without consulting me."

"What about calamari?" Tag said. Then his face brightened. "I'm so glad to see you." He said the same to me. I tried to intercede to give Lucinda a moment to calm down and told him the group was crocheting butterflies.

"It's monarchs everywhere," he said. "Sit, you two. How about some coffee or food?"

Lucinda seemed a little calmer when she sat down. "Casey told me all about the fisherman. I know you're trying to order calamari."

Tag seemed totally baffled. He turned to me. "When did you see me making a deal for calamari?"

Lucinda answered for me. "Last night. You've been acting strange for weeks," she said. "I told Casey about it, and then she said she saw you talking to the fisherman and thought there was a connection."

Tag swallowed so hard his Adam's apple bounced. "There is absolutely nothing for you to be concerned about. Everything is fine. There was no fisherman and no order for his squid catch."

"No, it isn't fine. You seem nervous right now. What's going on?" Lucinda asked.

"You have to trust me. I can't talk about it. But I promise you there is nothing wrong." She tried to pry whatever it was out of him, but he was absolutely resolute and would say nothing more.

Lucinda was shaking her head, muttering to herself as we walked back to Cadbury Yarn. "I see our happily ever after crumbling right in front of me. I can deal with him straightening forks and having to wash his hands three times before he starts work. I can accept all his eccentricities, but I can't deal with him keeping secrets."

13

"That was a wonderful experience," said the retreater who always wore a gray wool poncho. She held up her finished butterfly proudly. "It turned out that crocheting wasn't so hard after all." She had a bag on her arm and showed me that she'd bought a bunch of crochet supplies.

I was waiting on the porch as the group came outside in good spirits. I could see that some of them were still in line to pay for their purchases, including the two Danish women, who were admiring each other's monarchs.

Crystal walked outside with the last of them. "It looks like it was a success all around. The retreaters seem happy, and the store made a lot of sales."

Crystal and I had become friends, and I considered mentioning the man in the storage room. But then I thought of the mess I'd stirred up with Lucinda when I'd brought up the man I thought was a calamari fisherman. I decided to keep it to myself.

The retreaters were anxious to spend some more time wandering around the main part of town, so I took them back to the bus to drop off their packages and then let them go off on their own, setting a time to meet back at the bus.

"Coffee at Maggie's?" I said to Lucinda.

"Yes. I am too upset with Tag to want to go back there." As we walked down Grand Street, I mused about how, with the strip of greenery down the middle, it really deserved to be called Grand Boulevard. I looked down the street toward the Butterfly Inn. The imposing yellow Victorian took up a whole corner.

"Poor Sammy. He can't go back to his room," I said. Lucinda turned to me, perplexed, and I continued. "I never got a chance to tell you the whole story. His parents are staying at the Butterfly Inn. And he told them we're living together."

Lucinda winced. "Now I get why he can't go to his room. I'm guessing you're letting him stay with you." She knew my history with Sammy and smiled. "I wouldn't say poor Sammy. It sounds like he's got his dream come true."

"He's staying in the guest house," I said. "But you're right, he doesn't seem that upset."

We continued on to Maggie's. Walking inside the small coffee place always gave me an instant lift. The scent of coffee was part of it, but it was mostly the atmosphere Maggie had created. She waved at us from the counter with such warmth that I felt instantly welcome. We started to get in line, but as she handed a customer their drink, she gestured for us to just sit down. "I'll bring you your regulars," she said with a smile.

Lucinda pointed out a table in the corner near a window, and I sat and looked out at the street.

After a few minutes, the line died down and Maggie came over, carrying a holder with three drinks. "I love it when you two come in and give me a reason to take a break. Okay if I join you?" she asked, setting the paper cups in front of us and then waiting for our nods of approval before adding hers. Lucinda and I made a move for our wallets, and Maggie laughed. "Don't even waste your energy going any further. You know I won't take your money. It's professional courtesy."

"Thanks for keeping your regular order

for the muffins," I said. "I really appreciate your support." Though she hadn't said anything, I was sure that, like the others, she hadn't sold all the muffins the day before. I knew she knew why, too.

"No problem," Maggie said with a warm smile. I looked over at the basket on the counter she used for my muffins. There were still half of them left, when normally by this time of day they would have been sold out long ago.

She saw me looking. "It doesn't mean a thing. Like I said before, everything is off-kilter this week. The power of Butterfly Week is amazing. Nobody is even talking about Rosalie's murder. They're just going about their business as if nothing's happened." Maggie had dropped her voice, though there was no one else around to hear.

"What do you mean?" I asked.

"It's not like they dropped the investigation or anything, but I heard the funeral isn't going to be until next week. They're saying her family can't get here until then, but I think it's the work of the town council. This is Cadbury's week to shine. You can imagine what a damper it would put on the festivities to have a funeral procession parade through the center of town."

"What about her family?" I asked, realizing I knew almost nothing about them.

"There's her husband, Hank, and two sons. Both of them went to college on the east coast and never looked back. I'm not sure if it was because of the small town or that they didn't want to have to deal with her." Maggie took a swig of her coffee. "Her husband is an okay guy."

"I wonder if I've ever seen him," I said.

"Maybe not. He's on the quiet side and never makes himself the center of attention, the way Rosalie did. Plus, he has an odd schedule."

"I think he might have come in the restaurant once with Rosalie," Lucinda said. "It was right after we opened, and Tag dealt with them. They seemed to be checking out the place, and they didn't even stay to eat. I got the feeling she dismissed us as outsiders." Lucinda seemed to be searching her memory. "I don't have any memory of him other than he was present. Everything seemed to be about her."

"Sounds right," Maggie said. "But you never really know with someone like him — if he was really that easygoing, or if he just let her be the heavy and was behind everything she did." Maggie sounded like she was talking about something specific, but when

I asked her, she seemed uncomfortable with the question and just said no.

"I suppose his true colors will come out now," Lucinda said. "Now that he can't hide behind her."

I saw several of the retreaters pass the window. They had pinned their crocheted butterflies to their jackets. I pointed them out to Maggie and mentioned what a good activity it had turned out to be. I thought about mentioning the vanishing man in Cadbury Yarn, but I decided if Gwen wanted to rendezvous with a secret boyfriend in the stockroom, I wasn't going to spread the word around town.

"I didn't realize how late it was," I said as Lucinda and I approached the small bus. When I looked inside I saw that most of the seats were already full and there was a din of conversation.

"There are two people missing," I said after doing a quick head count. Someone called out who they were and said she'd heard them say they had to pick something up at the drugstore.

"I'll go round them up," I said.

It had been a long afternoon, and I knew the group wanted to get back to Vista Del

Mar for a little free time before dinner. Like everything else in Cadbury, Cadbury Drugs & Sundries was an independent shop. It wasn't like the big chain drugstores that were almost general merchandise places these days, although it seemed to be pushing the envelope when it came to the meaning of sundries, and it sold some food items and souvenirs. I noticed a couple of paper replicas of monarchs hanging from the ceiling as I walked in.

To say the store was packed with merchandise was an understatement. The shelves were higher than my head, and every inch of wall space was taken up. I almost expected to see merchandise hanging from the ceiling along with the butterflies. The way the store was laid out, there was no way to just stand in the entrance and look for my retreaters. I started down the maze of aisles, checking out the shoppers. The aisles were narrow, and a man in a white jacket was blocking the one that had actual drug supplies with a red plastic bin filled with assorted products. He was about to put some of the stock on one of the shelves, but when he saw me, he started to move out of my way. I saw that his hands were full.

"Go on and finish what you're doing," I said, stopping next to him.

"I appreciate your patience," he said when he'd finished. "We're such a small store, there isn't room for a large supply of anything. Not good for a shelf to be empty." I glanced down at the shelf as he added a container of tropical-flavored antacids to the ones already there, filled an empty space with some small boxes of laxative pills and finished by putting two bottles of bright pink stomach medicine in front of the one bottle left. He picked up the bin and started to move away. "Let me know if I can help you find anything."

I laughed. "More like anyone." I explained who I was looking for. I was sure he was the pharmacist and owner. I'd never met him, but I had heard about him. His name was Larry something; he'd bought the business about eight months ago and was divorced with a teenage daughter. But that wasn't what made him the topic of conversation. He looked like a shorter version of Clint Eastwood — younger, too. I guessed that he was in his forties. What made it even more newsworthy was the fact that the real Clint Eastwood had a ranch nearby.

There were a lot of jokes about what would happen if they met up, particularly since Larry had taken some of Clint's taglines and made them his own. I'd heard the most popular one was something like "Hey, let Dirty Larry make your day," when he handed someone a prescription.

I introduced myself, and he did the same, just giving his name without any tagline. "Nice to meet you, Casey," he said, extending his hand. "I think you'll find the women with the butterflies in aisle three. They were looking for tooth care supplies." I waited to see if he was going to add a tagline now, but he just pointed toward the aisle. When I found the pair, I saw they'd been susceptible to all the store's extra merchandise, and they had a lot more than toothbrushes. I walked them to the front to check out, but not without picking up a bunch of stuff, too.

Lucinda poked through my bag of things when I got back on the bus. "Cat toys?" she said with a laugh.

I shrugged. "I thought maybe if Julius had something to amuse himself with, he wouldn't be so anxious to wander."

With everybody on board, the bus pulled away from the curb.

Lucinda brought up Chloe and asked if I'd made any headway in clearing her. I was glad she seemed to have let up on her upset with Tag. I shook my head, realizing I'd been too preoccupied with calamari and crocheted butterflies to think about her. "If you had another suspect to throw Lieutenant Borgnine's way, he might not be so sure Chloe was the killer," Lucinda said as the bus left the downtown area and passed through a street of houses.

I shrank back against the seat as I recalled my earlier encounter with the cop in the rumpled jacket. How had I managed to so successfully put it out of my mind? "There is one other suspect he has," I said. Lucinda let out a gasp when I told her it was me.

The ride back was too short to discuss more. In no time we were on the Vista Del Mar grounds again. As Lucinda got off the bus, she seemed concerned and asked if I wanted to talk about it more. But this was her time off, so I urged her to join the others as they headed back to their rooms to drop off their purchases and get ready for dinner. Cadbury was hardly a hustle-bustle town, but it was still far more peaceful on the rustic grounds of the resort. If only I could have let go and enjoyed the fading afternoon.

I was on a mission when I got home. I didn't even stop to give Julius his toys. No matter, he was already poking around the bag where I left it on the table. I was sure he'd probably like them better if he pulled them out of the bag on his own.

I sat down and grabbed my landline. Frank wouldn't be at the office now. He'd said never to use his cell number unless it was an emergency, but I decided being a suspect in a murder case qualified. I had hidden my panic from Lucinda, but now that I was alone, it came out in full force.

I punched in the number and tried to get my breath to sound regular.

"Frank, I'm a suspect," I said as soon as he answered.

"Feldstein," he said, sounding surprised. Then what I had said sunk in. "I can't say I'm surprised. I figured that cop with no neck would come up with something. Cops don't like it when you make them look bad by showing off that they were wrong and then solving their cases." Frank let out a chortle. "You didn't do it, did you?"

"Of course not. This isn't a joke. Lieutenant Borgnine wasn't smiling when he started questioning me. And I'm sure you're right that he would love to get rid of me by sending me off to prison."

"Calm down, Feldstein. We're not going to let that happen." I heard some sizzling noises in the background, and Frank begged off for a moment. "Some of us are cooking our dinner," he said when he returned.

"You cook?" I said, surprised. I had no doubt he ate, and a lot. He had the body to prove it. But somehow I'd pictured him living on sub sandwiches, cold French fries and donuts, with a liter of soda thrown in.

"Feldstein, I am a Renaissance man. I'm making a stir-fry over jasmine rice. And it's almost done. So here's my advice. Unless you can come up with some more suspects, you might have to just let him have the girl with the bright hair. Honestly, I'm thinking she really might have done it. The woman humiliated her in public and threw her out of the Princess Court. You said yourself the girl threatened her. You said the weapon was a kitchen knife from the place where the dinner was, which means she could have had access to it. And you make her sound like a tough tootsie."

"But Frank, she said she didn't do it."

I heard him laugh so hard he snorted. "Feldstein, really — just because she said it, you believe it?"

"Wait, Frank, there's someone else. Rosalie's husband."

"You didn't mention she had a husband. Now we're cooking with gas. Spouses make excellent suspects. That's what you've got to do — give that cop another suspect. Dinner's ready, got to go." He clicked off.

I can't say his advice gave me much comfort, but I had to put it on hold while I went back to being retreat leader and sat through dinner with my group. Afterward, most of them broke off into smaller groups to make more butterflies. A few were more interested in the evening events put on by Vista Del Mar. There was a sing-along by the fire pit and the screening of *Butterflies Are Free* in Hummingbird Hall. The movie had nothing to do with monarchs, but I guess since it had butterflies in the title someone thought it fit in with the plan for the week.

When I stopped back at home, there were messages from my muffin customers saying that they wanted to continue with the half orders. I suppose I should have been glad that they didn't cancel entirely.

I gathered up the supplies for the night's muffins and put them in a couple of recyclable grocery bags. Frank's words echoed in my mind. I had to give Lieutenant Borgnine another suspect, but how?

As I was loading everything into the Mini Cooper, I heard music coming from down the street. That meant that Dane had some of the local kids over in his garage for karate lessons. Dane would know what to do.

I walked down the street and up his

driveway before knocking on the door to the garage. Our houses were a similar style but not quite the same. The music and karate yells covered up my knock, and I tried again. When nobody seemed to be responding, I opened the door and went inside. The floor was covered with mats, and the walls had mirrors, which made the space seem larger than it was. A bunch of boys were kicking their legs and moving in some kind of routine. Dane was in a white karate suit with a black sash, walking around and correcting their form. He was almost next to me before he realized I was there.

His angular face softened into a smile, and he held my gaze. He was definitely glad to see me. The boys gave me the once-over. I noticed Crystal's son, Kory, was among them. He gave me a little wave, but the others began teasing Dane, calling me his lady and saying they bet he liked my muffins.

Laughing, Dane told one of the other kids to take over and led me outside. There were some catcalls as we walked away.

"Don't mind them," he said. "I'd rather they tease me than grumble about the loss of that homecoming game. This is the first time they've been here since the game. I'm glad to see them back in action."

"Are the players who got sick in there?" I

asked, and Dane nodded.

"They were the ones making the catcalls." Dane had his teasing smile.

"I heard someone yell out something about muffins. I suppose they blame me for getting sick," I said.

Dane rolled his eyes. "I don't think they were referring to the muffins you bake. Teenage boys are kind of crude."

"Oh," I said, realizing what they meant. I also realized that I'd gotten distracted from my reason for coming over. "There's something I want to talk to you about — regarding the case."

"I'm all ears," he said, leaning against the wall and folding his arms. The door opened, and a couple of the boys came out.

"Sorry to interrupt, but we were wondering if you made some of that spaghetti." Dane told them that he had, and they went back inside, only to reappear a moment later.

"Everybody is asking how long till we eat?"

"In a few minutes — it's all ready," he said, urging the boys to go back inside. Then he turned back to me. "Sorry. You were saying?"

"This was a mistake," I said. "Maybe we can talk later."

His face warmed. "Much better idea." He

glanced toward his house. "You could come back when you're done, if you don't mind Chloe."

"That's not good. It might be hard to say things in front of her."

"There's your place," he said.

I shook my head. "Not with Sammy in the guest house." Dane got it and agreed. I suggested he come by when I was baking, but he said feeding the crew and the cleanup was going to take a while. "Those boys are like bottomless pits, even more so after a workout. I make them help with the cleanup, but it's more about teaching them to be responsible than speed at getting it done."

"Maybe we should just wait until tomorrow," I said.

"Not so fast. We'll work something out. How about when you finish baking? We could meet by the entrance of the boardwalk at, say, midnight?"

"Perfect," I said. "It's a date." I meant it just as confirmation, but he took it literally, and his mouth curved in a teasing grin.

"Oh yes it is."

14

Tag was waiting for me when I got to the Blue Door and followed me as I carried my bags into the kitchen. "How's Lucinda? Is she mad at me? Why is she mad at me?" he asked. The cook had already left, and the place would have been mine, except that Tag didn't make a move to leave.

"She'll get over it," I said. I looked over at the dessert case. There was a half of a chocolate cake left.

"Lucinda insists we have you make the normal number of desserts. The leftover chocolate cake will probably go at lunchtime," he said.

I told him I was making pumpkin cheesecakes for the desserts and pumpkin muffins to keep to the orangish theme. "Do you think the town council would go crazy if I called them Monarch Muffins?"

"They might be okay with that, but why take a chance? Just call them what they are

— pumpkin muffins," he said. Still, Tag didn't leave, and eventually he started helping me. It seemed like I was never going to get to bake alone. At least I was sure all the measurements would be exactly accurate, I thought, watching him pouring sugar into a measuring cup.

"She's upset because she thinks you're keeping secrets from her," I said.

"You mean all that nonsense about putting calamari on the menu without consulting her? I would never do that. What possessed you to tell her I was sneaking in squid?"

"I thought I saw you talking to a fisherman last night."

"You must have been hallucinating. I wasn't talking to anyone about fish."

"The man on the porch in the Windbreaker and rubber boots . . ." I said, trying to jog his memory.

"Him?" Tag said. "I noticed the Windbreaker, but I didn't notice his footwear."

"If he wasn't here making a deal for calamari, who was he and why was he here?" I asked, opening a can of pumpkin.

Tag appeared stricken. "I can't talk about it. If she was upset about a menu change, she'd go nuts if —" He cut himself off. "I'm not going to say another word." He found another measuring cup for the pumpkin.

"Don't tell Lucinda what I said," he said. "Tell her it really was all about calamari. You can say I admitted I was going to put it on the menu, but since it made her upset, I canceled the plan."

"But that's not true, and then she's going to think you lied to her," I said.

"Better all that than what it is," he said cryptically. He handed me the measured pumpkin and left without another word.

I finished up the rest of my baking without incident and left three pumpkin cheesecakes in the cooler. I packed the muffins in plastic trays that fit into two carriers and got ready to make my rounds.

The sidewalks and streets were deserted, so I got a little nervous when a lone car stopped next to me and the window went down.

"It's kind of late for you to be out alone. Hop in and I'll give you a ride," a man's voice said.

"Next you're going to tell me you're looking for your puppy," I said sarcastically. I'd grown up in Chicago and was streetwise. I made an abrupt turn and started to go back the other way, knowing the car couldn't make the same move, and taking out my cell phone just in case.

I hadn't considered that he would just back up and keep pace with me. "That's it, I'm calling 911. The police station is around the corner." I was about to press the button when he called out, "It's me, Dr. Bernard Glickner. Sammy's father."

I still kept my distance until he stuck his head out the window. Oops. I apologized profusely, and when he offered me a ride again, I explained I preferred to make the deliveries on foot. In reality, I just didn't want to be a captive audience. It didn't work.

"You shouldn't be out here alone." He pulled the car to the curb and shut it off. "I'll just walk with you," he said, getting out of the rental car.

It was useless to argue. He wanted to take both of the muffin carriers, but I insisted we each carry one. He had the same lumbering sort of build as Sammy, but none of the teddy bear quality. I noticed he was alone and asked where he was coming from.

"You know we just want the best for you and Sammy," he said, clearly ignoring my question. "I'm sure you want the best for him, too. There's lots going on in urology in Chicago. The big thing now is doctors doing seminars. Sammy would be great."

We crossed the street, and I went up to

my first stop. I pulled out one of the covered trays and slipped it in a delivery slot. The empty one from the day before had been left outside. Sammy's father kept talking. "At least he seems to have given up all that nonsense about magic. I've been hearing for years that it was all my fault, because I gave him a magic set for his eleventh birthday. He usually didn't like anything I picked out. Who would have guessed the magic set would be the one thing he loved?"

This was an awkward moment. Personally, I thought Sammy should just tell his parents what he was doing and let it go. I was almost going to say it for him, but I reconsidered. It was overstepping. "Sammy's a grown man now, so it's up to him to decide what he wants his life to be," I said. "He has to decide for himself what he wants and doesn't want."

"I shouldn't be surprised that you have that kind of attitude. How many careers have you gone through?" He looked over at me carrying the plastic containers. "And now you're wandering around this town in the middle of the night. A town so small and ridiculous they make bets on when butterflies are going to arrive. What kind of living is that?"

Stay calm, I told myself. Don't engage. I

didn't need his approval. He wasn't really almost my father-in-law.

"I don't agree with my wife," he continued. "She thinks you're just playing with him and that you're going to break his heart." We'd gotten to Maggie's, which was all closed up for the night. I opened the small door she had for deliveries and pulled out the empty container she'd left for me and then slid in the full one. "You're not going to break his heart, right?"

"Of course not. I love Sammy." The words were out of my mouth before I knew what I was saying. Did I mean that? Well, there were different kinds of love. I was thinking about that when Sammy's father said something that made me stop in my tracks.

"What are you now, around thirty-five? And where is your life? You're not a wife, or a mother, and what exactly do you call your career?" He sounded just like my mother. Apparently, he wasn't waiting for an answer and just continued on. "It's time for you and Sammy to step up the plate and quit living like a couple of college students."

I was relieved when we finished the deliveries. He drove me back to the Blue Door, where my car was parked. I was afraid he was going to insist on following me home, but I saw that he'd turned his car around and was headed back to the Butterfly Inn. I never did find out where he had been coming from.

I drove home and pulled into my driveway. I saw Sammy looking out at me through the open shutters. I waved and held up the container of muffins and pointed across the street in a pantomime that I was going to deliver the muffins. I didn't want to mention what I was going to do after or who I had just talked to.

There was nothing to mask the sound of the ocean, and I could hear the waves as I crossed the street. I always liked walking on the grounds late at night like this. Most everyone was asleep, and it felt like my own private little world.

The clerk gave me a sleepy yawn as I walked across the Lodge. The lights were on, and a fire was going in the big fireplace, but there wasn't another soul in the big room. The door to the gift shop was shut, with a big CLOSED sign hanging from it. The café was closed as well, and I left the container of muffins by the door. I'd pick up the empty the next day.

If the clerk noticed that I exited by the other door, the one that went out onto the deck and faced the sand dunes that bordered the property, he didn't say anything.

This side of the Lodge was even more mysterious than the other. The moon provided some light, and I could just make out the grass circle with its sprinkling of trees, and beyond that, the entrance to the boardwalk. I passed the small chapel, which was still shrouded from view, and went on to the beginning of the boardwalk. The white sand around it reflected back the moonlight, and I could see no one was there.

Had I been stood up? I was about to give up and go home when Dane stepped out of the shadows.

"Oh," I squealed, startled by his sudden appearance. I had kept a few muffins aside, and after I recovered, I held them out for him. "I hope you're not afraid to eat them."

"Of course I'm not." To prove the point, he took one out of the little shopping bag and took a bite of it. "Satisfied?" he asked, taking my hand. "Let's get situated before we get down to business."

I saw his point. It was so quiet, it seemed wrong to break it by talking as we walked. We started down the boardwalk. Tall bushes grew out of the white sand, and a deer stepped from behind one and then stopped to look at us before soundlessly disappearing.

We reached the end of the Vista Del Mar

property and crossed the winding street. The air coming off the water had a chill dampness but felt fresh and clean.

The beach ahead was empty, but as I looked back toward the posh resorts along 17-Mile Drive, their lights shined in the darkness. We were about to walk onto the sand when Dane stopped.

"I have a better idea," he said. I followed his lead, and we walked along the deserted street as it rose up a gentle slope. Finally, we reached the destination he had in mind.

I'd been there before. A bench sat on a small cliff above the waves as they lapped on some rocks. Ahead there was only dark water.

"This is the very tip of the land," Dane said as we both sat down. Instinctively, we turned to the right and saw the beginning of Monterey Bay.

"At last," Dane said. He pulled a small thermos out of his jacket pocket. "Hot cider," he said, opening the lid. It smelled of apples and cinnamon. "There's only one cup, though, so we'll have to share." He poured some of the steaming liquid into the top and handed it to me. "Ladies first."

I tasted it, and as I expected, it was great. "This is all very nice, but I wanted to talk about the case."

"Sorry, I got lost in the romance of the moment. This is kind of perfect." I didn't say anything, but I had to agree.

"Romance over and out," he said, giving a mock salute. "Of course, you're right. We should be talking about the case. Have you been able to come up with anything, like hopefully some other suspects?"

"There is one. Me. Lieutenant Borgnine seems to think I might have taken offense at Rosalie's comments about the muffins, because they were going to ruin my business."

Dane put his arm around me. "He doesn't really believe that, does he?"

I let the cool air refresh my senses. "Well, one thing is right: her comment has definitely put a dent in my business. The sales of all my baked goods are down."

Dane tried to sound encouraging. "I'm sure it's just temporary."

"That's what Maggie said, but what if it isn't? Another career bites the dust." I told him about running into Sammy's father. "Maybe he's right."

"About what?"

"That I'm wasting my time here."

"I suppose he was suggesting that you and Sammy get married and move back to Chicago," Dane said, sounding unhappy.

"Yes, but then he doesn't know that Sammy and I aren't really together." I let out a sigh. "I don't want to talk about it anymore. There's another possible suspect in Rosalie's murder. My old boss brought it up. Frank said I ought to try to get Lieutenant Borgnine to consider Hank Hardcastle."

"I'm sure Borgnine talked to Hank. But he could have dismissed him as a suspect because he's so sure Chloe did it." Dane punched his fist in frustration. "Just because she has blue hair, or whatever color it is this week, it doesn't make her a killer."

"I was thinking that if I talked to Hank Hardcastle I might be able to find something out. But I don't think I've ever met him."

"Hank works nights, so your paths might not have crossed. The more I think about it, it sounds like a good idea for you to talk to him," Dane said.

"I heard that before, about him working at night." I knew the streets of Cadbury were practically rolled up at night, so there weren't a lot of late-night opportunities for work. "What does he do?"

Dane pointed out into the bay. In the distance I saw a tiny green light and something brighter near it. "That could be him."

I was totally confused. "Doing what?"

"Fishing for calamari." Dane went to refill my cup with the cider.

"Calamari?" I repeated. Dane misunderstood and thought I wanted to know how they fished at night, and he went into describing how they caught the squid.

But I wasn't interested that they went out in two boats, with one shining a bright light into the water to attract the animals and the other boat actually catching them. Apparently they were like moths that way — drawn to the light. I just wanted to get back to Hank.

"What does he look like?" I saw Dane shrug his shoulders in the darkness. "Like just any regular guy. Five-ten, brown eyes and hair and no discerning features that I know of."

I told him about the man I'd seen Tag talking to outside the restaurant. Dane nodded.

"Sure, that could have been him."

"But Tag insists that it had nothing to do with getting squid for the restaurant."

"What did it have to do with, then?" Dane asked.

"He wouldn't say," I answered. Dane seemed more excited than he'd been before.

"Good work. All that skulking around sounds like someone who is guilty of something." He turned to me. "I can't talk to him since I'm barred from the case. But you could," he said. "Once we have something, we'll find a way to get it to Lieutenant Borgnine."

I looked out at the green light bobbing in the water. "What am I supposed to do, swim out there?"

"Very funny. We'll figure out a way for you to meet him." Dane moved closer and nuzzled my neck. "Now that that's done, let's get on to the date part."

15

Wednesday morning, the sky was a flat white. Sometimes it was a very bright white, but this bordered on gloomy. I didn't lounge in bed, and Julius seemed surprised when I abruptly threw back the covers, knocking him out of the spot where he'd nestled. I smiled thinking of the date part of Dane's and my evening. It was really sweet the way we'd just huddled together at the end of the earth. He'd said he was sure Lieutenant Borgnine didn't really consider me a suspect and that he was just trying to harass me. I hoped it was true.

I was on my way out the door when Sammy showed up with breakfast for both of us. He seemed disappointed that I wasn't staying. All the stuff his father had said rumbled through my mind, but I kept it to myself.

"I'll give Julius his stink fish," Sammy said, turning to the cat, who was parading in front of the refrigerator. Sammy knew the way to Julius's heart and was trying to win him over. Julius started to ignore him but quickly figured out who was the source of the stink fish and went over to do figure eights around Sammy's ankles.

I had breakfast with the group. My eating had been pretty spotty, so I decided the best thing to do was to make the most of the meal. As I went through the cafeteria line, I took a waffle, eggs and fruit. Thinking of the other night, I made a point of looking in the kitchen as I went down the line. As the server handed me my plate of food, I saw a knife block with an empty slot. I remembered that the knife used to stab Rosalie was from the Vista Del Mar kitchen and had probably been on a cheese tray. But what if it hadn't? How easy would it be for someone to slip in and take a knife?

The food server was busy looking at the people coming through for their food. The rest of the staff was occupied with preparing more. Curious, I set down my plate on the metal counter and walked into the kitchen, waiting to see if anyone noticed me. No one stopped me as I went toward the knife block. I had my hand up, ready to see how easy it was to take one, when a voice snapped me to attention.

"Ms. Feldstein. What are you doing in there? Who are you planning to stab this time?" Kevin St. John said. I groaned. Was there a chance that he wasn't going to mention this to Lieutenant Borgnine?

I lost my appetite after that and went back to the table without even picking up my food. Lucinda gave me a worried look. I had already decided not to tell her that I thought Tag's visitor was Hank Hardcastle until I knew what was going on.

After breakfast, Lucinda and most of the retreaters joined a power walk around the grounds. I went ahead to the meeting room, in anticipation of the workshop. I was surprised to see the number of finished hats sitting on the tables. I congratulated myself on the choice of loom knitting for this retreat. I sat down and picked up my round loom and the tool used to move the loops of yarn. I didn't find working with the loom as meditative as using needles, but it was still relaxing. I wrapped all the pegs and went back and began to slip the bottom loop over the top of each peg. I was quickly realizing that the secret was wrapping the pegs not so tightly that the loops were hard to manipulate, but not so loosely that the loops slipped off the pegs.

I was still working when Wanda, Crystal

and the retreaters all came in and gathered around the tables. Lucinda gave me a thumbs-up when she saw what I was doing. Everyone picked up their work, and a bunch of conversations started. I was glad to see that everyone seemed happy working with the looms. I gave myself another pat on my back for making a good choice.

I had taken a seat near the window and, out of the corner of my eye, saw someone lurking on the other side. When I turned, Dane motioned for me to come outside. I did what I could to not disturb things, but my loom went clattering to the floor, and everyone turned to look at me.

I put my hand up in an apologetic gesture and said I'd be right back. Dane had on his off-duty uniform of a hoodie over jeans. He gestured for me to step away from the build-ing to an empty spot.

He took my hand and looked into my eyes with a grin. "Last night and then now. This is a record." He looked around. "And there's no audience saying what a cute couple we are or a tourist choking on a piece of chicken to ruin our moment," he teased.

"Is that what this is about? What, next you suggest we find a doorway and make out?" I said, smiling. I was still keeping him at arm's length, but it was a real challenge. The night before, during the date portion of our meeting, there'd been a lot of electricity going on between us as we sat there on the bench. Eventually, it had erupted into a make-out session that almost boiled over into something more.

"Sounds like a good idea to me," he said with a wiggle of his eyebrows. Then he got serious. "I know how you can run into Hank Hardcastle. You're taking your group to the natural history museum tomorrow for the play, right?" I nodded. "Hank is going to be there for the ceremony about something they donated to the museum."

"You mean the pavilion that isn't really even a room? More like a stuffed bear," I said.

"Oh," he said with a smile. "Well, I just wanted to give you a heads-up on a chance to 'run into him.' Maybe you can find a way to start up a conversation. Only don't try any of that pseudo-flirting of yours. It would be inappropriate, since his wife just died, and he might think you have some kind of tic."

Flirting was definitely not my thing. In the past, Frank had suggested I use it to get information from Dane. It turned out to be more comic relief than seductive moment.

I made a playful swat at Dane, and he added, "And I might get jealous."

When I went back inside, Wanda and Crystal had taken the long looms and were demonstrating how to make a double knit scarf. I sat at the table, trying to absorb what they were saying while continuing with my hat.

The plan for Wednesday was like a sea day on a cruise. No butterfly outings, just the workshops and the evening activities at Vista Del Mar. I think everyone was glad to be staying on the grounds after the busy day before. By the afternoon workshop, they had all started working on a scarf and I was a little further on my hat. When the workshop broke up, Sammy and his parents were waiting outside the meeting room.

"Case, I wanted my folks to see you in action." He pointed to the trail of retreaters walking away. "She's in charge of all this," he said. They walked into the room and looked at the looms lying on the table, as I explained how this retreat was different from the others I'd put on. Not that they seemed very interested.

"We came here to spend time with both of you," Estelle said. "But you always seem to be rushing off. Can't we get dinner together? At that place you bake for?"

I was going to beg off, but I saw the pleading look in Sammy's eyes. "I guess my group will be all right without me," I said. But I quickly added I didn't want to eat at the Blue Door.

"What about here?" Bernard said, looking over the grounds. "I understand that meals come with the accommodations, but you can buy a ticket for one meal."

Sammy nixed that plan. He didn't give a reason, but I knew that since he actually had a job doing table magic in the dining hall on the weekends, he was afraid someone might bring it up.

We finally agreed to a place on the water in Monterey. I mentioned having to make desserts and muffins afterward. Bernard looked at his son with a troubled expression.

"I don't get it, Sammy. You let her wander the streets at night alone."

Estelle seemed surprised at the comment. "How do you know she was out in the street alone? Did you go out last night?" she said in a snippy voice.

"What's the difference? You took a sleeping pill and were dead to the world."

Sammy herded his parents away and said we'd meet back at our place.

■ ■ ■ ■

Julius watched from a chair as I got ready for my evening with the Glickners. They were in the living room having glasses of wine. Sammy had set them up on a winery tour earlier, and they'd bought some of the wine they'd tasted.

I hoped this dinner would satisfy them and that they would go back to Chicago and leave us all alone. I sighed. Who was I kidding?

The restaurant was near Fisherman's Wharf, and we had a table overlooking the harbor. It was one of those traditional steak and seafood kind of places, and Sammy's parents seemed happy with it. We'd all helped ourselves to the salad bar and were waiting for our entrées. They were discussing their food. Bernard and Estelle were very pleased with the caviar on the salad bar. I was more interested in looking out the window. There was a mass of small boats bopping in the harbor. I saw the green light on the mast of a fishing boat nearby. It was the same kind of light I'd seen on the boat Dane pointed out the night before. Could it be Hank Hardcastle's boat? I watched the activity as men moved on and off the boat, seeming to be getting ready to leave.

"What are you so interested in?" Estelle said, noting that I had moved closer to the window to get a better look.

"It's a long story. I'm curious about a squid fisherman," I said.

Estelle made a face. "It sounds better to say calamari. Why would you care about a fisherman?"

Sammy answered for me. "Casey has been using what she learned when she worked for the PI firm in Chicago to do a little independent investigating here. That's it, isn't, hon?" Sammy said.

"Independent investigating?" Bernard said, rolling his eyes skyward. "You certainly seem to have trouble settling on something. Your retreats, the baking at night and now you're a detective, too?"

"Variety is the spice of life," I said with a smile. I was never so glad to see dinner arrive. Thankfully, Bernard and Estelle were very into manners and didn't believe in talking with food in their mouths, so dinner proceeded in silence.

By coffee and dessert, I sensed that Bernard was anxious to get the meal over with. I was right there with him. He waved the server over and asked for the check.

"Nice place," he said, taking out his credit

card. He glanced toward his wife. "Estelle, you look exhausted. I'm sure you can't wait to get back to the room and go to sleep."

She looked at her husband with an arched eyebrow. "I know what you're planning. You have a problem." She turned to Sammy and opened her mouth to say something, but Bernard interrupted.

"Why don't the three of you go on outside. I'll just sign the bill and join you."

Sammy had already gotten the car, and we were waiting when Bernard came out. The drive to my place was silent, and I almost jumped out of Sammy's BMW when we got to my driveway. He backed out and headed on to the heart of town to drop off his parents at the B and B. I got in my yellow Mini Cooper and drove to the Blue Door.

For once I had an uneventful night of baking, and no one came knocking at the door. I left three pumpkin pies and took the pumpkin muffins around alone. After dropping off the batch at Vista Del Mar, I went home and fell into bed. Julius seemed to notice that I was still in my clothes and gave me a disapproving stare, but when he realized I wasn't going to get up and change, he curled up next to me and we both went to sleep.

16

"Are you okay?" A voice cut into my dream of monarchs fluttering around and a squid waving its tentacles. I opened one eye and saw that Lucinda and Sammy were standing over me. Julius was asleep next to me, completely ignoring their presence.

"When you didn't show up for breakfast, I got worried," Lucinda said. "And then when you didn't answer the door, I really got worried."

"Luckily, I was just leaving the guest house," Sammy said. "I used the key you gave me." I'd opened both eyes now and saw that he was holding it up. "Are you sure you're okay?" He gestured downward, and I remembered that I was still in my clothes. "I thought you might have passed out or something. I can give you medical aid if you need it."

He put his hand out as if he was going to feel my forehead but instead did some fluttering of his hand. "A penny for your thoughts," he said, making a coin appear.

He glanced around the room with a guilty look. "I'm sorry, I couldn't help myself. It's been a real strain not doing any magic while my parents are here."

I sat up, which seemed to reassure them both. The only one unhappy with the move was Julius, since it deposed him of his spot. He gave the three of us a stare with his yellow eyes before jumping off the bed and walking out of the room, swishing his tail with annoyance.

"I'll give him some stink fish on my way out," Sammy said. "I have a bladder surgery this morning."

Lucinda watched him go. "I always forget he's a doctor." I assured her I really was fine and urged her to go back across the street. I promised to join the group soon.

I showered and got dressed and was on my way in no time. People were just heading to morning programs when I got to the Vista Del Mar grounds. I didn't know much about what other groups were holding retreats there that week, but I was guessing at least one of them had to do with insects. Butterfly Week had to be a huge event for them.

I saw a cluster of people beyond the dining hall, at the edge of the grounds. They seemed to be working on something, and I realized it was the tarp-covered thing I'd seen earlier in the week. The brush blocked a lot of the view, and all I could see was a huge rendition of a monarch, with its stained glass coloring hovering at one end. I was sure it was connected to the parade.

I went right for the coffee and tea service when I got to the meeting room, and then I took my spot at the table. They were all working on their projects, and other than Lucinda, nobody seemed to notice I'd just come in.

They didn't want to stop at the appointed time, so we stayed in the meeting room until the lunch bell rang. For once I didn't have to rush off anywhere and stayed through the meal and the afternoon workshop.

There was a lot of excited talk about going back into town for the play. I was more excited about the prospect of finally getting to meet Hank Hardcastle.

After dinner, I directed my group to the driveway in front of the Lodge. The small bus was waiting for us. Lucinda and I sat together in the front. I looked over the seat to make sure everyone was there. "All accounted for," I said to the driver, and we were on our way.

The bus dropped us off at the natural history museum. The lights were on, and the doors were open. I led my group into the entrance hall, where we joined a crowd. Most of the people headed for the main exhibit hall for the dedication. My group wasn't much interested in this part and went off into the rooms devoted to the monarchs.

The crowd for the dedication was already overflowing into the entryway, but I squeezed into the room, determined to get a good view of Hank Hardcastle.

A woman with a microphone introduced herself as the chief docent. She was dwarfed by the hulking stuffed grizzly bear next to her.

"We are all saddened by what happened to Rosalie Hardcastle. This was supposed to be a happy moment for her. She had particularly wanted to place the plaque during Butterfly Week." She turned to the giant creature and seemed a little flummoxed. "We don't really have grizzly bears around here, but it's good for the museum to have a broader appeal." She looked at the towering bear. "And for any of you concerned, the bear was found already deceased, so it's not like he was sacrificed for an exhibit." A relieved sound went through the crowd, and then she introduced Hank Hardcastle.

I laughed thinking back to Dane's description of Hank. It sounded like he was describing somebody for a wanted poster. You'd think as a cop, he'd pay more attention to the whole person. Right away I picked up that he wasn't comfortable dressed in slacks and a sport jacket by the way he stood. He tugged at his shirt collar a few times, and I got that wearing a tie was definitely not his thing, either. He had longish hair, but it was slicked back, probably with the help of some men's hairdressing product. I looked at him for a long time, trying to match him up with the man Tag had been talking to. But then I'd only seen his back, and the man had been wearing rubber boots and a Windbreaker and had seemed a whole lot more comfortable in his clothes. Hank thanked the docent for the kind introduction and then turned sideways to gesture toward the bear. I almost gasped out loud. I couldn't be one hundred percent sure he was the man Tag had met, but when I saw his profile I was sure he was the man from the storeroom at Cadbury Yarn.

I looked back at the audience, surveying the crowd until I found Gwen. She was looking right at him with a furrowed brow. I had no idea what that meant.

Hank talked for a few minutes about Rosalie wanting to leave a legacy to the town, and how she'd expected this to be just the beginning of their gifts to the museum. "She had planned to have a whole Hardcastle Pavilion added on to the building in the future." He looked over the crowd. It seemed like he smiled at a few people, but I couldn't tell who. He held up the plaque. "It was supposed to have both of our names, but after what happened, I had a new plaque made up saying the bear was in memory of Rosalie Hardcastle." He bowed his head in respect for a moment.

"You all know I'm a fisherman and not much of a speaker, so that's all I have to say."

Everyone erupted in applause, and he walked into the crowd. The docents started directing everyone to the multipurpose room. I followed along with them and saw that the room had been set up with rows of folding chairs facing the stage. I saved seats in the front for my group and waved them over when they came in. With them all situated, I went to stand in the back to see where Hank sat.

He took a seat on the end of the back row, and I grabbed the chair next to him. I had hoped to start up a conversation before the play, but the lights dimmed and the curtain opened. Cora and Madeleine Delacorte were standing with the Princess Court. The princesses were now all wearing orange tunics over black leggings. With them all dressed in the same clothes, it was hard to tell one girl from the other. Except Chloe. With hair streaked with orange and heavy makeup, she definitely stood out. Chloe couldn't just go along with the crowd.

The docent who had introduced Hank joined them on the stage and welcomed the crowd to another Butterfly Week tradition. She did the whole number on how it wasn't a beauty contest as much as a competition to be an ambassador for the butterflies.

I saw that Dane had come in but was hanging in the shadow by the doorway. He was in uniform, but I suspected he was there to see his sister.

The docent turned over the microphone to Cora Delacorte, who said she was going to introduce each of the princesses and give her a chance to say something. As she started through the group, most of them said pretty much the same thing about how lucky Cadbury was that the monarchs had chosen the town and how they viewed their job as protecting the butterflies and taking part in the activities throughout the year. I held my breath when Chloe stood up. She turned to face the crowd.

I couldn't believe it when she said almost exactly the same thing. Then she hesitated. "Forget all that flowery stuff. I really want to be queen, and I think I'd make a good one. Take my word for it, if I'm queen, nobody will mess with the monarchs." I had never thought about it, but apparently she'd picked up some of the karate moves from her brother. She proceeded to demonstrate her power by doing kicks and jabs. Lieutenant Borgnine had come in now, too, and was standing at the side of the room, glaring at her. She was definitely not doing herself any favors.

I didn't get to see Dane's reaction. When I looked over to where he'd been standing, the spot was empty.

The "play" came next. I'm not sure what I had expected, but certainly not something put on by the elementary school and called *The Flight of the Butterflies*. It was hardly high drama. A bunch of kids wiggled on the ground, pretending to be caterpillars before being wrapped up in blankets. The lights went off, and when they came back on, they had all turned into butterflies. I kind of lost track of it after that, but they seemed to be making plans for the winter, and then the Lord of the Butterflies joined them and said he was going to lead them to their new home.

It ended with the docent inviting everyone to have punch and cookies. When the lights came up, I turned to start up a conversation with Hank, but he was out of his seat before I could say a word. I saw that Hank was headed toward the door, and I rushed to catch up with him.

I had no idea what I was going to say to Hank, but I hoped I still had the touch from working for Frank.

When I caught up with him, I started with how nice his words about his wife had been. Flattery always opens doors. He was no different.

"I'm not much of a public speaker," he said. "But thank you." I quickly added my condolences about Rosalie, though it felt rather strange, since I was hoping that he was the one who killed her, as I was trying to get the spotlight off Chloe and me.

"I wish I had been there," he said, hanging his head in regret — or maybe to hide his expression. "I could have protected her."

"So you weren't there for any of the event?" I asked.

"I don't know what you've heard about

Rosalie, but she was a special person. That's how I want her remembered." I wondered what Hank's alibi was and if Lieutenant Borgnine had checked it out. The cop had left by then, so I couldn't even ask him.

Hank was beginning to get that body language that said he was going to leave. I went right to the heart of things. "Were you at the Blue Door the other night?"

He stared at me for a moment and blinked a few times. "What makes you say that?"

"I saw Tag Thornkill talking to someone on the porch of the restaurant, and you resemble the person I saw."

"Us fishermen all look the same — must have been someone else." He had an uncomfortable smile.

"What about in the stockroom of Cadbury Yarn?" I asked. The color drained from his face, and he swallowed hard a few times.

Coach Gary without his wings stepped in next to Hank. "Sorry to interrupt, but Hank, I just wanted to say the bear is a great addition to the museum. I'm just sorry Rosalie couldn't be here to see the plaque." He gave Hank a pat on the back. "C'mon, let's get some of that punch."

As they walked away, I overheard their conversation.

"Thanks for saving me," Hank said.

"It looked like she'd cornered you," Coach Gary said. I couldn't quite hear what Hank said after that. Just the word *trouble.*

Lucinda caught up with me at the punch bowl. Since part of the thing with Hank involved Tag, I couldn't even talk to her about the aborted conversation. I gathered up the group and loaded them on the bus.

"So, how'd you enjoy the play?" I said in a cheerful voice as the bus pulled away from the curb. There was the silence of disapproval, then somebody in the back shouted out, "It wasn't exactly *Annie.*" I made a mental note that if I had a retreat the next year to coincide with Butterfly Week, I would not include the play again.

Even if they weren't that happy with the play, everyone seemed to have enjoyed doing something at night, and they all thanked me as they got off the bus.

"We're having a night-owl session," Olivia Golden said, gesturing toward the Lodge. "I know you have to do your baking. Bree, Scott and I can handle everything," she said. Lucinda overheard and said she would be backup, too. Even so, I walked in with them.

I was so grateful for their help. I simply couldn't have managed without them. I watched for a moment as they moved to the long table and started to gather chairs around it.

As I got ready to leave, Kevin St. John came up to me. "I need to speak to you, Ms. Feldstein." He went back and forth between calling me Casey and Ms. Feldstein, but using my last name was never a good sign. He'd been so busy with all the extra things going on, he hadn't had much opportunity to give me a hard time, but I had a feeling all that was going to change. There was a smile on his usually placid moon-shaped face. It was the kind that said to me he was looking forward to giving me some bad news.

"There's a matter of a bounced check," he said. "I'm sure when the Delacorte sisters hear about it, they will be very distressed. They're insisting that I give you a tremendous break on the rooms, and then you don't even pay that."

He'd caught me off guard, and I didn't know what he was talking about for a moment. Then I remembered the check Liz had given me for the Danish ladies. I had hoped that the manager would never find out that it had been returned before by the clerk.

"That's old news," I said. "It was just an error, and I gave the clerk another check."

Now Kevin St. John looked really triumphant. "Ms. Feldstein, it's that second check I'm talking about. When it came back, the clerk you talked to felt obligated to tell me what was going on."

He didn't seem to know all the details about the check. Once he heard I was connected with it, he probably didn't wait for the rest of the details. I wondered if I should mention that it was actually a check from Liz Buckley that I had signed over to them. I took out my checkbook, wrote out and tore off a new check and handed it to him.

"A third check? What guarantee do we have that this one will go through?" This was definitely the time I could have explained that the two bounced checks were actually from Liz Buckley, and that I had signed them over to Vista del Mar, but it seemed immature to try to pass the blame — besides, ultimately it was on me anyway.

"Can I use your phone?" I asked, doing everything possible to not grit my teeth. "To call the bank," I added when he hesitated.

"Good idea." He handed me the cordless phone and stood next to me as I called the automated line for the bank. I held out the phone as the mechanical voice announced my balance. He took the check before I had a chance to click off.

I was definitely going to have to have another talk with Liz Buckley.

17

I woke up Friday morning thinking about the situation with Liz. This simply was not right. She had made a point that she would be watching how things went with the Danish ladies before she pushed more business my way, implying that it was like an audition for me. I hadn't thought it was an audition for dealing with her as well. Now that I had workshop leaders I could depend on and the early birds' assistance as well, I could handle more retreaters. But what was the point of getting business from her if I ended up having to pay for the guests' stay? I didn't want to believe it was deliberate, but having two checks being returned made me wonder. And now that Kevin St. John knew, I worried what he might do with the information.

Julius seemed to understand I had something on my mind and stayed out of my way. He had figured out that he had a more agreeable source for stink fish anyway. When I went into the kitchen, Sammy was spooning some in his bowl.

Sammy stood up and rewrapped the smelly cat food with a surgeon's precision. "Case, what's the matter?" I hadn't said a word, but he knew how to read my expression. Oh no, Sammy really did *get me.* He'd brought coffee and breakfast sandwiches again, and we sat down together.

I told him about the returned checks. "I don't expect to make a lot from the retreats, but I also don't want them to cost me," I said.

Sammy offered a sympathetic ear. "I can help you out if you need any money. The only things I spend money on are props for my magic show." He gave me a warm smile, trying to cheer me up. "If you want backup when you go talk to her, I'm available."

"Then you know that I'm going to talk to her?" I said, surprised, because I hadn't said anything about a plan of action.

Sammy cocked his head. "Case, you would never just throw in the towel and let yourself be a victim. You're a woman of action."

I couldn't believe how much better I felt after what he said. "Thank you, Sammy. Of course you're right. I am going to confront her this morning." He took out his phone and started to check his calendar, thinking I was going to take him up on the backup offer.

"You go on and do your doctor thing. I'll be fine on my own."

He stopped with the calendar and looked disappointed. "I know you will."

I made an appearance at breakfast and waited until the retreaters were in the morning workshop, then I slipped out without telling anyone, sure that I would be back before the workshop ended.

As I drove into the heart of Cadbury, I was thinking about what I would say to Liz. I couldn't come on too strong, but still, two checks had bounced. I would let her talk first. Then I would lower the boom.

I parked my car almost in front of Cadbury Travel. When I walked into the travel agency, I saw that Liz was with a client. I stood at the front, hoping to catch her eye. She and the client were deep in conversation about the details of a European river cruise. When Liz looked up and saw me, her friendly expression changed to concern. Obviously, she'd figured out there was something wrong, and that was not a good vibe when she was about to make a big sale. She turned her attention back to the client but kept glancing nervously my way. After a few looks, she handed the woman some brochures and said she'd be right back.

She left the desk and came over to me with a businesslike manner. "I'm going to be a while," she said, as if I was another client there to plan a trip. "Is there some kind of problem?" she asked, in almost a whisper. When I nodded, her eyes widened in distress. "Can we deal with this another time?"

"I do have to get back to Vista Del Mar," I said firmly. She glanced back at her client and then regarded me. Her eyes were panicky.

She was trying to keep her tone businesslike. "Can we set a time in half an hour?" she said. I wanted to straighten out the check business, but there was no need to make a scene in front of her client. I also didn't want to be rushed through it — I had to make sure it was taken care of properly this time.

Liz seemed relieved when I agreed to meet later. I went down to Maggie's to get a cup of coffee while I waited. The green strip down the center of Grand Street was filled with activity. Booths were being set up for the street fair that started later in the day and went through Saturday.

Maggie's place was busy, but then it was

never really slow. The view of the counter was blocked by the line, and I waited until someone moved, then I held my breath as I checked out the muffin basket. Maggie saw me looking at it.

"We just sold the last ones. I told you nothing is normal during Butterfly Week." She gave me a thumbs-up, and I let out my breath, hoping the same was true at the other places that sold my muffins.

Maggie gestured for me to find a table. A few minutes later, she let her assistant take over and came to sit with me, bringing a cup for each of us. I didn't have to lift the lid to know it was a cappuccino made just the way I liked it, so that the taste of the espresso wasn't lost in too much milk.

Maggie had a red sweater on and a red bandana tied around her black hair. "They tried to get me to wear orange and black for the week, but I wouldn't budge. Those town council people ought to lighten up on the control." She took the seat across from me.

"I probably have coffee running through my veins by now," she joked as she picked up her cup. "Where are all your retreat people?" She made an exaggerated gesture of looking around me.

"Back at Vista Del Mar," I said. I didn't want to tell her about Liz and the bounced

249

check, so I just said that I had to talk to Liz about something and we'd set a time. I quickly changed the subject to the previous night.

"I wasn't there," Maggie said. "I've seen that play too many times."

"That wasn't the only event. They put the plaque on the exhibit the Hardcastles donated."

"Do you mean that grizzly bear? I think the only reason Rosalie picked it was because it was bigger than anything else in the museum." I was a little surprised by Maggie's harsh tone. It must have shown in my face, because she softened a little.

"I'm sorry if that sounds harsh since she's dead now, but it just makes me sick to hear all this nonsense about her caring so much for Cadbury and its residents. All she really cared about was making herself important."

"I finally met her husband," I said, not knowing how to react to what Maggie had said. "He seems like an okay person." I played with my cup. "You do know that spouses are the first ones most cops consider when there's a murder." I looked up at her. "He said he wasn't there for the event that night, but that doesn't mean that he wasn't on the grounds. Getting a knife from the kitchen wouldn't have been hard. That sort of covers opportunity and means," I said, hoping she saw where I was going. "The real question is, did he have a motive?"

"He had to live with her — maybe he just snapped," Maggie said. "I know everything changed when his mother died six months ago. They inherited the family's real estate holdings, and Rosalie seemed to have taken charge."

When I didn't seem to understand, Maggie continued. "Maybe he wasn't happy with the way she was handling things."

I saw her point, but I knew Frank would say I needed more specific information. There was no time to pursue it now though. It was time for me to go back to Liz's, plus a wave of customers had come in to the coffee shop.

Maggie was already taking the next customer's order as she headed behind the counter. I took a last sip of my drink and tossed the cup in the trash before going back outside.

When I got back to the travel agency, I was relieved to see that Liz's customer was gone and Liz was still there. She had to know why I was there and might have disappeared in an effort not to deal with it. She directed me to the seat by her light wood desk.

"I'm sure I'll be sending you more business. I've already heard from other travel agents wanting to know about future retreats of yours." She couldn't quite cover the nervous warble in her voice.

I ignored her ploy of dangling the promise of future business. I was all about taking care of the business we had. I laid the check on the desk.

Liz was a rather pale woman with blondish hair cut into a short wavy style, and suddenly her face was so red, I thought she might pass out. "Oh no," she said, picking it up. "I just don't understand. I know there was money in the account."

I suggested she call the bank to check. She appeared terribly embarrassed, and I stepped away from the desk while she made the call. It wasn't that I could really hear anything, but it seemed appropriate to give her some privacy.

Even so, she turned away. I pretended to be interested in the action on the center divider of Grand Street. I heard her make an unhappy noise. I can't say I was surprised. I know banks make mistakes, but bouncing two checks seemed like a real stretch.

She'd hung up when I turned back. "I'm so sorry," she said. "I've been so preoccupied I didn't realize he had made those withdrawals." And then she began to come undone.

She moaned and put her head down on her arms. It seemed wrong to stay standing, so I sat in the chair next to the desk.

"Do you want to talk about it?"

I was pretty sure that she did. Now that I understood it wasn't deliberate, I felt sympathetic. When I had worked for Frank in the detective agency, he had me do phone interviews, because I was good at getting people to open up to me. I thought it was both because they sensed I would really listen, and they had stuff on their minds they needed to unload.

After a moment she picked her head up and tried to regain her composure. "What you must think of me. Some businesswoman I am." She glanced around the empty office as if there might be someone hiding and then blew out her breath. "I've just been so worried." Her eyes darted furtively around the small office again. "I suppose it's okay to talk now. She's dead."

Was she talking about Rosalie? I sat forward so as not to miss a word or innuendo. I wasn't sure what was coming next. She paused again and seemed hesitant to go on. "What can she do now?"

"You might feel better if you talked about it," I said, trying to encourage her.

"You have to swear not to tell anyone. She said the deal was off if I told a soul. I didn't even tell Gary." Liz was sitting up, but she still seemed unglued.

"You're new to town, so you probably don't know about Rosalie. She was the Butterfly Queen when I was a kid. The way she acted, you would think she was queen of the universe. She was always trying to make herself important. She bad-mouthed the Delacortes, but it was only because she envied the way everybody in town put them on a pedestal."

"Kind of like they were royalty," I said, and she nodded.

"That's exactly it. I never thought of it that way. No wonder Rosalie made such a fuss about being Butterfly Queen. Then she actually was royalty — in the insect world anyway." Liz took a breath before she continued. "I'm not going to bore you with all the details, but here are the important ones. Everybody but Hank knew that Rosalie picked him because she could run him and he came from a well-off family. But whatever dreams of grandeur Rosalie had were quickly squashed, because Hank's mother controlled everything. She was low-key and fair. And then everything changed when she died six months ago and Hank inherited all the properties."

"I get it," I said, remembering the comment Rosalie made at the dinner about her and Hank's new position in town and putting it together with what Maggie had said about the grizzly bear exhibit.

"The town used to be a lot different. In those days the town council was all about modernizing things. Hank's family kept buying up buildings that were going to be demolished so they could preserve them. When I started the travel agency and rented this space, the Hardcastles were very fair about the cost. Two weeks ago I got a notice that the rent was going to double." Liz's face collapsed into worry. "There was no way I could stay in business. I was pretty sure it was all Rosalie's idea, even though it seemed to be coming from both of them." Liz stopped to regroup. I could see she had been holding this all in and that it was a relief for her to talk about it, yet clearly exhausting at the same time.

"I called her and told her it would put me out of business, so she said maybe there was a way we could work things out." Liz hit her fist on the desk. "Yeah, really work things out. She said if I made her a partner and gave her twenty-five percent of the business, she'd convince Hank to keep the rent at what it had been. I had two weeks to think about it, and in the meantime I was not to contact her husband or tell anybody, and if she found out I did, the deal was off."

Liz was spent and leaned back in the chair.

"Did you consider just moving?" I asked.

She let out a sigh. "Where? There's not an empty store in Cadbury. Besides, Cadbury Travel's identity is linked with this space."

"So, what happens now that she's dead?" I asked.

"I don't know. I guess the deal for the twenty-five percent is off. Maybe I can reason with Hank about the rent increase."

The mention of his name stirred something in my mind. "Do you know what other properties the family owned?"

"Lydia Hardcastle was not a show-off kind of person, so I don't know, but I think they were other buildings like this."

"Do you think Rosalie tried the same thing with all of them?"

Liz shook her head. "No, she said she was just making the special offer to me."

"Special offer? More like extortion."

18

I had intended to go right back to Vista Del Mar after I talked to Liz, but what she had told me about Rosalie changed everything. I walked past my car, down Grand Street, ignoring all the preparations for the street fair. The Cadbury by the Sea Civic Center was on a side street. I bypassed the police station and crossed the street to the Spanish-style city hall.

The paver-tiled floor was smooth and shiny from years of being walked on. The Cadbury seal was embedded in the floor. It featured a monarch fluttering over a cypress tree with the ocean in the background.

I headed directly to the Hall of Records, though it was more like a room than a hall. The clerk looked up from behind the counter.

"How can I help you?" she said in a friendly voice. I had learned while working for Frank that when you wanted information, it was better to have a story about why you wanted it rather than just to ask for it directly. It seemed like even better advice for dealing with someone in a small town.

I'd already come up with my story on the walk over. I began by introducing myself.

"You're the baker," the woman said. "Too bad about your muffins. I heard there was something wrong with them and that's why the Monarchs lost."

I set aside my real purpose for a moment and took the opportunity to do some PR for myself. "That was just a false rumor," I said. I assured her there was no way the corn muffins could have been responsible. "And the rumor seems to be dying off." I thought of the muffins that had sold out at Maggie's. The woman seemed happy to hear the news and said she'd spread the word if anyone asked.

It was time to get down to why I was really there. "I'm wondering if you can help settle a bet I have going," I began in a friendly voice. "Who owns more property in town — the Delacortes or the Hardcastles?"

"It's the Delacortes, hands down," she said. I was disappointed with her quick answer. I had hoped she would say she would have to check, and then I could get a list of the properties. I was really only after what the Hardcastles owned.

"That's what I thought," I said, not giving up. "But if I'm going to win the bet, I really need absolute proof. Like maybe a list of the properties each family owns."

The woman was definitely on my side now. "We want you to win that bet," she said. She turned, and I saw the huge books of records on the shelves and thought she was going to have to go through them. It would take forever. What a relief when she didn't even glance at the old books and went to a computer. I heard the printer start up, and a few moments later I had what I was after.

I folded up the list of the Delacorte holdings and stuffed it in my bag. It was the other one I was interested in. I read down the addresses of what the Hardcastles owned and swallowed hard.

"Frank, there's been a new development," I said.

"Feldstein, how about a 'Hello, how are you' before you jump into whatever you're calling about. New development in what?"

"You remember the death of the old Butterfly Queen? Dane's sister was the suspect and then so was I?"

"Hang on a second," he said. I heard the

squeak of his chair as he moved around. Then I heard the rustle of a paper bag. He was talking to someone there in the room, but I could still hear what was going on. "Hey, this is egg salad. I ordered the Chicago meat special sub." I heard some mumbling, no doubt the delivery person. There was more rustling of paper and finally something that sounded like Frank going, "Aah." "Don't go away Feldstein, I'm coming back. There are important sandwich negotiations going on here."

I was doing my best to be patient, but after what I'd heard and seen, I was bursting to talk to someone who could advise me and who wasn't involved.

"Okay, shoot," Frank said finally. I could hear he was chewing, which was perfect, as it would give me time to tell him everything before he got impatient and wanted to hang up.

What had taken Liz a long time to tell me, I told Frank in a few sentences. It was really pretty straightforward. The dead woman had been trying to muscle her way into a local business. I gave him a little background about how Rosalie had tried to accomplish it and that it seemed she'd been running the show.

"So the dead woman was into extortion,"

Frank said. "Finally, the kind of crime I can understand. So, that charming town that sounds like a candy bar has a dark side."

"*Had* a dark side," I said. "She's dead and hopefully took it with her."

"Don't be so sure, Feldstein. You keep saying how easygoing her husband is. That could all be a front. Maybe he let her do the dirty work, but he was the brains behind it."

"There's some more," I said.

"There always is. Don't keep me in suspense." I heard Frank take another bite of his sandwich.

"The travel agent thinks she's the only one who was offered the special deal, but I wonder if that's true." Frank continued to work on his sandwich, and I told him that in addition to the travel agency, the Hardcastles were the landlords for the Blue Door, Maggie's coffee place, the yarn store and the drugstore.

"What if all the tenants got the same rent raise, followed by the same offer with the same warning not to tell anyone?"

"Feldstein, now you're cooking with gas. Why would she stop with trying to get a piece of just one of the businesses if she thought she could get a piece of all of them?"

"Maybe you're right about the husband being behind it all," I said. "Though neither one of them will admit to it, I'm sure I saw the owner of the Blue Door talking to the husband." I said "the owner of the Blue Door" rather than "Tag" to keep my sanity. Frank was already on overload with all the people in my life, and whenever I used a name, every five seconds he'd ask me who they were again.

My ex-boss took his last swallow. "Aha, Feldstein, what did I say? I bet he's the brains behind it and he's making the rounds to tell them the deal is in force. Maybe he even killed her because now that she'd done the dirty work of setting it up, he wanted to reap the benefits all for himself."

"Now, how to find out for sure?" I said.

I heard Frank crumpling the wrapping from his sandwich. "This should be a piece of cake for you. You already know most of those people. Just scoot off and talk to them."

"It might not be that easy," I countered. "I told you the Blue Door owner wouldn't admit to talking to the husband. And the Cadbury Yarn woman actually lied to me and said that there had been no one with her. Frank, I saw the man with my own peepers. I believed that he was a boyfriend she was trying to keep secret until I realized who he was."

"*Peepers?* Feldstein, really. We're not in some old gumshoe TV show. Even I call them eyes." He chortled to himself as he repeated my word choice. There were more sounds of rustling paper. "So maybe I was wrong and you really have your work cut out for you. I want to hear about this one." Any second I expected the change in tone that meant good-bye would be coming soon, but he surprised me by continuing on in a chatty voice. "Say, what's up with your magician boyfriend?"

"Friend who is a boy — well, he's really a man, Frank. His father is acting like he's already my father-in-law. His father and his mother seem to be fighting about something. One thing is clear, they're trying to marry us off."

Frank let out a chortle. "I can't believe I'm still on the phone with you, but you're my comic relief for the day. What's with the muffins? Are the townspeople still up in arms, thinking you're responsible for the lost game?"

"No. Today was good. I think they've forgotten about it. The muffins are moving close to normal again."

"Too bad for the magician. If your baking

business collapsed, he might have talked you into leaving town with him. Remember Feldstein, if you come back to Chicago, you come work for me."

"Aw, Frank, that's so nice," I said.

"There's nothing nice about it. You were the best detective's assistant I ever had."

"You mean assistant detective," I said.

"Whatever," he said before he clicked off.

19

It was only when I walked back on the Vista Del Mar grounds that I realized I was still out the money from Liz's check. Lunch was in session, so I went directly to the dining hall and headed to the tables that had become the group's regular spot for the meals.

Lucinda got out of her seat and came over to me. "I was worried about you, again," Lucinda said. "I thought maybe . . ." She left it hanging, but I knew what the rest of it was. She was worried that Lieutenant Borgnine might have moved me up to chief suspect and arrested me.

I held up my hands to show that they were free and tried to sound breezy, but inside my brain was churning. There was so much to process. I glanced at my friend in her Eileen Fisher outfit and realized she had a real reason to be concerned about the secrets Tag was keeping from her. The worst of it was that I really couldn't say anything.

"When you didn't come back, I handled lunch," Lucinda said. The remnants were still on the round wood table, though everyone had left. Most of the rest of the dining hall was empty as well.

"You better get your food before they close up shop," she urged.

When I got this busy I tended to forget to eat. The smell of food reminded me that I was hungry. There was no line, and the kitchen staff was in the process of clearing up the lunch food.

"Excuse me, am I too late?" I said, trying to get someone's attention. A young woman in a white uniform looked up. She waved for me to come into the kitchen.

It was warmer in there, and the smell of hot food was stronger. It seemed like all the steam trays were empty except for some scrapings around the edges of the metal containers.

"They really cleaned us out today. I can make you a grilled cheese sandwich," she offered.

It sounded good to me, so I gave her a quick nod, and she dropped some butter in a skillet, where it instantly began to melt. While she assembled the sandwich, I looked around.

Everything Frank and I had talked about had just been supposition. I needed evidence. Looking around the kitchen made me think of the murder weapon. The knife had come from the Vista Del Mar kitchen, but there was some confusion as to whether it was on the cheese plate that was ordered by the butterfly people or if the killer had gotten it some other way. I figured I might as well see what the cook knew while she was making my sandwich.

"I suppose the police already asked you about the knife," I said. I didn't have to give it any more description for her to know what I meant. She dropped the sandwich in the melted butter and turned around.

"I know somebody said it was from the cheese plate, but I don't think so," she began. "We were really busy that night with the regular guests and the special dinner with the butterfly people. We had to make two different dinner menus. The woman in charge of the butterfly committee insisted we serve their people steak." She stopped and checked my sandwich. "We do a good job with food like this." She flipped it so the browned side showed. The cheddar cheese was beginning to ooze out of the sides, and my stomach rumbled in anticipation. "But steak." She made a hopeless gesture. "Most of the people just fought their way through it with the knives on the table, but someone did come back here asking for something sharper. We don't have steak knives, so I gave out one of our cooking knives."

My heartbeat picked up in anticipation as I asked her who it had been.

"The cop asked the same question — that one that wears the rumpled jacket and has no neck. Like I said, we were really busy in here. I barely looked up as I gave it out. I remember it was a man's voice asking for it, but that's all."

"Well, that should get Chloe off the hook," I said, mostly to myself. The server seemed perplexed, and I explained who Chloe was.

"You mean the girl with the tattoo?" When I seemed surprised that she'd seen it, the young woman explained that when people were going through the line, mostly all the servers saw was their shoulders and down. "You'd think it would get her off the hook, wouldn't you?" the young woman said as she put my sandwich on a plate and cut it on the diagonal. "But the cop seemed to think it didn't mean anything for sure, because the man could have been getting the knife for someone else."

Lieutenant Borgnine was really a piece of work.

I took the food back to the table. By now the staff was circulating around the sea of round tables, clearing off the dishes. Lucinda sniffed the delicious scent of my lunch. "That looks much better than the sloppy joes they served us." Lucinda, ever the restaurant person, grabbed the pitcher off the lazy Susan and filled my glass with iced tea. Or maybe it should have been called lukewarm tea. Either way, it quenched my thirst.

I offered her a bite, but I think she saw the way I was wolfing it down and realized how hungry I really was. Between bites, I told her what I'd just learned in the kitchen.

"Maybe Lieutenant Borgnine really is having second thoughts about whether Chloe is the main suspect. She *is* still out and about." Lucinda poured herself some of the tea.

"There might be another reason for that — one that's not so good for her. I saw Maggie this morning, and she made a point that butterfly week changes everything around here. You remember when she told us about Rosalie's funeral being put off until after the festival is done? Maybe Lieutenant Borgnine has been urged not to arrest Chloe because she's in the Princess Court."

Lucinda considered what I said and then

nodded. "That sounds right. It would certainly put a damper on the celebration to have one of the princesses arrested for the murder of a former queen. Life in a small town," she said with a sigh. The tables were almost all clear now, and all that was left of my sandwich was a few crumbs. The woman had added some carrots and celery sticks on the side, and they'd disappeared as well.

"Is that why you left this morning, to go talk to Maggie?" Lucinda asked. It did seem kind of lame that I would abandon the re-treaters just to grab a cappuccino. Lucinda knew nothing about the returned checks or even that Liz had put me on notice that she'd be watching how things went with the two Danish women. My friend did so much to help me with everything that I had wanted her to have some illusion of being just like the other retreaters, and not having to deal with what went on behind the curtain.

But what I knew now changed that. "I went to see Liz Buckley," I began. "It was about a bounced check." Lucinda's eyes widened with interest.

"That puts you in an awkward spot," my friend said after I'd finished the story. I had mentioned Liz's being distracted, but I didn't say by what. Until I knew what was going on with Tag and the Blue Door, I didn't want to say anything to Lucinda. I'd already caused more problems than I'd solved with the whole calamari story. It felt uncomfortable not telling Lucinda everything, and I think she had a sense I was leaving something out, but she let it go.

"I hope that once butterfly week is over and things go back to normal, she'll get it straightened out," I said.

Lucinda's expression clouded. "But for now you're still out the money."

Hoping she wouldn't connect the dots and think what I was asking was connected to Liz, I changed the subject to the Blue Door, and then after a few minutes brought up the question of their landlord. I was eager to find out what she knew without telling her what I knew.

Lucinda seemed disgruntled. "You'd have to ask Tag. I wanted to be an equal partner in everything about the restaurant, but Tag hovers over the business end and won't tell me anything. It's usually okay with me, since he's so good with all those little details. The food has always been my domain. That's why I was so upset when I thought he'd added the calamari without telling me."

I had to bite my tongue to keep from saying she ought to wish that was the problem.

"Time for the workshop," Lucinda said, checking her watch. "Will you be joining us?"

I gave her a weary smile as I got up. "Definitely. I think I need a retreat more than the rest of you."

As I walked over to the meeting room, I saw the sun had burned through the clouds and was making an appearance. It was amazing what the change in the light did to the surroundings. The weathered dark brown buildings didn't look so foreboding, and the dried golden grass had a glow. But by the time we'd walked the short distance to the meeting room, strands of shimmering white were blowing in from the dunes, and the sun looked like a copper coin under a veil.

Wanda and Crystal were already stationed at their respective tables already, and the others were coming in and taking their seats. I glanced toward the counter and saw that a coffee and tea service had been brought in. I looked with regret at the empty space next to it — the spot where I usually put homemade cookies. Maybe tomorrow, I thought hopefully.

My hat still had a long way to go until it

was finished, but I welcomed the mindless repetition of winding the yarn around the pegs on the loom and using the pick to move the loops off the pegs. I'd hoped the workshop would give my mind a rest, but instead all kinds of thoughts kept popping up. Now I understood why Maggie seemed so harsh about Rosalie. She must have gotten the "offer," too. And I understood why Gwen had been so worried. I wondered about the Clint Eastwood look-alike who owned the drugstore. I remembered that he'd opened eight months ago, when Lydia Hardcastle was still running things. Was he part of Rosalie's plan, or did she somehow leave him out?

I couldn't understand why Maggie hadn't said anything about Rosalie's offer. She had made it clear she didn't like her, so why not spill the beans? Could she have somehow escaped Rosalie's clutches?

Then another thought hit me. Maybe none of them were talking because they were worried about being a suspect in her murder. Or worse, what if Tag, Maggie, Dirty Larry or Gwen had killed her? And I couldn't rule out Liz. She was there that night. Sure, she was doing her narration when the lights were off, but she had one of those battery-operated microphones. She could have been anywhere. Over and over I'd heard that the Blessing of the Butterflies followed such an exact plan, you could set your watch by what was happening.

Liz could have been standing outside and known just when Rosalie's back would have been exposed by the open door.

I was so deep in thought, I didn't notice what anybody else was doing until the woman from across the table leaned toward me. "I just want you to know I was definitely against using a loom for knitting, but now that I've tried it, I think it's great. I'm not giving up my needles, but it's another avenue."

Inside, I let out a sigh of relief. When the woman had started talking, I thought she was heading for some kind of complaint. "Thank you for telling me," I said.

Now that I'd been pulled back to the present, I started paying attention to what was going on around me. Wanda and Crystal had demonstrated some advanced stitches at the beginning of the workshop, but after that they were really just there to help fix mistakes. The rest of the time they were working with the group on the same projects. A length of navy blue knitted material hung below Crystal's round loom. She had stopped adding to it and had taken out a needle.

"It's for Kory," she said, referring to her son. "Now that he's working on the grounds here, it'll keep his head warm and be stylish at the same time."

Her comment made me think of her mother's yarn store. Crystal might know something about what was going on without realizing it.

"Does your mother own or rent the building?" I asked Crystal. She gave me an odd look, and I realized it did seem like an out-of-the-blue question.

Crystal had cut the yarn, leaving a long tail, and threaded it through the needle. She began taking the loops off the pegs with the needle. After she took off the last loop, she pulled tightly on the yarn, closing the top of the hat. "I think she rents it." Her face lit up in understanding. "I know, you're thinking of opening your own bakery and you want to know about getting a space."

"That's it," I said, glad that she had provided just the cover story I needed.

"You should talk to my mother. I just help with arranging the yarn, giving lessons and ringing up sales." Wanda threw Crystal a disapproving look from the other table.

"Doesn't your mother talk to you about

the business end of the yarn store?" Wanda said. "I would certainly know everything about everything if I was working with my mother."

"So then you don't know anything about the rent and if there was recently a big raise in it?" I persisted.

Crystal suddenly appeared guilty. "I'm afraid I've been far too self-absorbed. I should be more involved in things." Wanda looked stunned that Crystal had actually agreed with what she said.

"Hey," Kory said as a greeting as he came inside and walked over to his mother. She was just weaving in the last strand of yarn.

"Here it is," she said, and her son put it on. His cheeks were ruddy from the cool air. He modeled for the group, and they all gave their approval.

"Were you just talking about the store?" Kory asked. He had his mother's looks, but there was a stableness about him that reminded me of Gwen.

"Yes, and I was embarrassed to admit that I don't know much about the business end of it."

I was surprised when Kory gave his mother that universal look of disbelief, as if asking how she could be so clueless. Crystal seemed like such a cool parent, I thought she would somehow have managed not to get that kind of treatment. "Do you mean that you don't know that Gamma has wanted to buy the building for years from the Hardcastle family? It seemed like she was going to manage it, but then something happened. That's one of the reasons I wanted this job. I thought I could help out." He bobbed his head with pride. "It's so cool with school out this week that I could get all these hours."

Crystal gave her son a squeeze. "You got the good genes," she said. "You're nothing like your dad." The rest of them didn't know what she meant, but I did. Her ex was a rock god jerk and had all the stereotypical traits that went with the title. She'd hung on as long as she could, but in the end, he'd been the one to cut the string when he went off with a younger woman. I noticed that Kory made no move to defend his father.

I watched it all with a strange feeling. I was still the only one who knew that Kory was actually the great-grandson of Edmund Delacorte, and that his grandmother, sensible Gwen, was Edmund's love child. He had definitely inherited Edmund's love of Vista Del Mar. Once again I thought of showing Gwen the evidence I had. I could almost hear Frank telling me to leave it alone. And for the moment I was going to. There was too much on my plate.

Kory had an ease with adults that impressed me. He worked his way around the table, checking out everyone's work. When he got to Scott, he stopped.

"High five," he said, holding out his hand. "I knit, too." He seemed unusually comfortable in his skin for a kid of around fifteen, even though he looked gangly, like he still had to grow into his body. When he got back to the front of the room, he looked in my direction. "I just want you to know that the guys on the team don't think it was your muffins that made them sick. Those pumpkin ones were really good."

I was going to correct him, as the ones I'd brought to the dinner had been corn muffins, but he was already on his way out. "Back to work," he said, sounding upbeat. "I'm on garbage detail."

"Love that kid," Crystal said when he'd gone out the door. I could certainly see why.

20

When the workshop ended, Crystal and Wanda were done for the day and headed off. The retreaters took a few minutes to freshen up before meeting outside the Lodge. The small bus was just pulling in. I was hoping the late-afternoon activity would be more successful than the play the night before.

"A street fair, how fun. This is the best retreat," Bree said as she got on the bus with a woman wearing an almost identical outfit. If I was naming looks, I'd call it "mother with young kids." The jeans and hoodies with school names on them seemed comfortable and worked for a lot of different activities.

Olivia stopped as she passed me. "I agree with Bree. The retreats where we didn't leave the grounds of Vista Del Mar were wonderful, but taking part in all the Butterfly Week festivities is different and fun."

More retreaters passed me, and they all had the same excited look. Scott took up the end of the line.

He seemed a little less enthusiastic — he said he liked the escape of spending the whole retreat away from it all. Lucinda and I got on the bus last and took the front seat. "I am absolutely not stopping by the Blue Door while we're in town," she said.

The sun had made another appearance as the afternoon waned. The bus let us off at the edge of downtown, near the post office.

"They've done so much since this morning," I said to the group, amazed at the transformation of the downtown area. The whole parklike center of Grand Street was filled with little white tents. Strings of lights hung from the trees, and giant monarchs were suspended from the tree limbs.

The plan was that the retreaters were free to wander as they pleased until it was time to meet back at the bus. They all took off, including Lucinda, leaving me to check things out on my own. Traffic had been blocked on Grand Street, so I walked along the pavement, curious about the little tents. The fronts were open, and I saw that there were little booths with games and crafts. I noticed something else — there was a young woman wearing a crown working in each of them. Another of the princess tasks the contestants were being judged on, no doubt. Sure enough, I saw Cora and Madeleine with a few other people walking along the street, making stops on the way. Several of them had clipboards. I continued on behind the committee, wondering what kind of booth Chloe had been given.

I laughed to myself when I saw it. Whoever had done the planning had picked the perfect one for her. The sign above it promised face painting and temporary tattoos, and a line of kids was waiting. Chloe was definitely a good advertisement for it. Her orange hair stood out, and she wore a barely there skirt that made me hope she wouldn't have to bend over for anything. Her fleece jacket was open, and I caught a glimpse of something red and shimmery. Her own face had butterflies painted on the checks. A teenage girl was sitting inside the booth, sheltered by the enclosure. She'd taken off her jacket, and Chloe was applying the tattoo stickers on her arms. Her face had already been made up to look like a cat.

I stood for a moment, watching, until I sensed someone next to me. When I turned, I realized it was Lieutenant Borgnine.

"Thinking of getting your face painted?" I

said, noting that his gaze was glued to Chloe. That nonsense about me being a suspect was probably just a bluff to scare me off. He was clearly still focusing on her, and I was probably right that someone had told him not to arrest her during this important week in Cadbury.

"Very funny, Ms. Feldstein. I'm not here for fun. I'm just keeping an eye on things." He turned to face me. "What about you? Are you here for fun?"

"Of course," I said. I had the uneasy feeling that he'd read my mind and knew that I had already planned to make use of my time at the fair to check out a few things.

I waited for him to walk away and then moved closer to the booth. Chloe looked up from her work. "Here to check up on how I'm doing?" Her tone had an edge, but I was beginning to accept that was just how she talked, and I didn't take it personally. She handed the girl a mirror to see herself as she talked. "The two sisters and their mothball committee have already been by." Chloe gave a triumphant smile. "Let them put this on their stuffy old clipboard." She gestured with her elbow to the line of people waiting for her booth.

I felt for Dane. Hard as he tried to soften Chloe's edges, it wasn't going to happen.

Before I could mention Lieutenant Borgnine's presence, she brought it up. "And I don't know what Lieutenant Rumpled Jacket thinks he's going to see, hanging around staring at me all the time."

I let her talk and didn't bring up my theory that he was keeping an eye on her for now and probably planned to pounce on her after Butterfly Week ended. No doubt he was sure that she wouldn't be made queen.

"Look who's here," a woman said from over my shoulder. I recognized the voice and turned, putting on a smile. Sammy's parents had stopped on the grass behind me.

I greeted them with a hello, but Estelle grabbed me in a hug. "You're just about family," she said. She turned to Bernard. "Aren't you going to hug your almost-daughter-in-law?" He looked cranky but gave me an awkward hug.

Chloe observed the whole thing and gave me a dirty look. "I'm not going to tell my brother about that." She used her elbow again to point. A new girl was in the seat, and Chloe was holding a paintbrush, ready to start. "My brother is a good guy, and I think you're just a tease."

Sammy's parents heard what she said and

gave me dirty looks in unison. Estelle looped her arm in mine and started to walk, pulling me with her. "Young lady, we need to talk."

Young lady? Wasn't that reserved for thirteen-year-old girls?

We walked on, with Bernard trailing a few steps behind. She stopped when we reached the next booth. Crystal's daughter, Marcy, was the princess in charge of this one. There were some folding chairs inside, along with a small table. The sign hanging off the front announced MAKE AND TAKE. Several of the seats were taken, and I saw a lot of glitter, construction paper and pipe cleaners.

While I waited for the inevitable lecture from Estelle, Coach Gary strolled by, wearing his Lord of the Butterfly wings, black hood and antennas. He held out a fistful of strips of blue tickets toward us. "Get your tickets! All the money goes to support the Monarch Sanctuary and the exhibit at the museum. Have some fun, help the butterflies."

"Sammy's not here now, so you can tell us what's really going on," Estelle said, ignoring Coach Gary. That was a pretty open-ended statement, and I wasn't sure how to answer.

"What do you mean?" I asked. Estelle's

expression said she saw right through my question.

The strings of lights hanging between the trees blinked on, giving the whole area a charming look, and Estelle pointed ahead to the next booth. The princess in charge was dispensing hot drinks and donuts. A sprinkling of chairs sat out front.

I had no choice but to agree to go along. Estelle grabbed some chairs and told Bernard to get us all drinks. Bernard came back a moment later with a crankier expression.

"What kind of nonsense? They won't take cash. She said we need some kind of tickets."

I pointed out Coach Gary, and Sammy's dad went to flag him down. "Men in butterfly wings," he muttered when he returned, shaking his head at the absurdity.

I was glad for the delay, as it gave me time to think, but finally the three of us sat facing one another, each with a cup of hot cider and a donut with orange frosting.

"Sammy is a grown man, and he needs to be able to live where he wants and do what he wants," I said. "Like follow a hobby if it makes him happy. You need to let him make his own choices." I covered up my emotions by taking a sip of the spicy cider. I felt good about what I'd said. It was all true, and I hadn't made any false claims about our relationship. I should have known they wouldn't just accept it.

"We are not going to just stand by and watch Sammy throw away his career," Bernard said.

"He's not throwing away his career. People around here need a urologist," I said, and Estelle rolled her eyes in annoyance.

"We heard that your baking career is on the skids," she said. "Something about some of your muffins poisoning some kids? Both of you are being ridiculous. I don't know why Sammy is the way he is about you, but I can't change that. We know Sammy isn't the problem about a wedding." She paused to let it sink in and looked at the donut, making a face at the sweet icing. She shook her head and pushed it back over to her husband.

I couldn't help it — I just lost it. "Where did you hear that about the muffins? It isn't true. There's no way some corn muffins could have given anyone food poisoning."

Estelle looked at her husband. "Bernard, honey, where did we hear that?"

He thought for a moment. "It was in that coffee place. Someone came in and was buying a bunch of muffins, and a person in line mentioned they'd been baked by Casey and hadn't they heard about some people getting sick."

"I thought that was over with," I said, mostly to myself. Then thinking out loud, I muttered, "I'm going to have to find out what really happened." I spoke directly to them. "My baking career isn't on the skids. There was a temporary dip, but that's all. Why can't you let Sammy and me decide about our own happiness?"

I set the drink and donut down and left in a huff. Did they think their behavior was making me want them as in-laws?

They had gotten me riled, and I needed to calm down in order to deal with everything else going on. I walked the length of the booths and then crossed back to the sidewalk. All the stores were staying open extra hours, and most had some kind of sidewalk sale going on in front of their places.

I passed several of my people, and they all seemed to be having fun. Finally, I turned off on a side street. I hadn't really thought about where I was going until I realized I was in front of Cadbury Yarn. Even though it was off the main street, Gwen had strung lights and set things up on the front porch. All the chairs were full of people knitting and crocheting. There was a table of yarn bargains to the side.

I went inside. Gwen was working the register and had extra help with the customers. I looked around the converted bungalow with new interest, knowing the connection it had to Rosalie Hardcastle. It almost struck me as funny that I'd thought Gwen had a secret boyfriend when I'd seen her with the man I now knew was Hank.

I was always amazed how things seemed to go in waves. As crowded as the porch and store had been, it suddenly emptied out, leaving only a couple of browsers.

Gwen greeted me as I walked up to the counter. "The store looks great," I said.

"We try to do something special during the street fair."

"You'll probably get some of my people wandering in." I told her that I'd bused them in as part of the activities.

I took a deep breath and then said, "I know who the man in the storeroom was."

Gwen looked like she'd gotten an electric shock. "I don't know what you mean. There was no man in the storeroom. It must have been a shadow or something."

"I know it was Hank Hardcastle," I said.

Gwen appeared panic-stricken. "Please, just let it be."

I leaned closer to make our conversation

288

seem more personal. "I know you're probably afraid to talk about it. I talked to
somebody else in the same situation."
Gwen's eyes opened wider in surprise.

"What? You mean I'm not the only one?"
I nodded, and she sighed in relief. "I don't
know why it should make me feel better that
someone else is in the same boat."

I wanted so badly to say, "And that boat
is?" so she'd tell me exactly what had happened to her. I really had no idea if it was
the same thing as what had happened to
Liz.

It must have been terrible for Gwen to
have to keep everything to herself. Just the
few words from me seemed to have lifted a
tremendous weight off her shoulders.

"I had no idea there was anybody else.
Rosalie said it was only me." Gwen took me
into the storeroom and offered me a chair.
"It's much more private in here." She suddenly looked worried. "Crystal doesn't
know, does she? Or Kory?" I assured her
that I hadn't said anything to them.

"When Rosalie came to see me, I thought
it was to talk about me buying this place.
It's no secret that I've been trying to do
that for a long time." Gwen looked angry as
she relived the moment. She took another
of the chairs and sat. "All these years and

289

there was never a problem with the Hard-castle family. They were fair about the rent and took care of the bungalow. And then Rosalie took over." Gwen's voice was full of disgust. "I have to tell you that when she was killed, I was sure they were going to come after me. That somehow the police knew that she had told me she was raising my rent to an impossible amount unless I took her in as a partner in the store."

Gwen had left the door open so she could see into the store in case there was a sudden rush of customers. It surprised me to see how angry she was. She was usually so calm. "Talk about making a deal with the devil. I knew if I made her a partner, even if she was only a minority one, she'd try to run things. Since she owned the building, who knows what she'd threaten."

There was a partially done scarf on some circular needles on the shelf next to her. She picked up the ball of royal blue yarn and the needles and began to knit as she talked. It was a complete aside from what was going on, but I watched in total amazement at how fast she worked without having to keep track of the stitches. Before I could blink she was on the next row.

"I certainly wanted to kill Rosalie. My mother started this store in this location, and that miserable woman was going to put me out of business. I knew what her game was. She was trying to make herself important to be like the Delacortes." She turned to me. "By the way, I told her no deal on the partner business. I didn't know how I was going to raise the money for the higher rent. I'm embarrassed to say, I was relieved when I heard she was dead."

When Gwen mentioned the Delacortes, I wondered if this was the time to tell her about the proof I had that Edmund Delacorte was really her father. I imagined the shock on her face if she realized Vista Del Mar was meant to belong to her. Of course, I didn't know what the outcome would be. Edmund had been dead for a long time. I had no idea if the sisters would choose to honor their brother's wishes or fight to hang on to it.

She went on talking, having no idea what I was thinking about. "Hank said he needed to talk to me, but I wasn't to tell anyone. At first I thought that he was going to take over for Rosalie and try to make the same deal." Her needles continued to click as she moved on to another row.

"But he didn't," I said.

"The poor man seemed shocked at what his wife had done, but at the same time he

291

wanted to preserve her memory for all the good things she'd done in town. He said everything would go back to the way it had been, but only if I'd give my word not to let anybody know about what Rosalie had tried to do, or even that we'd talked." She suddenly looked stricken. "But I just told you."

I waved off her concern. "I won't tell anyone." I'd had a thought. "Do you think he was really trying to protect her memory, or the Hardcastle reputation?"

Gwen stopped knitting and put the yarn in her lap. "I never thought of that. Hank is very well liked, and the Hardcastle family has always had an impeccable reputation, which means everything in a small town. He kept telling me that he knew nothing about what Rosalie had done and how as soon as he found out, he knew he had to do something about it."

It was as if Gwen suddenly heard her own words. "Could that mean that *he* killed her?"

21

I left the yarn store feeling uneasy. Gwen had been quick to accept that Hank might have killed his wife. Did she believe it, or was she trying to cover up the fact that she could be a suspect?

I still had some time before I met up with my group, so I headed for Maggie's. Now that I figured Rosalie had probably tried the same with her, I really wanted to talk to her. And I could use another cappuccino.

I had to pass back through the street fair area. Light was fading, and the cool breeze made me glad I had on the blue fleece. The whole area had gotten more crowded. I couldn't help myself from checking on Chloe. The line in front of her booth had gotten even longer. I passed Coach Gary, who appeared to be taking a break from his ticket-selling duties and was sipping a cup of cider.

"Those wings must get heavy," I said.

"I'm used to them," he said. He rolled his shoulders to demonstrate that the wings didn't weigh him down. "I keep getting the gig because I'm the only one who volunteers."

Kory came by. "Hey, Coach, don't fly away with those wings."

The coach gave him a mock salute, and Crystal's son kept going. "He's a good kid," Coach Gary said. "He comes from a good family."

It was hard for me not to smile at the last part of the comment. If he only knew what family he really came from.

From where we were standing, I had a good view of Chloe's booth. No surprise, she seemed to be a natural at face painting and applying the temporary tattoos.

"She's certainly raising some money to help the butterflies," I said.

Coach Gary didn't look impressed. "I'm surprised that she's going through all the princess tests. I'd bet money she not only won't be queen, but won't be in the top three. And when Monday comes around and things go back to normal, I expect that Lieutenant Borgnine will do his job and arrest her."

"You seem pretty sure she did it," I said.

"I was there," he said. "After what Rosalie

said to the girl, and then kicked her off the court . . ." He put his free hand up with a shrug that made his wing move. "That certainly counts as motive. And on top of that, she did threaten Rosalie, and once Rosalie was out of the way, she put herself back on the court."

"What I heard was Rosalie didn't really have the authority to throw her out of the Princess Court in the first place." I didn't know if it would do any good to try to defend Chloe to him, but I felt obligated to try.

"I'm sure you must know that Rosalie doesn't seem to have been well liked, or liked at all," I continued. "I wouldn't kill her over it, but she made a comment about my corn muffins making your players sick, and overnight my baking business hit the skids."

"I thought you said your muffin sales had recovered." I was surprised by his comment. "I didn't mean to eavesdrop, but I heard you talking to Dr. Sammy's parents." His glance moved over the crowd — a woman was coming toward him with a fistful of long streams of tickets.

"It sounds like they just want the best for both of you. Sammy is a good guy. And I'm sure the opportunities for both of you would be better back in Chicago." He smiled at me. "As the saying goes, you could do a lot worse."

How did we go from talking about murder suspects to discussing who I should marry? I think Coach Gary saw my face and realized he might have overstepped his boundaries. "Sorry, but I'm so used to hearing the kids' problems and giving them advice, it's become automatic." The woman caught up with us and handed him the tickets.

"Break time over," he said, tossing the paper cup in the trash can. "The Lord of the Butterflies is back on duty."

Life in a small town was certainly different. Everybody was in your business. I never would have expected to be getting relationship advice from the high school football coach.

I considered buying some tickets from him before he fluttered away, but what I really wanted was that cappuccino. I continued down the street to Maggie's.

Plus, in light of the new information I had, I wanted to talk to Maggie. Not that I was going to give her any specifics of what I'd been told. I wasn't sure how I was going to ask her about it without breaking my word. I didn't want to jeopardize Gwen's deal with Hank, particularly since I'd had the thought that he might have killed his wife either to save his reputation or to save the town from her. Once someone had broken that boundary and killed once, killing a second time probably wasn't so hard. The last thing I wanted was to be responsible for anything happening to Gwen.

I hadn't planned on the mob in the coffee shop. Even with the extra help, there was no way Maggie could sit down with me.

She saw me over the crowd and beckoned me to the side. "The usual?" she said with a wink.

I nodded and quickly added that I had some news that might interest her. It was like I had dangled catnip to her.

"C'mon back. We can talk while I make drinks."

It felt weird to be behind the counter, viewing it all from a different perspective. Apparently I spent too long admiring the faces turned toward me though, because they started yelling their orders at me. How did Maggie manage to keep them straight? By the time I'd heard decaf cap foam alone, extra hot chai latte almond, I was lost.

"What happened to your news?" Maggie asked. I was like a deer caught in the headlights, but she was able to juggle taking orders and handling payments and still notice that I hadn't started talking to her.

"I know she probably raised your rent and then tried to make a deal with you to be a partner. She told you not to tell anyone and gave you a deadline. I think you know who I mean." I had made a point not to mention Rosalie's name.

Maggie froze. "How'd you know?"

"Because you're not alone."

"That skunk," Maggie said. "She made such a point that it was only me. She even tried to tell me she'd be a strategic partner." Several people stepped up to the counter. "The deadline for letting her know is up, but after what happened, I was waiting to see if there would be further instructions."

"You mean from her husband?" I asked, and Maggie nodded.

"She said 'we' in all our dealings, but I was only supposed to talk to her. Hank has always seemed to be pretty low-key, but you never know. I always thought that while she got to play the heavy, he might be pulling the strings."

"I don't think so." I checked the area around us to see if there were any ears I had to be concerned about. "I can't say who, but I know that her husband has approached one of the others and basically told them to forget everything she said. The one requirement is that whatever she did was never to be mentioned to anyone."

"That seems kind of odd." Maggie marked an order on a cup and passed it down.

"Maybe not. He's claiming he wants to keep her legacy intact."

"Legacy?" Maggie said. Her eyes flashed with uncharacteristic anger. "What? That she was Butterfly Queen three times and tried to run everything she got involved with?"

She took the next order and marked it on the cup. "It must have been difficult being married to her. He could have found out what she was doing and been horrified. What if he tried to stop her and she wouldn't agree? Fishermen know their way around knives."

"He said he wasn't at the event, but that doesn't really mean anything," I said.

"He could have slipped in. I am sure he knows the script for the blessing service and knew about the lights going off. He could have stabbed her and been on his way out of the grounds before anyone even realized what had happened."

"You have a point," I said. The customers kept coming, and Maggie swiped another credit card.

"From what you're saying, I should be

expecting a visit from him soon. Maybe I can find something out. Just a thought though — if she was operating on her own and insisting no one talked, how did he find out what she'd done?"

With that thought I took my cappuccino and left. Maggie had her line, and I had my group.

Most of them were waiting when I got to our meeting spot. They were all talking, and I noticed that a number of them had visited Chloe's booth and were sporting all kinds of body decorations.

Lucinda came rushing down the street with a guilty look. "I know I said I wasn't going to do it, but I went to the Blue Door. I talked to the cook, and he assured me no calamari was ever added to the menu. What is going on with Tag?" I just gave her a hopeless shrug as an answer.

My retreaters were all energized by the afternoon adventure, and as soon as they got off the bus, they rushed directly to the dining hall while dinner was still being served. The rest of the evening was free for them to meet up in groups to work on their own projects or go to the screening of *The Butterfly Effect* in Hummingbird Hall. I would have been happy to do either one, but my day wasn't done.

I was going to go home for a little breather before heading back into town to bake. When I arrived, I saw that Sammy's BMW was parked in the driveway next to my Mini Cooper. His parents' rental car was parked on the street. They had been hinting about coming over again, and I guessed that Sammy had agreed. Poor Julius!

Seeing them once in a day was more than enough, but I had to get my baking supplies. It seemed crazy to have to sneak into my own house. It was dark now, and light was streaming out from the glass on the top half of my back door. I grabbed a peek and saw a bunch of take-out containers on the table. Julius was pacing around with his tail in angry mode.

Could I slip in and get my stuff without being noticed? I decided it would be better if I knew what was going on and who was where. It seemed like every light was on in the house as I crept around the side. I popped up for a moment outside the bedroom that I used as an office. Estelle was in there, looking around. I watched as she picked up the worry doll. Sammy was in the doorway, and I got the feeling he was telling her I made it. She gave it a disparaging look and dropped it back down on the love seat, so that the doll's dress came undone and she flopped over on herself. It took all of my self-control to keep from knocking on the window and telling Estelle that was no way to treat my creation.

They went out of the room, and I slipped around to the front just in time to see them go into the small living room. Estelle looked around with disdain. Bernard ignored it all and seemed engrossed in some game on television. Sammy was playing host and offered them glasses of wine. I was glad to see he'd found some proper glasses in the things my aunt had left.

When Estelle sat down with her wine, I thought I was home free. I could easily get in and out of my kitchen without them knowing. I was backing away from the window when somebody grabbed me from behind.

You don't live in Chicago without being tough, and I pushed back with both elbows, hoping to hit a soft spot. Instead, the next thing I knew I was on the ground.

"Sorry! It was just an automatic reaction," Dane said, crouching over me. "You're deadly with those elbows." I held up my finger to shush him.

"What's going on?" he whispered. I pointed upward, and he peeked in the window and returned to the ground next to me.

"It looks like they moved in."

"I'm sure they trapped Sammy." I was trying to get up.

"Did I hurt you? That move is supposed to disable an attack with no damage." He brushed off my clothes as I stood.

"Don't worry, I'm fine," I said.

"Do you mind telling me why you're playing Peeping Tom at your own home?"

I led him away from the window and around to the back. "I was trying to see what was happening without going inside. I took my group to the street fair, and Sammy's parents got me alone and had their way with me." I shook my head, trying to get rid of the memory.

"That bad?" he said, fighting a smile.

"They seemed happy about the problem with my baking business, because they think it will make me want to run away from here."

"You're not going to do that," he said.

"Well, it seems like the worst is over, but I still feel like I'm a tarnished brand. I keep thinking if I could clear the muffins unequivocally, things might go back to normal."

Dane put his arm around me supportively.

"There just might not be any way to do that. Besides, I heard your supply sold out today."

"Really?" I said, feeling encouraged. "I knew they did at Maggie's." We were back by my kitchen door now, and I stopped.

"What is it?" he asked.

"They're all in the living room. I could probably just sneak in the kitchen and get my baking supplies. It's either that or go to the store and buy all new stuff."

"Or maybe there's another way." He grabbed my hand. "Give me your car keys." I handed them over, and he crouched down and pulled me with him. He led the way to my car and opened the driver's side. He motioned to the other door. When I got to it, it was open, and Dane whispered for me to get in.

"You don't have to whisper now," I said with a laugh. "They're not even close. There's no chance they'll hear us."

"This is more fun." Still crouching low, he turned on the car and put it in reverse, and it began to roll down the driveway. When it rolled into the street, he suddenly sat up, turned on the headlights and stepped on the gas. We more or less burned rubber for a few moments until we landed in front of his house and he veered into his driveway.

"Help yourself to whatever you need," he said when we got into his kitchen. There was still a faint smell of spaghetti sauce in the air. He pulled open the door to the pantry. Since he did so much cooking for the kids who hung out at his place, his pantry looked like a storeroom. He bought pasta by the case, and there were several huge cans of tomato sauce.

"What are you making tonight?" he asked.

"I'm sticking with the orange theme and making carrot muffins." He'd watched me bake enough to know what I needed and loaded it all up in a couple of plastic shopping bags.

He noticed me sniff the air, and he shook his head. "You didn't eat again."

He pulled out one of the kitchen chairs and told me to sit. "Hope you don't mind leftovers." He put some water on to boil and some sauce on the stove to heat up.

"I'm almost afraid to ask, but have you found out anything that will help Chloe?"

His teasing face had turned serious. Even with our earlier talk about Hank being a suspect, I was pretty sure he knew everybody still thought she had stabbed Rosalie. And I was sure he wasn't happy that she was keeping such a high profile.

"As a matter of fact, I have," I said. His

face instantly lightened.

"Were you planning to tell me?" he asked. The water began to boil, and he swished some leftover spaghetti in it. At the same time, the sauce had begun to simmer, filling the air with a delicious smell.

He put a plate together and set it in front of me. "I just found out most of it," I said. The food looked delicious, and I picked up my fork, ready to dig in.

"Wait. You get the good stuff." He went to the refrigerator and came back with a block of hard cheese. He held a grater over my plate, and curls of Parmesan cheese hit the hot sauce. It was all I could do to wait until he finished to take my first bite.

He sat down next to me as I began to twirl the noodles on my fork. "I love a girl who eats." He gave me a few moments of eating time before he nudged me about telling him what I knew.

"Did you know about the Hardcastles owning some commercial property in town?"

He shook his head ruefully. "I guess that's why I'm still a beat cop and not a detective."

I told him the bits and pieces that I'd picked up. "I haven't talked to all the tenants, but I'm pretty sure Rosalie did the same thing to all of them. It seems like now that she is gone, they're all off the hook. That certainly gives them all a motive."

"There's something missing in what you said. Like names. Who are these people that Rosalie was squeezing?"

"The thing is, between Rosalie swearing people to secrecy and now Hank asking them to keep it quiet as well, the people I've talked to don't want their names made public."

"I'm not the public," he said. "We're talking about my sister's future here. I already feel like I failed with her. The hair, the clothes. But prison?"

"You can't do anything with the information anyway. Remember, you're off the case. There are a few more people I need to talk to."

"You don't really think anyone is going to admit they did it, do you?" he asked.

"No, but I want to get the whole picture before going to anyone with my theory."

He reached over and touched my arm. "I trust you." He looked at the plate and the food still on it. "Go on and finish." It didn't take much urging, and in no time, all that was left was a smudge of sauce. I heard Dane laugh.

"I knew I'd figure out a way to get you to come over for dinner."

22

The food had done wonders for me. Dane walked me outside to the Mini Cooper, and I gave him a spontaneous hug, thanking him for dinner and the baking supplies. I'm not sure who was more surprised.

As I drove past my place, Sammy was just walking his parents out the door. I stepped hard on the gas and took off, hopefully before any of them noticed.

When I reached downtown Cadbury, the street fair had closed up for the night. The flaps were down, and the Lord of the Butterflies must have gone home. Only the strings of lights and the giant monarchs hanging from the trees remained. The stores were in the process of closing, and all the things from the sidewalk sales were being brought inside.

When I drove past the Blue Door, I saw there were still quite a few diners. Since I wanted to talk to Tag when he was alone, there was no reason to rush.

In the meantime I thought I'd make a visit to Cadbury Drugs & Sundries. Now that I knew it was part of the Hardcastle real estate holdings, I was curious to see what I could find out.

Since it stayed open all night, Cadbury Drugs was not winding down like the rest of the businesses. However, the table that held items for the sidewalk sale had been brought inside.

The interior was almost too brightly lit, and it felt out of sync with the stores around it. I asked the older woman handling the checkout at the front where the owner was.

"He's in aisle three, putting up stock. He's always putting up stock. That's what happens when you try to have too much variety and not much of any one thing." I found aisle three and saw Larry, who was wearing his white pharmacist coat and putting out boxes of bandages.

"Hey, Dirty Larry," I said, putting out my hands like they were six shooters. I expected a smile; instead, he looked at me like I was nuts. I should have let it drop, but I spent too much time explaining why I'd greeted him that way.

He stood up, and his eyes moved around the store nervously. "The town council came down on me for the whole Clint Eastwood thing. I didn't understand it, exactly, but they kept talking about how everything in Cadbury had to be authentic and I was a fake Clint Eastwood." Larry shook his head at the nonsense of it all.

I smiled inwardly. I hadn't been sure how I was going to break the ice with him, but he'd provided the perfect means. "It's tough being an outsider," I began. "They gave me the same business about my muffins. I had all these cute names for them like Merry Berry and Ebony and Ivory, but the town council said I had to call them exactly what they were."

I looked around the interior of the store. "Isn't this building owned by the Hardcastle family?"

He suddenly had a wary expression. "Yes, why are you asking?"

I remembered how Crystal had thought I was thinking of opening up a bakery when I asked about her mother's store. "I'm thinking of opening my own bakery, and I just wondered how the Hardcastles were as landlords."

"They seem okay to me." He had an impassive expression.

"I'm asking because I heard that everything changed recently and Rosalie Hardcastle was dealing directly with all the tenants. How was she to work with?"

He seemed uncomfortable, but the direct question left him nowhere to go — or so I thought.

"It's really irrelevant now," he said, "after what happened." He rocked his head in concern, though I couldn't tell if it was real or feigned. "And Cadbury seems like such a friendly town."

"I was at the Blessing of the Butterflies service," I said, as though it meant I knew some kind of secret. "What about you?" I noticed the clerk had come down the aisle with a customer in tow. They stopped next to us.

"I didn't go to the service. No time." He answered quickly and put the box of bandages he was holding on the shelf, as if to end our whole exchange.

"But didn't you go out to Vista Del Mar that night, right around the time of the service?" the clerk asked. I heard Larry suck in his breath, but his expression didn't change.

"Is there something you need?" he asked, glancing from the clerk to the man with her. Apparently, he thought by ignoring her comment, I would, too. But I don't think he expected the clerk to ignore his question about needing his assistance.

"He does everything around here," she chattered on to me. "He's a full-service pharmacist. When somebody at Vista Del Mar needed a prescription, he not only filled it, but delivered it." She turned back to her boss. "You can't have forgotten."

"Of course, that's right." He forced a weak smile.

"I suppose the cops talked to you and asked if you'd seen anything," I said.

He tried to brush me off by dealing with the clerk and the customer with her.

The clerk held out a strip of paper and a brown paper bag. "He wants to return this and get the cash back." The man had a determined expression, with his arms folded.

Larry read over the receipt and checked what was in the bag before shaking his head. "The best I can do is offer you a store credit," he said. He kept the receipt and merchandise and scribbled something on a card and handed it to the customer.

"Customers," he said with an annoyed tone when they had walked away. He showed me the receipt and the contents of the bag, and I understood why he was upset. It showed the customer had bought a box of allergy medicine. It listed the brand, the size of the box and even the dosage. The name on the credit card was there, too, though only the last four digits of the credit card number appeared. The item in the bag was a bottle of generic aspirin. It was obvious he wasn't going to respond to my comment about the cops, so I repeated it.

"You didn't say if you had to talk to the cops," I said.

He seemed uncomfortable. "No. Nobody at Vista Del Mar knew I was there except the person I brought the prescription for, and I think he left the next day." He seemed to have realized what he just said. "I try to steer clear of trouble. I didn't realize my clerk knew where I went," he said half to himself. "You're not going to go off and tell the cops anything, are you?" His tone sounded almost threatening.

Before I could respond, two women came down the aisle, and he recognized them as business. "Well, it was very nice talking to you. And you're right about us outsiders sticking together. You never know what can happen."

No, you don't, I thought to myself. "I just put you on my suspect list," I said out loud, after I'd exited the store.

I walked back to the car and got my muffin ingredients and carried them to the Blue Door.

In the time I'd spent at the drugstore, the restaurant had emptied out, and Tag was looking through the menus, making sure they were all pointing in the same direction. I checked the dessert counter. There was some cake left, but knowing that the muffins were selling out again, I didn't take it as a mark against me. With no name attached to the cakes, they were just generic and probably didn't seem special. I would talk to Lucinda about putting my name back on them.

The cook had his backpack slung over his shoulder and gave me a wave as he headed to the door.

Tag looked distraught. "Did you tell her all the secrecy was really about adding calamari?"

"No, I just left things as they were," I said. I took my supplies to the kitchen and came back into the dining room. He was sitting at one of the tables and pulled out a chair for me.

"You don't think that Lucinda isn't going to come home after the retreat?" The poor man seemed almost panicky. Even so, he thought to straighten the fork on the place setting in front of him.

"She'll get over it," I said. The idea of me being a relationship helper seemed pretty funny considering my own difficulty with managing them. "She's not upset about whether you really added calamari to the menu — it's that you left her out of something." I glanced up at him and hoped that I was giving him a knowing look, thinking that if he thought I already knew about why Hank had been visiting him, he might start talking.

It seemed he was too busy checking over the other place settings, and I realized I was going to have to be a lot more obvious. "I know who the man really is and why he was here."

Tag appeared stricken and sucked in his breath. "I didn't tell you," he said. "You have to make that clear." He started muttering worriedly to himself, and I put my hand on his arm to reassure him.

"You're not the only one this happened to," I said, and his head shot up.

"There were others?" He seemed surprised and relieved at the same time. Then it was like somebody unzipped his mouth and the words just tumbled out. "I didn't want to tell Lucinda about the rent increase until I'd worked out a solution. I thought if I found a way to increase the business, I could compensate. I was trying to drum up some catering business. I brought the cheese tray for the butterfly group to give a sample of what we could do. And I was talking to the manager of the Cora and Madeleine Delacorte Café about letting the Blue Door supply some sandwiches and salads."

"So that's what you were doing when you dropped Lucinda off on the night of the murder."

He flinched at the word murder. "I couldn't tell her what I was doing at Vista Del Mar. I mean, I would have had to tell her eventually, if it worked out." He stopped and seemed overwhelmed with it all. "It was such a terrible time after that Hardcastle woman told me about doubling the rent. And then when she made me that offer — I certainly wasn't going to let her be a partner in the business." He put his hand up and began to run his fingers through his thick brown hair. "I just thought I was protecting Lucinda. Isn't that what men are supposed to do?"

"Maybe in the old days," I said. "But now we women are right there with you guys, taking care of business. Lucinda isn't some frail flower who wilts at problems. She's helped me out of lots of sticky situations."

"Right," he said with a sigh, and then his

expression changed. "I should have figured it out. You're probably investigating Rosalie Hardcastle's death. I thought it was a given that it was the princess with the tattoo." He'd begun thinking out loud. "But she's Dane's sister. You'd be trying to defend her by finding another suspect." I watched his mind begin to churn. "Another suspect like me. But if what you said was true about other people getting the same offer I did, one of them could have done it."

"Why don't you just tell me what happened," I said.

"What happened when?" he asked. I should have known. Tag was such a precise person, he needed exact questions.

"Let's start with the night she was killed."

"After I dropped off the cheese tray and Lucinda, I talked to the manager of the café, and then I went home and spent the night worrying," he said. "I was supposed to give Rosalie my answer on Monday."

"And then?" I urged.

"When I heard she was dead, I didn't know what to do."

"Did Hank Hardcastle contact you?"

Tag was sitting up straight now. "No, I got in touch with him. I wanted to make it clear that I wasn't going to take that offer. He's a hard one to connect with since he works nights. We arranged to meet here." Tag looked toward the front door and the porch beyond. "That's when you saw him."

Tag started to play with a spoon and then caught himself. He seemed terribly upset by what he was doing and quickly put it back into perfect alignment with the rest of the silverware. "I was shocked. He didn't know anything about the deal I'd been offered. Or the rent increase. He told me that when they inherited the property, Rosalie had insisted on handling it and he'd let her. He apologized for what she'd done, over and over. He seemed terribly embarrassed and went on about her ruining the Hardcastle name. Said that his mother would be horrified if she knew what he had let happen. That's when he told me there would be no rent increase as long as I agreed never to tell anybody what she had done." Tag froze. "This can't count, because you already knew, right?"

"No, he can't blame you for me finding out. He sounds like a desperate man. Desperate to cover up what she'd done." I didn't say anything, but this time Tag got what I meant.

"You mean he could have killed her?"

"He could have just been pretending he didn't know when he talked to you. He could have found out what she was doing, and maybe he thought there was no other way to stop her."

Tag didn't seem to want to think about it. "Well, now that it's out in the open, maybe you could tell Lucinda what happened. Be sure to tell her I did it all for her own good."

"I think she would much rather hear it from you."

"You're right," he said. His spirits seemed a whole lot lighter when he got up. He put on his jacket and left.

23

The ringing of a phone cut into my sleep, and I sat up suddenly, not sure of what day it was. As the room around me came into focus and I saw an annoyed looking Julius, who had been displaced, I realized it was Saturday. I looked at the clock before I answered and let out a sigh of relief — it was still very early, and I wasn't late for anything yet.

"I didn't want to wait until Sunday to call this week. I didn't wake you?" my mother said. Who did she think she was kidding? There was no way my doctor mother didn't know that it was two hours earlier here in Cadbury and that I never got up at six in the morning.

"No," I lied. Why did I always do that when she called too early? Did I feel some kind of shame that I was still asleep? There was no time to analyze my emotions, because she got right to the meat of her call.

"Are Sammy's parents still there?" she asked. I groaned to myself. I knew she knew they were still here. I uttered an uh-huh and she continued.

"So how is the visit going?" she asked brightly.

"You want to know the truth?" I asked. Of course she said she did. "While they're busy fussing around with Sammy, Bernard and Estelle seem to be having their own battles going on."

My mother was all ears as I recounted hearing Estelle tell Bernard that something he was doing was a problem and he insisted he did whatever it was to relax.

"And she didn't give any hint to what it was? I hope it isn't drugs." Then my mother quickly added, "I'm sure Sammy is nothing like that, except for that nonsense with the magic."

"I'm not worried about Sammy being like his father. We're just friends," I said.

"To you, you're just friends. But I bet he'd make a justice of the peace magically appear if you just said the word." She paused for only a moment. "I know this is a cliché, but you could do a lot worse. Everybody loves Sammy."

She paused, and when I didn't say anything, she spoke with a knowing tone to her voice. "Isn't this the place where you say, 'Except me'?" When I didn't protest right away, she laughed. "Maybe you didn't say anything because you do love Sammy."

"Maybe I do, but only in the friend way," I said, and she made a hopeless sound. "If Sammy would just tell them the truth about his magic gigs, we could stop this charade."

"You don't really believe Sammy wants to stop playing your boyfriend," my mother said with a chuckle. We did a few more back-and-forths about Sammy, but meanwhile, I was thinking about something else. I knew she'd see Sammy's parents when they got back, and I knew they would bring up the rumor about my muffins. Who could predict what they would say? They already weren't happy with me. By then they could want to bury me. Better that she heard it from me.

"There's something I need to tell you."

I could hear the anticipation in her breathing. "I'm guessing by your tone that it isn't good."

I spilled the whole problem with the sick football players and how Rosalie had implied it was my muffins and now she was dead. "Don't worry, I'm not really a suspect," I said. "I think it's getting better, but the rumor is still out there."

"Back up," my mother said. "The woman is dead? How did it happen?"

"Sammy's parents aren't likely to bring up the dead woman. The whole town is keeping it quiet because it's Butterfly Week."

"Casey, I can't believe how much you leave out of your life when we talk. I didn't know about any of this. You said you're not a suspect. Then who is?" As soon as she heard it was Dane's sister, she knew I was involved with the investigation.

"Remember, I offered to send you to that detective academy so you could get a private investigator license. The offer is still good."

I was going to remind my mother I had a profession as a baker, but with what I'd just told her, that seemed a little shaky at the moment.

"Thanks for the offer. I'll think about it," I said. I heard my mother laugh.

"Do you think I don't know that's a brush-off? I'm just saying it's there if you want it. Now tell me why that woman thought your muffins made the boys sick."

I told her the details again.

"How many boys got sick?" she asked.

"I only heard about two," I said.

"This is where I put on my doctor hat," she said. "It seems to me that if there was something wrong with the food, more people would have gotten sick. And even if it was some bug going around, more people would have been affected. It sounds like there was something wrong with just their food."

"Mother, I didn't think of that. I guess nobody did." She seemed pleased that she might have been helpful, and we got ready for our good-byes.

"Your life continues to mystify me," she said. "When I was your age," she began, and I thought, Here we go with the usual, and interrupted.

"I know when you were my age you were a wife, a doctor and a mother, and then you always say, 'And you're what?' "

"Maybe that wasn't what I was going to say this time. Actually, I was going to end it with, for better or worse you're my daughter, and although I don't always agree with your choices, I will respect them."

I looked out the window to see if any pigs were flying by. Had my mother really changed?

I fell back asleep with the phone next to me. Eventually, a wonderful smell drifted through my dreams, and I opened my eyes with a start. Sammy was standing in the doorway, holding a container with food and coffee.

"It looks like you overslept. I finally get to bring you breakfast in bed," he joked.

I looked at the clock and freaked. "Put it in the kitchen. I'm late." I got up and started grabbing clothes and heading for the shower. He was sitting at the kitchen table when I came in.

"Julius has had his stink fish," Sammy said, reaching down to pet the cat. Julius surprised me by leaning into his hand and then jumping on his lap. Sammy seemed thrilled. I flipped the lid off the coffee and started to drink.

"This is the last day with my parents. And then everything can go back to normal," he said. He sounded a little down, and I thought of what my mother had said.

"Good. I never thought I'd say this, but I miss you making things appear out of my hair, my ears, my hands and whatever else." I hoped it would cheer him up.

"Like I always say, Case. You're the only one who gets me." His eyes brightened, and he reached down toward the cat. "Oh, look what was in your ear, Julius." A quarter seemed to have come from nowhere. The cat wasn't impressed.

"Now if you could make a can of stink fish appear," I said, and we both laughed.

■ ■ ■ ■

A few minutes later Sammy and I walked outside together. "I'm meeting my parents this morning and taking them to the Monterey Bay Aquarium. Want to come along?"

"Sorry, I've got retreaters to deal with," I said. "Otherwise, I'd be there." My tone was clearly sarcastic.

"I wish I could just drop them off." Sammy seemed forlorn, and I hugged him, hoping it would make it better.

I followed along as he backed his car down the driveway and waved as he pulled onto the street and drove away.

"I hope that wasn't as cozy as it looked," Dane said. I hadn't noticed that he was standing in the street. I could tell by the shorts that he was out for a morning jog.

"I actually have stuff to tell you."

"How about we talk about it tonight? You could be my date to the Butterfly Ball."

"I have a date," I said. His face fell, and I realized he thought I meant I was going with Sammy. "With a bunch of women and one man — my retreaters," I added quickly. "I hope it's one of those things where people just get on the dance floor by themselves and move around."

"Why don't you just tell me what you know now? Please, please let it be something good." His tone was light, and I was amazed how he managed to keep it together with his sister still being the prime suspect.

"It's sort of good, but not that good. I told you before about the Hardcastles owning commercial property and Rosalie trying to muscle her way into the businesses."

"Yes, and you wouldn't tell me who they were."

"Well, now I'm ready to." I named names.

"I like that you have a list of suspects. Though convincing Lieutenant Borgnine that there are other suspects is another story. We'll have to come up with a way you can let him think he figured it out himself, and soon. I'm sure he hasn't arrested Chloe because it's Butterfly Week. He's just keeping an eye on her though. She keeps complaining to me that wherever she goes, there he is." Dane started to run in place. "Speaking of Lieutenant Borgnine, he'll be at the ball with Mrs. Borgnine."

"Really! There's a Mrs. Borgnine? Now I'm really looking forward to going."

I started to leave, but he didn't move. "What?" I said, looking at him.

"You gave him a hug," he teased. "Don't I

get one, too?"

Lots of people were walking around the Vista Del Mar grounds. Breakfast had just ended, and a crew was working on the float for the parade. There was too much activity to keep it hidden anymore. Kevin St. John drove past me in his golf cart with the Delacorte sisters.

I stepped into the Lodge and noticed Liz Buckley was hanging by the counter. Her manner was a lot different than when I'd met her here at the beginning of the retreat. She'd seemed efficient and businesslike then. She still wore business wear, the same as when I'd seen her before, but she looked like she was just barely keeping it together.

"I thought I might run into you here," she said. She led me off to a corner and then took something out of her bag.

When I looked down, she pressed a heavy envelope in my hands. She seemed a little nervous. "It's all there. I didn't want to give you another check."

The envelope was thick with bills and a handful of change. I noticed a lot of the bills were singles. My first thought was it looked like it had come from a piggy bank. "You can count it if you like. I wouldn't blame you for not trusting me."

"That's okay," I said, putting it in my tote bag. "The Danish women seem very happy with the retreat."

"Good. I hope you won't hold this against me and we can do more business. It will benefit both of us. I promise it won't be like this next time."

I nodded as if I was agreeing, but I wasn't so sure there would be a next time. She was definitely on my suspect list. She'd certainly had access to Rosalie at the service, and she'd had a motive. The way she seemed now could be the aftermath of killing someone. Maybe she'd felt justified in killing Rosalie, but then afterward her conscience kicked in.

I could just hear Lieutenant Borgnine say, "She *could* have done it, but that didn't mean that she *did* do it." Without evidence, it was all meaningless.

We parted company, and I went on to join my retreaters. I thought it would be hard to segue from thinking about Liz being Rosalie's killer to being with a bunch of knitters, but it turned out to be easy.

The room was ready for us as usual. A fire warmed the space, and the window looked out on the flat light of another white sky day. I walked around admiring everybody's work. It was impressive how much they'd done with the looms. Most were still working with the looms, but a few of them had made enough items and had gone back to the traditional way of knitting with needles. A group of retreaters were gathered together, crocheting butterflies. They were all chatting as they worked, and the atmosphere was warm and friendly.

Crystal nodded her approval when I took my seat and began working with my loom. "It looks like I'll have to finish it after the retreat," I said, holding up my work.

"You don't seem particularly enthused about making a hat," Crystal said, and I nodded in agreement.

"I noticed that you wear a lot of cowls," Crystal said.

"They're all my aunt's creations," I said.

Crystal took a bright red cowl out of her bag and showed it to me. "Maybe you'd be happier making one of these." I loved the color and tried it on at her insistence.

"You're right. I would rather make a cowl." I took it off and handed it back to her.

"It's even easier than the hat," Crystal said. "I'm sure you won't have any trouble with it, but you know where to find me if you do." She showed me some written instructions and a skein of the red yarn.

"My gift," she said, putting the yarn and instructions in my tote bag. She pulled out the set of round looms in the bag and pointed out the one I should use.

"I'm sorry I've missed so much with the group," I said to both Crystal and Wanda. Crystal looked forgiving, but Wanda didn't seem so anxious to let me off the hook.

"The retreat seems to have worked out okay, but only because I — well, and Crystal, too — kept it together. Next time, I think I should have more say in the plans."

Crystal wrinkled her eyebrows in consternation at Wanda's comment. "How about the three of us should work together," she said. I could see their point and agreed. Wanda had continued wrapping and then moving loops off the pegs as she stood there talking. She saw me staring at her work.

"It's a hat for my son. He saw Kory's and wants one," Wanda said, continuing to manipulate the navy blue yarn.

Crystal had a pleased smile. "Wanda's son is still in middle school, but Kory is kind of a hero to him — especially being on the football team and now working at Vista Del Mar." Wanda didn't say a thing. The two workshop leaders left me and made the rounds of the room to see if anyone needed help.

Lucinda was sitting next to me, working on a round loom as well. The way she was using the pick to pull at the looms made it obvious she was upset.

"What gives?" I asked, almost in a whisper. She stabbed at a tight loop and then dragged it up the peg.

"It's the Butterfly Ball." Her expression sagged. "I don't know how I'm going to deal with Tag being there. I just don't want to see him right now."

"About that," I said, keeping my voice low. "He has something to tell you. I know you're upset with him, but when you know all the facts, I'm sure you'll feel differently."

She stopped working and looked at me. "Why don't you just tell me?"

"He said the same thing. I don't want to go into detail here; just trust me. Everything is okay with him."

The conversation at the table had turned to the Butterfly Ball.

"It's the last big event for the princesses," Crystal said. "The Butterfly Queen committee gets together after the ball and votes. They don't notify the winner until just before she's getting on the float. I'm so excited for Marcy," she added. "My daughter has never done anything like this before. I was shocked when a girl who wouldn't run for student council suddenly announced she wanted to be part of the Princess Court. It would reinforce she did the right thing if she ended up being chosen queen."

"My sister really wants it, too," Wanda said. "She's older than most of the others, but she thinks her maturity will help." Wanda stood up and did her teapot pose. "But I heard Larry Benson's daughter is trying really hard to impress the committee." She glanced around at the group. "The family is new to Cadbury. He's the pharmacist and owner of Cadbury Drugs & Sundries."

I hadn't thought about Larry Benson having a family, and I certainly hadn't realized his daughter was one of the princesses.

"If I was on the committee, I'd have second thoughts about choosing a queen who hadn't even lived here for a year," Wanda said.

"Don't worry, the committee is taking everything into consideration." Madeleine Delacorte had come into the room and overheard. "I am so sorry to have missed this retreat, but duty calls." No denim for Madeleine today, but she was still shunning the old way she had dressed and had on a pair of purple slacks with a matching top. She walked around between the tables, admiring the women's work.

"How did Rosalie feel about Larry Benson's daughter being a princess?" I asked.

Madeleine shrugged. "She was only there for the first interview. But knowing Rosalie, she would have been very negative, since they were newcomers."

Madeleine returned to the front of the room. "I just stopped by to make sure you were all coming tonight. The Butterfly Ball is always an exciting event."

The women all nodded in enthusiastic agreement. Scott leaned back in his chair, and I had the feeling he hadn't decided. Madeleine waved and said she'd be looking for them and then left, just as Kory came into the room.

His dark curls were hidden under the hat his mother had made for him. The whole group recognized it, and he walked around the tables, showing it off again.

"No more garbage detail," he said. "I'm working in the dining hall now, busing tables." He laughed. "Maybe it's not such a step up from garbage detail."

When he mentioned the dining hall, it made me think of the chili dinner and what my mother had said. While the group broke for tea and coffee, I called Kory to the side. I made a little small talk before I got to what

I really wanted to discuss.

"You said you sat at dinner with the two players who got sick, right?" It took a moment for my question to register, then he nodded.

"I was curious. How did they arrange the seating?"

"You mean like were there place cards or something?" he asked. I nodded and he continued. "No, we just sat wherever we wanted to. The team all sat together at one of the long tables, and the parents and other people were at a different one."

"Did you go up and help yourself?" I asked.

"No, it was a big deal that we were served. They came around with a tray full of bowls." His eyes lit up. "I know why you're asking. It's because of your muffins." He seemed to be getting ready to go. "It's okay. You must have noticed that they're really moving again." It seemed an odd comment, and I was going to ask about it, but before I could, he was out the door.

24

I made it a point to sit down and have lunch with the group and was just settling into the idea of spending the rest of the day with them when I saw Sammy come into the dining hall. He stopped in the entrance and surveyed the room. I figured he was looking for me and waved. As he crossed toward my table, I heard several of the staff members ask if he was there to do a show. Sammy seemed pleased and nervous at the same time.

"Case, my mother's all upset," he said when he reached me. "My father disappeared before our trip to the aquarium. My mother is a wreck, insisting we have to find him. She's saying we have to do an intervention and the more people there, the better chance he'll listen. She said since you're almost a family member that you should come along." His eyes were apologetic. "I tried to talk her out of it. I hate to ask you for another favor . . ."

Lucinda overheard. "Go on," she urged. "By now everybody knows what to do. I hope you'll be back in time for the Butterfly Ball."

"You can bet on that. Lieutenant Borgnine is going to be there with his wife. I can't wait to see what she looks like." I took a moment to tell the group I would catch up with them later, then I headed out.

Sammy was already almost to his BMW when I caught up with him. I saw that Estelle was in the passenger seat, so I got into the back. Sammy pulled away as soon as I shut the door, and I was still putting on my seat belt as we turned out of the Vista Del Mar driveway.

"Do you have any idea where he went?" I asked. I couldn't believe they were planning to just drive the streets looking for him.

"Yes, we do," Estelle said. "He slipped out this morning without saying anything, as if I wouldn't notice."

"So then he isn't actually lost," I said, trying to make sense of what was going on.

"No, Bernard knows exactly where he is, but *we* don't know where he is."

Sammy didn't go through the heart of Cadbury but instead headed for the highway that led to Monterey and beyond.

"I heard you say something to Bernard about his having a problem with an activity. Does that have anything to do with where he went?" I asked.

"Does it have anything to do with it? How about it has everything to do with it!" Estelle was leaning forward, as if it would make the car go faster. "When we find him, I'm going to give him a piece of my mind."

"Okay, but could you give me a hint about what?"

"Sammy, tell her," Estelle said. "It just makes me too angry."

Sammy caught my eye in the rearview mirror and rolled his. "We're going to check out the local card rooms. My father likes to play poker."

"Likes to play," his mother said, indignant. "He's obsessed. This is the third time he's slipped away this week. The man has a problem."

Sammy was biting his lip to keep from smiling. I'm pretty sure he was thinking that the one with the problem was her.

The highway ran along the water of Monterey Bay, and the waves were small as they lapped up on the sand. Not being a card player myself, I had no idea that card rooms even existed.

Sammy was consulting a map on the car's

small screen. He pulled off the highway, and we began driving through the streets of Bayside. He followed the directions, and we entered the parking lot of a strip mall that had an Old West look to it. Next to a lounge, there was a sign that said POKER CASINO, with some dancing spades and diamonds around it.

Sammy pulled into an empty spot. Estelle was out of the car before Sammy cut the motor, and she marched through the door of the casino. Sammy caught up with her, and I took up the rear. I was expecting some kind of razzle dazzle in the decorations, but it was just a big wood-paneled room with a bunch of round card tables. It must have been mostly a nighttime activity, because there were only three tables in use. I was amazed how no one even looked up as the three of us walked around the players, searching for Sammy's father. Not that it would be easy to recognize him. All the players had on baseball caps, or hoodies, or hoodies and baseball caps. A few were wearing sunglasses. Not one of them broke their expression, even with Estelle practically putting her face in front of theirs.

"He's not here," she announced, and marched toward the door.

After we all piled back into the car,

Sammy punched in something on the GPS and we were off again. "How many of these are there?" I asked, looking at my watch. "I do have a retreat going on, and tonight is the big event of the week."

Estelle looked around the front seat. "This is much more important than a dance. Family comes first, and it's your duty as an almost-Glickner to help with Bernard."

I looked up at the rearview mirror and saw that Sammy was sending me an "I'm sorry" look. I felt terrible. I should have been with my retreaters or trying to hunt down Rosalie's killer instead of going on a wild-goose chase. Time was going by quickly. Butterfly Week was almost over, then Lieutenant Borgnine would lower the boom on Chloe unless I did something fast.

I didn't even know where we were by now, beyond that we were in one of the small communities that hugged the bay. We passed one similar area of fast-food places and convenience stores after another, and for the first time, I realized why the town council was so adamant about keeping chains and big-box stores out of Cadbury. As we drove on I felt like we were in a personality-less Anywhere, Small Town, USA. The second card room was located in an old car dealership. I had a feeling the colorful banners that flapped along the outside of the parking lot were left over from its previous tenant.

Sammy parked, and we all marched toward the place. This was a much bigger setup, with many more tables and even a restaurant at the end. But like the other one, afternoon didn't seem to be their busy time, and only a few of the tables were full. Estelle was ready to lead another trip around the tables to check for her husband, and I could see it was going to pose the same challenge as the last place. All I saw as I looked at the players were a bunch of head coverings. Then one of the players turned his head. Beneath the black baseball cap with *Cadbury by the Sea* embroidered in red across the front, I recognized Sammy's dad. It was almost as if Bernard had some kind of radar that told him his wife was in the building. He instantly began to shake his head in annoyance and held his hand up to stop us. He threw in some cards and gathered up his chips before turning to the man next to him. He gave him a friendly pat, which seemed to be a sign of good-bye and good luck.

The three of us retreated outside, and a moment later he joined us. Before he said a word, Estelle began. "Bernard, you have a problem. You need to face it."

Bernard took off the hat and looked skyward for help. "Are you crazy?" he said, moving his gaze down to his wife's face. He glanced toward Sammy and me. "I'm sorry your mother dragged you along on this."

He wanted to leave, but she was insistent on dealing with it right then and there. She turned to Sammy and me. "You two be the judges." Then she confronted Bernard. "We have been here for not even a week, and how many times have you played cards?"

"You're being ridiculous. So I played a few times." He seemed annoyed to have to do it, but he explained to Sammy and me that he had a card fund that he played with. "It's not like I'm losing the mortgage money."

Sammy was shaking his head now, too. "What's wrong if he likes to play cards? As long as he does his day job, so what if he has a passion for something else?"

Was Sammy going to say more and finally tell them the truth? That he was working nights and weekends performing magic and that was why he was in Cadbury? I gave him a little nudge, and I think he knew what I meant, because he vehemently shook his head and whispered, "Not now."

"We might as well go back," Sammy said.

There was a minor argument over who was going to drive with who. Estelle insisted she didn't trust Bernard driving alone, that he would just circle back or go on to another card room, and he didn't want to drive with his irate wife. So, I was called into duty.

Bernard turned on the radio, and I expected the ride back to be a silent one, but he started pleading his case to me. He kept talking about the guy sitting next to him as if I knew him and how he was a different story. "I've played cards enough to recognize the guys like me, who play as a diversion, and the guys like him, who have a problem." I assumed the point of his telling me this was so I could pass it on to Estelle. I mostly tuned it out and watched the passing scenery. We were driving along the bay, and I could see some fishing boats. It made me think of Hank Hardcastle and how far I was from saving Chloe.

25

I expected Bernard to drop me off and leave, but he pulled into my driveway and shut off the motor. "Maybe I can hang out here for a while," he said, looking toward my house. I sighed. Lies always catch up with you. How could I say no to him, since as far as he knew it was Sammy's house, too? I couldn't say I blamed him, either. I'm sure Estelle was going to chew his ear off about his supposed problem.

"She just doesn't understand the difference between spending some vacation time doing something I like and someone with no control," he said.

Sammy's BMW pulled in behind us. I saw that the passenger seat was empty. I think Bernard did, too, and he let out a sigh of relief.

"I thought I'd hang out at your place for a while and give your mother some time to cool off," he said to his son. Sammy looked confused for a moment and then realized what his father meant.

Sammy must have seen the look on my face. "Casey has a lot going on right now. How about we go out for a beer?"

Bernard agreed, and I was relieved. Sammy pointed his father across the street and said they'd go to the Cora and Madeleine Delacorte Café.

"Thanks, Case," Sammy said, hanging back as his father walked down the driveway. "I owe you big-time."

I went inside, happy to have a few minutes alone. To make up for yet another absence with my group, I decided to bring them a treat. I always kept rolls of butter cookie dough in my refrigerator. I took out four of them and turned on the oven. I covered two cookie sheets with rounds of dough and then added a sprinkle-covered chocolate wafer on each one to make them special.

By the time I got back to Vista Del Mar, it was almost time for the workshop to end. I was surprised to see that Madeleine Delacorte had come back and Crystal was showing her how to use the round loom. "At least I'm getting a little taste of the retreat," Madeleine said to me. "The princesses are doing a nature walk, and I left Cora in charge."

She watched as I set down the plate of cookies.

"Casey's baked goods are the best," she said, taking one of the cookies. "I don't believe for a minute there was anything wrong with those muffins," she whispered to me. She held up the cookie to show the others before taking a dainty bite. "Hmm, that's delicious."

"I know you're trying to help, but I think the problem is ebbing. It was only for a day or so that the muffin sales dropped off."

"Really? Maybe you should talk to him." She pointed outside, and I saw Kory pass by. Crystal overheard and wondered why her son had been singled out. She followed me outside, and we caught up with the teen.

He was still wearing the navy blue hat as he pushed a hamper of dirty linens. "I get all the glamorous jobs," he said, and laughed until he saw the serious looks that Crystal and I wore. "Whatever it is, I didn't do it," he said, still in a joking tone.

Madeleine had come with us. "I saw him and some of his friends buying lots of your muffins. They had a bag full, and I saw them throwing them to the seagulls."

Kory swallowed so hard it made a boinging sound. "I know teenage boys are supposed to be like bottomless pits when it comes to food, but we ate as many as we could." Meanwhile, my face was falling as I realized the problem wasn't over with my baking and that something weird was going on.

"We were just trying to help," he said. When no one said anything, he went on. "It wasn't really our idea. Dane was behind it."

"What?" I said.

"He paid for them all and said we could do what we wanted with them. Like I said, we could only eat so many. The seagulls loved them."

"Why didn't you tell me?" Crystal asked. "I thought you knew we could talk about anything. I'm your friend and your mother." Kory made a face, and I gathered it was a one-sided plan.

He started to push the laundry cart and then turned to me. "None of the guys think it was your muffins that made anybody sick. About what you asked me before — I remembered the guys next to me said they got their chili already loaded."

When Madeleine didn't seem to understand, he explained. "Theirs had cheese and chips already."

"I'm sorry," Crystal said when he'd left. "I thought I had this open relationship with my kids. Now what else hasn't he told me?"

Madeleine was still a little dense in the ways of the regular world after living such a sheltered life, but she seemed to comprehend that she had created a problem. Crystal excused herself and went after her son.

Just then, the princesses went by. They were dressed for outdoor work, with only the little tiaras showing off who they were. Chloe was in the middle of the pack, and I heard her describing how the dunes were being replanted with native species. It would have been fine, but at the end she yelled, "Nailed it!" and put her hands up in triumph.

Cora stopped next to us and let the princesses walk on alone. She let out a weary sigh. "I'm glad we're almost done with this. Rosalie was a pain, but it's a lot harder without her."

The clipboard slipped out of her grasp and fell down. I rushed to pick it up and glanced over it. "It's no use trying to figure out who is in the lead," Cora said. "I use my own special code to give each girl a mark on the events." I saw some actual sentences next to the names. "Those are Rosalie's notes," she said, noticing where I was looking.

I thought she was going to take the clipboard away from me, but she shrugged and said since I didn't have a relative in the running, it probably didn't matter if I looked at it. I read over what Rosalie had said after meeting Chloe, and as expected, it basically indicated that she had no chance to be queen. There weren't really comments about the others, except for one.

"Who is Megan Benson?" I asked, reading over what it said. *Single parent, lives with father, but for how long? Too new to Cadbury to be queen.*

"Her father is the one who bought Cadbury Drugs. The one who looks like Mr. Eastwood," Madeleine said. "No way would she be queen if Rosalie was still around."

With that, Cora and Madeleine went on their way, and when I looked back to the meeting room, everyone had left. I went inside and picked up the empty cookie plate and saw that some kind person had put my partially done hat in my tote bag, along with the round looms. Then I went looking for the group. Most of them had moved on to the Lodge. I did a few more rows on the loom but mostly just talked with everybody. Because of the Butterfly Ball, dinner was served early, and then we all went our separate ways to get ready for the evening.

I was glad to go home and collect my

thoughts. So much had happened, and it was all churning in my brain. I kept thinking about Rosalie's notes on the princesses. What if the pharmacist knew that Rosalie had already decided his daughter wasn't going to be queen because of Rosalie's own personal prejudices? And what if she'd made him the same offer she had the others. It would be pretty easy for Larry to figure all his problems would be solved if Rosalie was out of the way.

But I needed proof. And now I had the Butterfly Ball to deal with. There was always some kind of event on the Saturday night of my retreats, but this was far bigger than even a dance at Vista Del Mar. The Butterfly Ball was for the whole town.

After giving Julius some attention, I dished out a generous portion of stink fish, which he surprisingly didn't seem that enthused about. The mystery was soon solved when I saw the empty can in the trash. Sammy was trying to win over the cat with the smelly treat and obviously had already offered him a huge portion.

I heard a car drive up and looked out the window as the BMW pulled in my driveway. Sammy got out and came to the back door. He was wearing a tuxedo and carrying a box from a florist.

"What's up?" I asked when I opened the door. He looked at my face.

"Maybe I should ask you that. You look worried."

Sammy had been out of the loop about Rosalie's death and all the intrigue I had uncovered, and I was going to leave it that way. He had enough on his plate with his parents. I forced a smile and asked what was in the box.

"I know you're going to be there with your group, but my parents don't understand at all. My mother got it in her head that this is like a town prom, and she said I ought to get you a corsage." He took a breath, as if he was getting to the bad part. "You saw how my mother is when she gets something in her head. She's insisting that we meet up here first for a glass of wine, since this is their last night in town," he said. "They're taking the red-eye from San Jose. So, this will be the last time I have to pretend I live here." He tried to make it sound like that last part was a relief, but Sammy would never make it as an actor.

The news that they were leaving perked me right up, and I said their visit was no problem. He handed me the box. Inside, two creamy white gardenias rested on some shiny green leaves. The fragrance was divine.

"Is that the tuxedo you wear for the magic shows?"

Sammy nodded with a smile. "The suit is the closest my folks are going to come to my performances."

The doorbell rang, startling both of us. We answered the front door together, and his parents came in, carrying a bottle of wine. I had a feeling they were still arguing, but they seemed to be putting on a front.

"I had no idea we'd be going to a dance," Estelle said. "I had to make do." She glanced down at her black dress with a cream-colored bolero jacket, obviously fishing for a compliment. I obliged and raved about how great she looked. She gave my jeans a sideways glace. "You're not going like that?" Her voice dripped with disapproval.

"Of course she isn't," Sammy said. Bernard had gone on to the kitchen and come back with the wine opener and glasses. He poured the dark red merlot into the glasses and took a seat on the sofa. A deck of cards was on the coffee table, and he took them out and started shuffling them and then laying out a game of solitaire.

"Bernard, not with the cards again," Estelle said, momentarily forgetting about my clothes. Sammy's father sat up a little straighter and glared at his wife. Then his glance went to me and Sammy.

"Sammy, why don't you help her get ready?" he said. When both Sammy and I seemed shocked at his suggestion, he almost laughed. "I know what living together means. I assume that means you've seen each other without clothes."

He almost chased us out of the room. When we'd shut ourselves in my bedroom, Sammy said, "Don't worry, Case, I won't look. Even though since I'm a doctor, I'm used to seeing people without their clothes. It doesn't mean a thing to me."

I wanted to say, "But they weren't me," but I was more interested in what was going on in my living room and had my ear pressed against the door. Sammy said something about me getting dressed.

"Go find something. You have good taste," I said, gesturing toward my closet.

Estelle and Bernard were having a heated discussion, and with us out of the room, they didn't bother to keep their voices down. I got that Bernard was still steamed about her intervention.

"I don't have a problem," he said. Estelle said something back, but I couldn't quite make it out, and then he continued. "Here's how you know when someone might have a problem. The guy sitting next to me was there all the times I played and, judging by how well the dealers knew him, was a regular. Now, it could just be that there isn't much to do in this small town and that's why he plays so much."

Nosy me wanted to know who in town he was talking about, and I kept my ear jammed against the door. "Here," Sammy said, handing me a hanger and subtly pulling me away from my listening post.

The pale coral dress had an overlay of cream-colored lace. My mother had sent it to me, and the tags were still on it. She knew about the weather in Cadbury and had sent along a short off-white jacket that looked like something Marilyn Monroe would have worn.

Hers would have been ermine; mine was fleece.

"Do I have to come up with shoes, too?" Sammy said, looking at the row on the floor.

"I can handle that." I grabbed a pair of sandals with low heels. I wanted to get back to listening, but Sammy had positioned himself in front of the door. I knew it was no accident. Who wants to have someone eavesdrop on their parents arguing?

"I'll turn around," he said.

"This is like something out of an old movie." I rolled my eyes but still waited for him to turn away. It felt weird to be getting dressed almost next to him. I pretty much shimmied out of the jeans and pulled off the turtleneck I'd been wearing and dropped on the replacement clothes.

"Let me know if you need anything zipped," he said, half turning toward me.

"Nope, and you can turn around," I said. He did and smiled.

"Wow, Case, you're the magician." I tried to act like I didn't care about the compliment, but of course I did. I excused myself to go to the bathroom to put on my makeup.

I could tell Sammy was about to say something, but I stopped him. "Don't worry, I won't listen."

When we came back in the living room, his parents were sitting together on the couch as if nothing had happened. Estelle didn't try to hide that she was giving my outfit her critical appraisal. She seemed okay with it. It figured, since my mother picked out the dress. "You can lock up," I said to Sammy as I headed to the door.

"I still don't know why you can't go with us," Estelle said.

I ignored her.

26

"Don't you look nice," Lucinda said as I came into the Lodge.

"So do you," I said, admiring her taupe silk dress. Her new bob hairstyle only added to the sophistication of her look. The whole group was waiting with her. It was fun to see the transformation of everyone from their casual clothes to totally dressed up. A number of the women had pinned the crocheted butterflies to their clothes. I was glad to see that Scott was with Bree and Olivia, after his earlier reticence.

"You left this when you were here before," Lucinda said. It was my tote bag, with the round looms and some yarn.

"It goes with the outfit," I joked. I was going to run it home, but the bus showed up, and everyone was anxious to get going, so I just took it along.

The bus dropped us on Grand Street, and we had to walk the rest of the way. There wasn't an inside space big enough for the ball, so the street around the natural history museum had been closed down and a big tent erected next to the building. I stopped at the long table in front of the entrance. Cora, Madeleine and several of the princesses were handling taking the tickets. I had them for my whole group, and it took a bit of doing to get them organized. Finally, Cora said it was best to just give each person their ticket, as they had to get their hand stamped. Another woman on the committee was distributing streams of tickets to some of the other princesses, explaining they were raffle tickets. One of them was Chloe.

Dane would have had a fit if he saw what his sister had chosen as ball attire. She had on a dress so short that it literally just covered her butt. It was stretchy material, so I guessed it would stay in place. It certainly showed off the tattoo and her orange hair, which she had done into a bun on the side of her head. She'd gone with heavy eye makeup and then some pale lipstick. Her earrings were so long they brushed her shoulders.

She gave my dress the once-over and seemed about to say something, maybe a compliment, but Sammy caught up with me. "Case, you forgot your corsage." He went to put it on my wrist, but the red tote bag was in the way. I had wanted to leave it on the bus, but apparently they couldn't guarantee the same bus would pick us up.

"Let me get rid of this." I saw that the museum doors were open, and there was a big sign pointing toward the restrooms. I went into the entrance hall and glanced around for a spot to stow the bag. The doorway to the butterfly room was blocked off with chairs, and the room was dark. The door to the multipurpose room and kitchen was simply closed. On the other side of the small hall, the doorway that led to the main exhibit areas had chairs blocking it as well. Nobody would even know if I stuck the bag in there. I moved the chairs aside and went into the dark room. I automatically looked around the large space. It wasn't completely dark, due to the emergency light on the wall, which filled the big room with creepy shadows and gave off just enough light so I could make out all the cases filled with stuffed animals. The giant bear seemed even more menacing in the almost-darkness. It had been posed so that the upper paws were outstretched, as though it were about to take a step and attack. I deposited the bag against the wall and slipped back out of the room.

When I got back to the entrance to the tent, Sammy was gone, probably off looking for his parents. I went inside to look for my group. The interior of the tent was decorated with lanterns and giant silk butterflies fluttering in the breeze. A floor had been added over the ground. Several princesses were manning a table with drinks and snacks, and a DJ was just starting up, trying to get everyone on the dance floor. As I had hoped, he said partners were optional. An upbeat song began, and the crowd divided into dancers and those standing around watching. I made my way through the crowd. It seemed like everyone was there, though I had to do a couple of double takes to recognize people in their fancy clothes.

Coach Gary had left the butterfly wings home and was dressed like a normal person in slacks and a dress shirt. He and Maggie were in the middle of the dancers. It was hard to miss her in her red long dress. Kevin St. John was hanging around in the background, and I almost wanted to pull him out on the dance floor just to see what he would do. Liz Buckley had found a post to lean against, and she looked like her mind was somewhere else.

The music changed to a slow dance, and the "partners optional" portion seemed to end. A bunch of my retreaters left the dance floor and hung out on the edge. I saw Kory ask his grandmother to dance. Gwen always wore what I called sensible attire at the store, but she'd gone all out and wore a long skirt and white shirt covered with a blue mohair wrap. I thought she was even wearing makeup.

I almost didn't recognize Larry the pharmacist without the white jacket. He swooped in and asked Crystal to dance. As usual, her clothes were full of color and her earrings didn't match.

"I bet he wouldn't give her any trouble if she brought back an item that wasn't on the receipt," I said, half to myself. Lucinda had come up next to me and only caught part of what I'd said. She responded with a "Huh?"

I quickly told her about the fuss he'd made about a return and how he could tell it was the wrong receipt because there was so much information on it. We both watched the way Larry seemed to have pulled Crystal closer. "I see what you mean," Lucinda said with a smile. "He does look smitten."

I didn't say anything, but I was thinking it would be better if Crystal didn't get too attached, since Larry might be a murderer.

I saw Tag come in and make a beeline for Lucinda. He linked arms with her, and I heard him say that they needed to talk. They stepped away, and I couldn't hear their conversation, but judging by the pleading look on his face, he was trying to make amends. My friend seemed to be holding her ground, but apparently they settled things quickly, as I saw them go out on the dance floor.

I glanced over the crowd. Wanda was there with her husband. I almost laughed out loud. They were about the same height and both stood in the teapot pose as they considered buying some raffle tickets from Wanda's sister. The slow song ended and the dancers left the floor.

Several couples headed to the refreshment table. I saw that Sammy and his parents were helping themselves to punch. His parents looked like they didn't want to be there but were making the best of it.

Some people moved, and I saw Dane huddled with a bunch of teenage boys, who I figured were the ones who hung out at his place. He seemed to be telling them something, and they fanned out and began asking lone women to dance, including some of my retreaters.

One of the boys was Kory, and he asked me to dance.

"It's very nice of you," I said, "but you don't have to. I don't mind standing around. I know Dane told you to do it." He took my hand anyway and led me onto the floor.

"Dane is always telling us to do nice stuff," Kory said. I was trying not to step on his toes.

"You mean like buying up all the muffins?" He answered with a nod. I still didn't know how I felt about what he'd done. It made me smile to think how he had wanted to fix things for me, but it really hadn't solved the problem. My thoughts moved to what my mother had said about only the two players' chili being tainted.

"Did the boys ask for their chili that way?" It was a bit of a non sequitur, and it took a moment for Kory to catch up to what I was talking about. "I was thinking maybe it was something with the cheese."

"I don't think so, but you could ask them. They both helped that night." He moved our hands in the direction of a couple dancing nearby. I almost choked when I saw Liz Buckley dancing with Hank Hardcastle. He was whispering something to her, and she practically had her head on his shoulder. The song ended, and Kory released me.

He'd been a good sport and managed to ignore the times I trampled on his toes. Hank and Liz walked into the crowd, and I lost them. So, Hank Hardcastle was at the chili dinner.

Another slow song started, and I walked to the side. Dane was looking my way from across the room, and our eyes met. I shook my head, thinking of the muffin business.

He, on the other hand, looked over my outfit and nodded in approval. He mimed dancing with a partner and then pointed at the crowd moving around the floor.

"You should have warned Kory about my dancing skills," I said when he reached me. Dane laughed and said something about how dodging my feet was probably good practice for football. He took my hand and led me into the middle of the dancers. "I know what you did about the muffins," I said as we assumed slow dance position.

"Who told?" He glanced over the crowd. Then he smiled. "It was Kory, wasn't it?"

"It doesn't matter. Thank you, but you'll go broke if you keep it up, and all the seagulls will get potbellies." Dane laughed at the image of tubby seagulls.

"The only answer is for me to show that the muffins weren't involved with the football players getting sick," I said.

"You're doing better in the dancing department," he said, looking down at our feet. "I don't think you've stepped on my feet once."

"That's because we're barely moving since there are so many people."

"Lieutenant Borgnine and his better half at twelve o'clock," Dane said, turning me so I could look.

"He's wearing a suit and it's not wrinkled," I said, watching as the gruff-looking man walked along the edge of the room.

"Don't let the outfit fool you. He's never really off duty, and I know he's keeping an eye on Chloe." Dane turned me again, and I saw that Chloe was selling raffle tickets near the cop. I wanted to get a good look at his wife. So far all I could tell was she was short and had dark hair. When I saw her face, I was surprised at her dainty features. I guessed opposites really did attract.

I was about to thank Dane for getting my people dance partners when I felt a tap on my shoulder. When I turned, Bernard was giving Dane a dirty look and cut in.

He held me at a polite distance and shuffled his feet in time to the music. "Estelle said I should dance with you," he said. Dancing with Bernard was pretty close to a chore for both of us. My mind started to wander, and random thoughts started popping in my head. I kept thinking about the chili and the players who had gotten the loaded bowls. I had assumed it was special treatment, but what if it was a way to mark the bowls of chili meant for them?

I was beginning to think the song was endless as Bernard and I moved around. I glanced up at his face to see his expression. I was surprised to see that he was greeting someone nearby. Who did Bernard know here? Then the earlier fuss came back to me. He'd talked about somebody he'd met playing cards who was from Cadbury. I followed Bernard's gaze and almost tripped over his feet when I saw who he was looking at. It couldn't be him.

I needed a moment to process everything and went outside to think as soon as the song was over. I thought over the last week and things I'd heard. And then it was like when you see an anagram and the word hidden in it jumps out at you. All of a sudden I knew who had killed Rosalie.

27

I went into the entrance hall of the museum.
Several women were exiting the bathroom
and passed me as they headed back outside
to the dance. As I was passing the men's
room, I heard the door opening. Anxious
not to be seen, I moved quickly into the
multipurpose room, letting the door close
behind me. I walked through the large
empty room to the kitchen.

I'd seen something before that hadn't
seemed to mean anything, but now I wanted
to have another look. The kitchen looked
untouched, and Rosalie's things were still
sitting on the counter where I had seen
them before. I began to unload the big pots
that were nested together. Before, when I'd
found the strip of paper stuck between two
of them, I had assumed it had gotten there
by mistake. But now I was sure it had been
a plan.

I pulled the top pot off, and there was

nothing there. The same was true with the second one. But when I took the third one out, I saw the strip of white stuck to the bottom of it. The first time I'd found it, I'd only given it a cursory look, and once I saw it was a receipt, I had just put it back in with the pans. This time I read it over carefully and was stunned to see what it was for: three boxes of chocolate-flavored laxatives. The pills would have dissolved in the chili and the flavor gone unnoticed. Marking the bowls by making them loaded would have made it easy to ensure specific people got them. It came back to me that Kory had mentioned who had been the one to serve him and the players next to him.

I thought back to what I'd heard Sunday night, when I'd been in line at the dining hall, trying to get my food ahead of the people there for a special event for Butterfly Week. Now it made sense. Rosalie had said she'd found something that explained what happened. She must have meant explained what happened to make the players sick. Then a man had asked her what she wanted. I had thought he was talking about her choice for dinner, but he was talking about what it would take to keep her quiet.

I shuddered when I thought of her answer. She'd said she would have to think about it.

I knew what she'd tried to do to the Hardcastle tenants when she thought she'd had them trapped. I could only imagine what she would have wanted to remain silent.

The person who'd bought the laxatives had paid with a credit card, and his name was on the receipt, clear as day. Gary Buckley.

Why would a coach feed laxatives to his two star players? The answer was obvious, even to me, a non-sports person. He wanted his team to lose the game. As for the why — I was sure it had to do with money.

Knowing all this would have to be enough for now. There was no way I was going to interrupt the Butterfly Ball. I backtracked to the entrance hall. I didn't want to keep the receipt with me and thought of the tote bag. Seeing no one, I walked quietly back into the main exhibit hall. I found my tote bag against the wall and slipped in the receipt.

I stood to go and heard a voice behind me.

"No one is supposed to be in here." Coach Gary was standing just inside the doorway.

"Then I better get out of here," I said, taking a step toward the doorway. He moved to block me.

"I heard you telling Dane you wanted to

settle what made my players sick once and for all to get the suspicion off your muffins." He stepped a little closer. "Then I saw you go in the kitchen. Any luck finding an answer?"

"No," I said with a hopeless sigh. "I don't know what I thought I would find anyway. Everything had been scrubbed clean." I shrugged, as if I was giving up. "Might as well get back to the dance."

"Why did you come in here?" he asked. He didn't sound so friendly now.

I held out my tiny white cross-body bag. "There isn't room for anything in this. I came in to get my makeup to do a repair job." I pointed at my face, trying to sound silly and girlish. It worked about as well as my pseudo attempts at being flirtatious. I made another move toward the door, but Coach Gary's gaze had stopped on my tote bag. I went to grab it, but he got it first. He picked it up from the bottom, and everything tumbled out, the round looms hitting the floor with a clatter and rolling away. The white receipt fluttered down and settled into the darkness.

"I better clean up this mess," I said, still trying to sound light.

"Let me help you," he said, coming up behind me. He leaned down and picked up the receipt.

"That's okay. I think I'll get it later." I made a move toward the door, but he wrapped his arm around me. My impulse was to pull free, but he was stronger than I was.

"So that is what Rosalie had," he said. Even in the semidarkness, he had recognized what it was. He muttered something about being careless.

"It doesn't prove anything," I said, trying to reason with him.

"Stupid Rosalie," he said in an angry voice. "If she hadn't said your muffins were to blame, you would have left this alone."

"We could just crumple up the receipt and forget about it," I offered. I was trying to sound calm, but my voice had the squeaking pitch you get during an adrenaline rush.

"But you still know." His voice was almost a growl. I made another attempt to pull away, fueled by the surge of energy, but he pushed something hard against my back. I was sure it was a gun.

He seemed at a loss for what to do as he glanced around the exhibit hall.

"I'm not trying to make waves in Cadbury. We can just forget all of this happened," I said, trying to reason with him.

"Shut up," he said harshly. He started to

drag me around the dark room. He stopped in front of a mannequin holding a spear. "This is a dangerous place to be wandering around in the dark," he said. "One false step and you could end up on this spear." He seemed to be taking a moment to figure out the logistics while I searched for a way out.

There was a sound of voices coming from the entrance hall as some people headed to the bathrooms. I thought of yelling for help, but the gun was stuck against my back, and if I startled him, he might shoot without thinking. The noise would get their attention, but I could be dead in the meantime.

He took a step back, looking for a shadow to hide in. The grizzly bear with its outstretched paws threw a big pool of darkness on the floor. He pulled us both back toward it, and my foot hit the fallen looms.

His cell phone began to ring. You know how they say don't use your phone and drive? The same is true when you're holding a hostage. His hold loosened, and he was distracted just long enough for me to use my foot to kick the looms away and pull free. He came after me, not realizing there was anything on the ground. He grunted as his feet got trapped in the looms. As he tried to pull free of them, he began to lose his balance and teetered back and forth, reaching out for something to grab on to. The only thing available was the outstretched paw of the grizzly bear, which, as it turned out, wasn't tethered to the ground very securely. Suddenly the giant bear lurched forward and then fell over, pushing Coach Gary with it and then landing on top of him.

"What's going on?" an angry voice said. The lights flipped on in the large room, and Lieutenant Borgnine walked in, drying his hands with a paper towel. "I was coming out of the little boys' room, and I heard some racket."

His gaze went from the grizzly bear sprawled on the floor to me. "Ms. Feldstein, what have you done? I didn't take you for someone who'd commit vandalism."

"Get this off me," Coach Gary said from beneath the giant stuffed animal. "I can't breathe."

Lieutenant Borgnine's eyes opened wider. The noise had attracted more people, and I saw Dane and another man come in. Dane and the other man lifted the bear off Coach Gary, and he stood up. I noticed that his hands were empty.

"Arrest that woman," he said. "I found her wandering in here, and when I told her this was off limits, she went crazy and attacked me with those." He pointed at the round looms and yarn scattered on the floor. "And then she pushed the bear on top of me." I think Lieutenant Borgnine might have been willing to go with that scenario, but Dane shook his head.

"There has to be more to it than that," Dane said. Coach Gary was looking around frantically, and I saw his eyes stop on the white strip of paper. He made a grab for it, but this time I was faster.

"I think if you look at this, everything will become clear," I said, holding it out. Dane started to take it, but Borgnine got it first. Coach Gary was edging toward the door, and Dane went to block him.

"He put the laxatives in the bowls of chili for the two star players and then marked them by adding the chips and cheese. When he brought the tray to the table, he knew exactly which bowls to give them." I gave it a moment to sink in.

I had never seen Lieutenant Borgnine get so upset. "How could you do that to your own team?"

Dane was angry, too. "You're supposed to be an example to the kids."

The other man shook his head. "How could you do that to the Monarchs?"

"He has a gambling problem," I said. I told them about my trip to the card room and how Sammy's father had been talking about someone he'd seen the times he played there who had a problem. When I'd seen Sammy's father nod like he knew somebody at the ball, I'd put it together.

The other man seemed impressed at my abilities, but Lieutenant Borgnine was clearly annoyed that I'd bested him again. I told them there was a gun somewhere on the floor and started to look for it. "We've got it, Ms. Feldstein." He glared at Coach Gary. "Let me guess — you owed somebody a bunch of money, and you connected with one of the bookies around here and bet against your own team."

Coach Gary's silence said it was true.

"You're missing the big picture here," I said. Lieutenant Borgnine gave me a look, but I continued anyway. "The receipt was stuck with Rosalie's chili stuff." I told them about what I'd overheard. "He killed her," I said, stunned that I was having to spell it out. "All he had to do was stab her before he made his entrance as Lord of the Butterflies."

"I did the town a favor. That woman was a monster," Coach Gary said.

With that, Borgnine put him under arrest and called a cruiser. They decided it was best to simply take Coach Gary out through the kitchen and not disrupt the ball.

Lieutenant Borgnine, Dane and the other man, who introduced himself as Arthur Reisling, one of the city council members, huddled in the kitchen. I followed them in, and Arthur took over. "We'll keep a lid on everything until Monday, when Butterfly Week is over." He looked at all of us. "Now, we all need to rejoin the ball as if we've done nothing more exciting than used the facilities."

I still couldn't believe that Lieutenant Borgnine had actually called it the little boys' room.

We started to file back into the entrance hall. Dane held me back and did a mock bow. "I'm in awe of your ability. You did it. You got Chloe off the hook. We'll see how I can repay you later." And then he gestured toward my dress and hair, indicating that I was somewhat mussed from all the action.

I let them all go back to the ball, and I made a detour to the women's room to repair the damage, which amounted to finger combing my hair, straightening my dress and adding a new coat of lipstick.

I took a deep breath and went back to the tent. Another no-partner-necessary upbeat song was playing, and the dance floor was packed with people. Bree, Olivia and Scott were dancing near a bunch of the retreaters. Everyone looked like they were having fun, and I didn't think my absence had even been noticed. Somehow, Sammy had gotten his mother to join him on the dance floor. When the song ended and the dance floor cleared, I saw Sammy and his mother going back to where Bernard was standing. I was on my way over to join them when Kory went up to Sammy. "You dropped this." He held out Sammy's magic wand.

Sammy froze, and Kory continued, not knowing anything was wrong. "Dr. Amazing, how about wowing us with one of your tricks?" Some other people had gathered and also called out for Sammy to do some magic.

Sammy shrugged, realizing the truth was out. He took the wand and acted like he was going to put it away, but instead he waved it over Kory's pocket, and suddenly a trail of silk scarfs started to appear. The crowd responded with delight.

It occurred to me that Sammy's tuxedo was probably always stocked with props. A moment later, Sammy pulled out a deck of cards and fanned them out, asking a bystander to pick one.

I thought both of his parents were going to pass out.

I went over to calm them — as if it was possible. They were battling with each other, each blaming the other for Sammy's magic "problem." Bernard had given him the first magic set, but Estelle had applauded when he put on shows when he was a kid, which Bernard said only encouraged him.

Sammy finished his impromptu show and finally looked at his parents. Seeing that they were in meltdown mode, he brought them outside, and I got carried along.

"So, now you know. I'm known as the Amazing Doctor Sammy, and I'm a professional magician." He looked at them both. "That means I get paid for doing magic," he said. "I have a career here. I have regular weekend gigs doing table magic at Vista Del Mar, and I'm talking to some other of the resorts about doing something on weeknights."

"Where does she fit in all this?" his mother said, glaring at me.

I let Sammy tell them that we weren't a couple and we didn't live together and that I wasn't why he was there.

"Good," Bernard said. "Then nothing is really keeping you here, and you can come back to Chicago, where you have a future in urology." He shook his head. "Who wants a doctor with a magic wand in his pocket?"

I was so proud of Sammy. Instead of throwing some emotional fit the way I might have, he spoke in a calm voice and told them that the decision of where he lived and what he did was his.

They still seemed to blame me for everything, but the fuss got cut short. Their flight was leaving from San Jose, and they had to drive to the airport. I stood with Sammy as they left.

"You did the right thing," I said.

Sammy smiled at me and took my arm. "Case, you're the only one who gets me."

The ball was winding down by then, and I found my group outside by the curb, waiting for the ride back. Tag walked Lucinda over to join the group and reluctantly let go of her arm. It seemed they had worked things out.

She looked at me. "Anything interesting happen?"

28

Sunday morning came too soon. For me, anyway. Julius was already up and waiting in the kitchen for his stink fish when I walked in, trying to will my eyes to stay open.

The retreaters had all been too wired to sleep when we got back from the ball, and they'd sat around knitting and talking until all hours. Lucinda and I had stayed off to the side, and I'd told her about what she'd missed and made her promise not even to tell Tag until Monday.

"All these secrets," she said with a shake of her head. She was much less concerned about the football game and more about the bad mark against my baking being removed forever.

Sammy could have gone back to his spot at the Butterfly B and B now that his parents were gone, but he'd wanted to spend a last night in the guest house.

I passed on calling Frank and was relieved that my mother didn't call me. I dressed quickly and went across the street to Vista Del Mar for the last day of the retreat and the final day of Butterfly Week.

Generally, Sunday mornings were quiet at Vista Del Mar. People slept a little later and were getting ready to leave. But today there was a buzz of activity as I walked to the Lodge. I saw a bunch of people around the float. The tarps were back on, and it was being hooked up to an SUV. I watched as it was carefully pulled off the grounds and taken into position for the parade. After the ball, the committee had gotten together and tallied their votes for queen, but no one would know the results until the grand finale of the parade.

I went to cut through the Lodge and was surprised to see Liz Buckley standing near the registration counter. She looked like she hadn't slept. Obviously, she knew what had happened.

"I just wanted to apologize for the problems. I know the powers that be are keeping everything quiet. Nobody even told me where Gary had gone until after the ball. I know you know what happened." She shook her head sadly. "I had no idea that Gary had such a problem and was taking money out of my business account. That's why the checks bounced." She seemed so distraught; I put my hand on her arm in a supportive manner. "I don't know what I'm going to do. Will everybody blame me for what Gary did?" She didn't wait for an answer. "And in all the weird twists of fate, Hank Hardcastle called me yesterday. He was working his way through their properties, trying to find out who Rosalie had put the screws on. Last night at the ball, he told me again that everything she'd done had died with her, but I had to keep it to myself. I was so relieved." Now I understood why she'd almost had her head on his shoulder when they were dancing. "The poor man really is trying to protect her memory. And he doesn't even know about the fall of the bear."

When I seemed surprised, Liz said she had already seen Gary in jail, and he'd told her about who had taken him down and how. I thought she might blame me for what happened, but she said that things hadn't been good between them for a while, and he had brought it all on himself. She seemed more concerned with how she was going to keep afloat financially.

"I can only speak for myself, but I certainly won't blame you for what he did," I said. "The Danish ladies seemed to have enjoyed the retreat. I'd be happy if you could send more people my way."

She looked like she really needed some support, and I gave her a hug. She thanked me again and then left.

When I went out the other side of the Lodge, people were coming down the path toward the Sea Foam dining hall. The smells of breakfast food and fresh coffee wafted my way, and I went toward them, almost in a trance. The air had its usual bracing chill, and the sky was thick with clouds that seemed almost gloomy.

Inside there was a clatter of dishes and a din of conversation. Lucinda was up and perfectly done up as usual. She was at our usual table and was filling her cup from the coffee carafe. The rest of the group came in and found seats. I noticed they all had the usual vibe of the last morning of a retreat — everybody always felt nostalgic now that that their time together was ending. A number of them were wearing hats and cowls they'd made during the retreat, but the most treasured of their projects seemed to be the crocheted butterflies, since they were what the week had been all about.

We had our last workshop after breakfast.

After everyone sat down, Wanda pulled me aside.

"I see you don't have your looms. It's really not good form when the leader of the retreat isn't prepared," she said. I had to force myself to take the rebuke without saying where I had left them.

At the end, everyone packed up their supplies and gave hugs and thank-yous to Wanda and Crystal. I was glad to see that while Wanda and Crystal still had their different opinions, they were learning to appreciate what each of them brought to the workshops. They were already discussing ideas for next time.

When the group came out for lunch, they all had their luggage with them. Kevin St. John for once had been agreeable about something and had arranged a place for them to stow their bags for the rest of the day.

By afternoon, the clouds had melted and the sky was a pale blue. I always felt like the sky was smiling when the sun came out. The bus picked up the group and deposited us on Grand Street. There was some time before the parade, and most of the group wanted to take a last look around town. I had a stop I wanted to make as well. I went past the drugstore as Larry Benson came outside.

He nodded a greeting at me and glanced toward the street. "It won't be long now until we find out who the Butterfly Queen is. I've known all along my daughter didn't have much of a chance since we're so new to town, but I can still hope."

I agreed and started to walk on, but he called after me. "I'm sorry if I was difficult when you came in the store. I had a lot on my mind, but it's all good now."

"Believe me, I understand completely."

I turned on the side street and walked down to Cadbury Yarn. Gwen looked up when I came in. "We're just closing," she said. "I want to watch the parade. It would be wonderful if Marcy is the queen."

"There's something I need to show you," I said. I pulled the worn manila envelope out of my bag and extracted the old photograph of the baby and a teddy bear. I laid it on the counter in front of her.

"That's the bear my mother made for me," she said. She looked at the infant next to it. "Is that me?"

"She's Edmund Delacorte's love child," I said, then I swallowed, waiting for her reaction.

"Me?" she said in a whisper.

"I have a sample of Edmund's hair roots and all. A paternity test would prove it was true."

What she said next totally surprised me. Her expression grew harsh. "I don't like the Delacortes. Why would I want to be one of them?" She pushed the photo back to me. "I have to go now."

I took the envelope back and prepared to leave. "Think about it. Not just for yourself, but for Crystal, Marcy and Kory. You must know how he feels about Vista Del Mar." And then I left.

When I got back to Grand Street, the sidewalk was thick with people in anticipation of the parade. The retreaters had stuck together, and I joined them. Sammy came out of the crowd and stood with me. The sun had stayed out, warming the air, and people started shedding their fleece jackets as a voice over the loudspeaker announced the beginning of the parade with the Lord of the Butterflies.

The figure with the giant wings made his way down the street, waving to the crowd. With the black hood, I'm sure no one realized it wasn't Coach Gary. No one had told me, but I was pretty sure it was Hank Hardcastle. Fishermen had strong shoulders, too. The rest of the parade was definitely small town all the way. The high school band came along, playing a few squeaky notes, while a bunch of young girls in short skirts twirled batons with a few missteps. The fire trucks came by with the firefighters waving at the crowd. Dane hadn't told me about his part in the parade. He and the kids who hung out at his place came by all dressed in white karate outfits, doing karate stances as they walked. The town council members rode by in butterfly-festooned golf carts. Arthur Reisling caught my eye and gave me a thank-you nod.

Next, a police cruiser drove by slowly, with a couple of uniformed officers walking alongside. I did a double take when I saw Lieutenant Borgnine taking up the rear. I didn't think I'd ever seen him smile before, and he was waving at the crowd, too. I checked the sky again for flying pigs.

"And now, for what we've all been waiting for," the voice over the microphone said. Crystal and Wanda appeared next to me as two decorated golf carts went by with the Butterfly Queen committee. Not only did the Delacorte sisters hold their handbags Queen Elizabeth–style, they had her wave down, too. Kevin St. John was in the back-seat. No waving from him, just very straight posture.

There was a break when nothing went by, and then some royal-sounding music began. The float turned onto the main street and started its slow procession toward the crowd. All I could see was a giant monarch on the front. A canopy with side panels covered the float. Just when it reached the beginning of the crowd, the covering was pulled back. I heard a gasp go through the crowd, and then Wanda and Crystal both started talking about how something was off. The court was always in the front of the float with the queen on a throne at the end. But the front of the float was empty, and there seemed to be a crowd at the other end, and no throne.

The voice over the loudspeaker finally explained. "The committee decided that it was too much work for one person, and so they have elevated all of the princesses to Butterfly Queens. They will be sharing the duties and honors. May they reign well." I heard a squeal of delight. I thought it was probably coming from Crystal, seeing that her daughter was one of the queens, but it was Wanda. She jumped up and down, yelling, "Yee-ha," while waving at her sister, who was another of the queens.

I felt someone step up next to me. It was Dane, in his karate outfit. "Have they an-

388

nounced the queen yet?" he said. He seemed ready for bad news, but I pointed to the float, which was just arriving in front of us.

I heard him make a surprised noise — Chloe was with the others. Somebody must have given her a dress to wear. I couldn't imagine her picking anything as plain and modest as the yellow dress that went to just above her knees. All the princesses had new crowns on now. Chloe was waving at the crowd, and then she saw Dane, and her face lit up as she gave him a double thumbs-up. I couldn't be sure with all the noise, but it sounded like she yelled, "Nailed it."

As the parade ended, shimmers of clouds were coming across the sky and blotting out the sun, and the air felt colder. The group loaded up on the bus, and we went back to Vista Del Mar.

I always felt a tug when it got to be time to say good-bye. This week I hadn't spent as much time with the retreaters as before, but I still felt an attachment. The Danish ladies were the first to say good-bye. They said they wanted to come again and bring some friends. Bree Meyers was next. She had a bag full of things about the monarchs that she was taking back to her sons.

"It's been great," she said, giving me a hug. "Having this time away really helps me

to be a better mother. And I made these."
She pulled out two small hats and one large
one, explaining they were for her boys and
their father.

Olivia had a huge bag of squares. "I love
the idea of using the looms to make them.
It's been another wonderful retreat, though
I wish I'd seen more of you. You'll have to
let me know what kept you so busy."

Inwardly, I smiled. So I *had* managed to
keep all the turmoil away from them.

Scott stopped next to me. "I appreciate
trying the looms, but I'm a needle man."
He held up a scarf connected to a pair of
circular needles to illustrate.

The van for the airport pulled up and
began to load. A few people who had driven,
headed for their cars. Everyone thanked me
and said they wanted to come back. I guess
that meant the retreat had been a success.

Finally, it was just me and Lucinda.
"Whew," she said. "This has been quite a
week. And they had no idea what you had
going on. Make the regular number of desserts for us, and if I were you, I'd make full
orders of the muffins, too. You'll see, tomorrow everything will go back to normal."

She pulled her coat a little tighter against
the chilly air. Her suitcase stood next to her.
"There's Tag," she said, as a Prius turned

off the driveway. "With the restaurant closed, he's planned a special welcome-back night for me. Being away really puts a new spark in things."

I waited until she'd gotten in the car and it had driven away. I felt at loose ends when I went back home. There had been so much excitement, and now it was all over. Julius was sitting on the stoop outside the back door, waiting for me. I was about to go inside when the door to the guest house opened and Sammy came out, pulling a bag.

"Thanks for letting me stay last night. It was kind of traumatic with my parents, and it was nicer to stay here."

"I'm sorry about the way it worked out," I said.

"It's okay. It's better that they know why I'm really here, instead of thinking it was because of you. No more pressure from them about when there's going to be a wedding." He looked at me with his soulful eyes and held my gaze for a little too long for it to be believable that he was really happy about it.

"I'm glad you made the parade," I said. His face lit up, and he let go of his bag.

"I have to show you what I'm planning for next year." He took out three red bean-bags and started juggling them. He did pretty well, only dropping them once. "By next year I'll be juggling flaming batons." It was probably good his parents weren't here for this.

One way or another, my life was intertwined with Sammy's. I went to give him a hug. "You know, if you want to rent the guest house, I'm still available as a tenant," he said.

He finally ambled down the driveway toward the BMW parked on the street.

The phone was ringing as I went inside. I knew who it was. I grabbed the cordless and said, "Hello, Mother."

"Huh?" the voice on the phone said.

"Frank?" I said in surprise. Then I got worried. "Is something wrong?"

"Feldstein, everything is still copacetic here. You left me hanging. I wanted to know how it all turned out."

"Nailed it," I said with a laugh. Then I told him all the details. Frank was as horrified as the other men at what Coach Gary had done to his team. He wanted me to let him know what they finally charged him with, and he thought it would be a long list.

"My muffins are off the hook, and it's going to be baking as usual," I said.

"Good for you, Feldstein. You make me proud. I guess this means you won't be moving back." Did I detect a little disappointment in his voice?

"You could always come for a vacation," I said.

I heard him chortle as his chair let out a protesting squeak. "Maybe someday I will."

That night, I made myself a frozen entrée and gave Julius some stink fish, and then I got my baking things together.

Grand Street was quiet, and all residue of Butterfly Week had been packed into a load of plastic trash bags that would be picked up the next day.

The Blue Door was dark, like all the other businesses on the street. I unlocked the door and turned on the light. After setting my things in the restaurant kitchen, I quickly turned on some soft jazz to cover the deathly quiet. I should have known it wouldn't last.

I planned on following Lucinda's instructions and making the full order of desserts. I began by taking out the ingredients for apple pie. I had lost myself in peeling apples when I heard a knock at the door. I went to answer it, expecting it to be one of the usual people who showed up. I was shocked to see Gwen, with her face close to the glass.

I opened the door and brought her in. Her

brow was furrowed, and she said she didn't want to sit down. "I'm still trying to process what you told me. If it was just me, I would leave everything as it is. But I have to think of Crystal, Marcy and Kory. I'll do the paternity test. Then maybe you can help me consider my options."

"Of course," I said.

"But it stays our secret for now." Gwen looked to me for agreement. Now that she'd gotten it off her chest, she said she just wanted to go home.

I went back to the pies and, when they were done, smiled at the row of them sitting on the dessert counter. I was ready to move on to the muffins when there was another knock at the door.

This time it was Dane in uniform. "No rest for the wicked," he joked. "I thought I'd take my break here." He held out a red tote bag. "I retrieved it from the museum. I think everything is in there, but it's probably a mess."

"Thank you," I said, looking inside. The work I'd done on the blue hat had fallen off the loom and come apart, but the skein of red yarn and instructions for the cowl were intact.

"I'm going to start on this when I get home tonight," I said. He nodded, though I doubted he knew what I was talking about.

He seemed more thoughtful than usual. "I don't know how to begin to thank you for what you did for Chloe."

"We couldn't have her in jail when she got her shot to be Butterfly Queen."

Dane smiled. "Chloe as a queen is going to be something to see. I hope Cadbury is ready for it." He watched as I unloaded the muffin ingredients.

"I was planning to make full orders even before Lucinda suggested it," I said. "And there's something else. I know the town council will go nuts, but I'm calling the pumpkin muffins Monarchs."

"You go, girl. And that is probably the one fancy name the town council won't mind anyway." He handed me the paper baking cups. "This shift isn't all bad," he said. "I could take my breaks here. That is if you don't mind. It could be almost like a mini date," he said with a wink.

PATTERNS

Crystal's Loom Cowl

Note: Looms come with tool and instructions on e-wrap cast on and stitch.

Supplies

1 skein Lion Brand Homespun, Candy Apple, 6 oz, 170 g, 185 yds, 169 m, 98% acrylic, 2% other fibers
41-peg round loom
Knitting loom tool (comes with loom)
F-5/3.75 mm crochet hook
Tapestry needle

Finished size: Approximately 26 inches in circumference and 8 inches tall

To cast on: Make a slip knot, leaving a tail. Take slip knot through middle of loom from top to bottom and place it on side peg. (This is just to anchor yarn. After a few rows, take off peg and let hang loose.) Working counterclockwise around loom, e-wrap pegs, keeping wraps loose.

Round 1: Working in the same direction as cast on, e-wrap pegs. After wrapping all pegs, anchor yarn by wrapping around side peg. There are now two loops on each peg. Working in same counterclockwise direction, use loom tool to lift bottom loop over top loop and off peg. After working the last peg, release the working yarn from the side peg.

Repeat Round 1 until knitted work is approximately 8 inches. To cast off: Work the cast off very loosely. Hold working yarn to inside of loom. Insert crochet hook in last stitch worked from bottom to top. Lift loop off peg, chain one by sliding working yarn through loop on hook (keep loop loose). Use crochet hook to lift next loop off peg, going from bottom to top. There are now two loops on hook. Slide new loop through other one, chain one, being sure to keep the loop loose. Repeat until last stitch. When there is one loop left on hook, chain one, cut yarn and pull the end through final loop, tighten loop. Weave in ends with tapestry needle.

GWEN'S CROCHET BUTTERFLIES

Supplies

1 skein Red Heart Super Saver, Carrot, 7 oz, 198 g, 364 yds, 333 m, 100% acrylic (enough to make a lot of butterflies)

1 skein Red Heart Super Saver, Black, 7 oz, 198 g, 364 yds, 333 m, 100% acrylic (enough of both yarns to make a lot of butterflies)

Size K-10.5/6.50 mm crochet hook

Size H-8/5.00 mm crochet hook

Tapestry needle

Stitches used

Chain (ch), single crochet (sc), double crochet (dc), triple crochet (tr), slip stitch (sl st)

Finished size: Approximately 4 inches across the wings

Wings

Using K hook and carrot yarn, ch 8 and join with a sl st.

Round 1: Ch 1, make 17 sc in the circle, join to first stitch with a sl st.

Round 2: Ch 3, sc in next stitch, *sc, ch 3, sc* repeat from * to * around. 8 chain 3 spaces made.

Round 3: *Sl st to move yarn into ch 3 space, sc, dc, dc, tr, dc, dc, sc (all in the ch 3 space)*.*. Repeat from * to * 7 more times. Sl st in first space. Fasten off.

Weave in the ends then fold the piece in half and the butterfly shape should be apparent. With K hook, attach black yarn to top side of one of the wings. Ch 1, working through both layers join by single crocheting around the wings. Fasten off and weave in ends.

Body

Using H hook and black yarn ch an approximately 10-inch strip. Fasten off.

Make a knot at each end of the strip, cut excess yarn (this will be top of each antenna). Fold the strip across the center of the butterfly (so that it shows on both sides), tie the top in a knot (the butterfly's head) leaving about an inch on each end to create the antennas.

MONARCH MUFFINS

2 cups unbleached all-purpose flour

2 teaspoons aluminum-free double-acting baking powder

1 1/2 teaspoons ground cinnamon

1/2 teaspoon baking soda

1/2 cup chopped walnuts

1 egg

3/4 cups buttermilk

3/4 cup canned pumpkin

2/3 cup packed brown sugar

2/3 cup melted butter

1/4 cup spiced pumpkin seeds (optional)

Preheat oven to 375 degrees Fahrenheit. Line 12-cup muffin pan with paper baking cups.

Sift flour, baking powder, cinnamon and baking soda into a medium bowl. Add nuts and stir.

In another bowl, beat egg lightly with fork.

Stir in buttermilk, pumpkin, brown sugar and melted butter. Make a well in the middle of dry ingredients, and add wet ingredients all at once. Stir just until moistened. Batter will be lumpy. Spoon into prepared pan. Sprinkle spiced pumpkin seeds over each muffin. Bake for approximately 20 minutes, until a toothpick comes out clean. Makes 12 muffins.

The employees of Thorndike Press hope you have enjoyed this Large Print book. All our Thorndike, Wheeler, and Kennebec Large Print titles are designed for easy reading, and all our books are made to last. Other Thorndike Press Large Print books are available at your library, through selected bookstores, or directly from us.

For information about titles, please call:
  (800) 223-1244

or visit our Web site at:
  http://gale.cengage.com/thorndike

To share your comments, please write:
  Publisher
  Thorndike Press
  10 Water St., Suite 310
  Waterville, ME 04901